KEEPER *of* TIDES

A NOVEL

BEATRICE MACNEIL

BREAKWATER

P.O. Box 2188, St. John's, NL, Canada, A1C 6E6
WWW.BREAKWATERBOOKS.COM

COPYRIGHT © 2014 Beatrice MacNeil

LIBRARY AND ARCHIVES CANADA CATALOGUING IN PUBLICATION
MacNeil, Beatrice, 1945-, author
Keeper of tides / Beatrice MacNeil.
ISBN 978-1-55081-483-5 (pbk.)
I. Title.
PS8575.N43K43 2014   C813'.54   C2014-900561-X

Originally published as *Box of the Dead* (McArthur & Company, 2012)

We acknowledge the support of the Canada Council for the Arts, which last year invested $154 million to bring the arts to Canadians throughout the country. We acknowledge the Government of Canada through the Canada Book Fund and the Government of Newfoundland and Labrador through the Department of Tourism, Culture and Recreation for our publishing activities.

PRINTED AND BOUND IN CANADA.

Breakwater Books is committed to choosing papers and materials for our books that help to protect our environment. To this end, this book is printed on a recycled paper that is certified by the Forest Stewardship Council®.

TO MY MOTHER AND FATHER,

BEATRICE AND NEIL MACDONALD,

WHO REST

PEACEFULLY BENEATH THE STARS.

ONE

THE CALICO'S MODE is eloquently striking. Old Rose, despite her seventeen years, is the queen of the hunt. Invisibly crowned, she creeps slowly, her chin low and sensual teasing the grass, shoulders in a sculpture of pure feline delight. Her yellow eyes feast on the slow movement on the path before she strikes and flips the mouse with her paws, cracks it open with her claws, sniffs warm spills and escorts her victim carefully between her teeth to the back veranda. The rodent shudders like a brown leaf on the blue welcome mat where Old Rose releases her gift. It expires on the letter O within minutes. Old Rose licks her lips. She loves the flavour of death.

"Be off with that business!" a voice through the screen door cries out. Old Rose's ears perk to the sound of her owner's voice, cracking like crushed ice between her teeth. Ivadoile Spears squints through the screen at the corpse the cat has brought to her veranda for its wake.

At ninety-two, she is a riot of blue veins and stains. Strands of loose white hair scatter as if in a wind fire, and fly off in every direction from a shrunken skull that has summoned a broken cherub for protection. Her round eyes, a fading day's blue, widen slowly behind a pair of cat-eye framed glasses. Thin limbs clamp her into a stooped half sphere as she opens the door holding her broom in one hand. She's not about to be scared off now. It's going to rain. Her joints speak to her in a stiff voice as rusty as her own.

Creaky old woman making sounds like the bend in the hollows.

Another voice crawls in her ear as soft as a cat's purr. It is a man's voice and the sound of it plays inside her head. He is calling her Iva. She pauses long enough to smile with gratitude. She feels hopeful under this darkening sky. Almost giddy like a schoolgirl who's received her first valentine with the promise of emotional tinkering when the time's right. But she must not pay too much attention to such things. Another man called her Iva. It came out of a drool and left a stain on her fine linen.

A raincloud strolls above her head, spitting rain down in slow drips. A gravel of thunderous notes breaks loose. Another sound crawls along the veranda. Iva pauses to listen. Risky at her age to be unable to identify what is wailing towards her. The cat turns towards the sound and stares alertly into thin air. The corpse, lying on its side between them, is ignored for now. The poor mouse has no need to fear any living creature at this time. Iva takes a couple of steps closer to the sound with her broom in hand. She refuses to be undone. She scrambles in her head for the sound of a wild animal and listens. She's heard everything that bends and sneaks into this pocket of Port Murdock. It is her piece of southeast Cape Breton hanging above an eroding lip of split cliffs.

Wildflowers and bogberries tag each other between the leaves around here. Remnants of bootleg pits and illegal stills emerge at the end of overgrown paths. The air of a tune begins in the fiddler's foot. Rhythm and warmth are his secret notes. The beginning of a brawl has a melancholy voice of fists and bones. Church steeples, nosing their way into infinity, ring their bells. They offer land warnings, *Your soul is sinking!*

The voices of young boys pierce the air like static as they dangle high above the rowdy Atlantic on the cliff's edge, daring one another to jump. The sea climaxes beneath their bare heels and seduces them into its depth with a roar. Only the dead in the rambling graveyards separate their bones in silence.

Iva hears another sound like a stick being slammed up against the barn door. She vaguely makes out the swaying motion of the rotting sign on the gate post, shaking loose in some energetic form of the life it once produced.

She scolds herself as she walks carefully down the steps towards the gate, broom held like a cane for support. A rusty chain dangles to the ground. She swipes at the wooden sign with the broom handle. The chains come loose and fall, rattling like spring snakes unknotting from winter's rest.

She musters up the strength to bend down and pick up the sign. Back on the veranda, she sweeps the corpse off the mat. Old Rose rushes over to retrieve the mouse between her teeth and scurries down the path out of sight and the sound of thunder.

Iva looks down the lane expecting to see Margaret LaMae, her nearest neighbour and former employee, coming around on her weekly visit. But the lane is as still as a freshly closed grave.

In her kitchen, she throws the decayed sign of the barely visible TIDES INN in the old wood box behind the stove where she keeps wood for the fireplaces she no longer uses. It showers splinters against the back wall.

How foolish have I been to keep this sign posted, she asks herself, having made new signs now and again. CLOSED is now made visible to keep strangers away from her door.

She cannot recall how many years ago she closed the inn to the public, to the parade of lodgers that slept soundly and frolicked madly on her clean sheets behind her numbered doors. She could always tell when something went on between her sheets the night before. People sat shifty-eyed at the table as if they were making plans for a holdup the next morning. They never looked her in the eye.

The numbers are still on the inn doors, left in place at Iva's insistence, preserved like the dahlia bulbs she fed to the earth each spring and pulled up gently in the fall with hands that obeyed the nature and sequence of beauty.

The sun seeps through the widow's peak on the west side of the inn where people took photographs of its grandeur in its heyday. The sun's rays filter through the curtains. Their lace hangs like rotting fishnets and spreads its lazy flames on the patchwork quilts and braided rugs and rests like an old dog on the wide plank floors where the spiders cross its path in a march of yellow glory. There are four windows facing the sea. Their outer casings peeled down to the raw wood, arched roofs acting as stages for the seagulls to give their high performances, winter and summer.

Above the main glass, four small panels of stained glass display an elegance of reds, blues, greens, and gold. Two of the red stained squares are cracked like a pair of old raw hands. Behind door number Four, an old doll named Victoria keeps a watchful eye on the sun's coming and going through these squares.

Rarely does Iva greet a visitor now except in spring when the rooms are scrubbed down by a couple of cleaning women from the village. One woman will not take the job alone because they believe there are ghosts that roam the halls of the Tides Inn.

Victoria, the doll, sits prim and proper in a white wicker chair in her bleached knickers and a faded linen dress, her little red shoes are pale and split as if she were a frequent visitor to the Land of Oz. She has two top and two bottom teeth behind her cupid smile. Her hair is auburn and her eyes are as green as a spruce. Pick her up and her dress would crumble in your hands. Iva paid little attention to this rag of youth given to her by her father one Christmas Eve when she was six years old.

Victoria was never meant to grow old, never meant to drown the devil out of her limbs with lotions that baptize brittle bones for the grave. Iva wanted something real for Christmas when she was a child. She had tucked in her mind a list of cat names should one snarl its way out from under the McLaughlin tree. Victoria is a sun goddess with the wind and the sea sneaking in a lullaby at the going down of the sun.

In the grand parlour, the old piano is silent. The lid is left open. A heavy fragrance fills the room. The piano itself is a corpse with musty air trapped between its yellow teeth. Perhaps it mourns for its own silence because it has not been touched in years. Margaret, the cook, played "Amazing Grace" once for a guest while her roast was cooking.

She showed off her ability to play the Protestant hymn— as her church's organist she could read music—while noting in her heart that God could hear all notes bellowing to the heavens every Sunday. Catholics had not hit a note of "Amazing Grace" on their organs at mass back then. "Amazing Grace" trembled from under her spiced fingers and sent shivers of repentance around the room.

One of the guests, an elderly woman who came to the Tides Inn for rest and serenity, wept violently under a blanket beside the window and cried out, "I am that wretch! I am that wretch!"

Iva came running into the parlour.

"Margaret!" hissed Iva, as if she had a broken syllable caught between her teeth, "The best thing about that hymn is that it comes to an end this minute."

Red faced, Margaret spun from the piano stool and hid her shame with her head in the oven while basting the roast. Ivadoile Spears was never musical, Margaret reminded herself to lessen her guilt. She disliked hymns and any reference to spiritual health. She believed Adam and Eve were Raggedy Ann and Andy, playing dress me down under a tree while bobbing for apples. Iva referred to this when

Margaret peeled apples for pies or made date squares. She had a way of keeping Margaret in her place with figs and apples.

The windows in the parlour have not been opened for months. Heavy green velvet drapes keep out the drafts and the sun. Shelves of old books lean against one another for support. King Lear is shrivelled. Four wingback chairs face each other, two by two in the parlour, like four heavyweight women engaged in a serious conversation.

The main dining room faces Iva's secret garden. She goes out through the kitchen door and walks along the veranda. Steps out into an overgrown path. Listens for garden voices. She can hear them whispering between the blades of grass in the garden that sprang from the earth like a maze when she moved here years ago.

She designed the gardens herself and had her caretaker fashion them to her satisfaction. There was something about a path that led a person forward to something yet unexplored.

A low wind beneath the tall stalks bend them into a curtsy. Iva smiles at the sound as they ripple an ode to a new season. A robin digs furiously for a worm in the damp soil where all the tulips hide until spring. Uprooted twigs scurry along the path. Singing is the petite bird as plump as a dumpling. It always sings on the fat garden cherub with the broken hand.

The cherub's sightless eyes are forlorn; heaven must have abandoned it to the four seasons for some innocent mischief. God's angels and men have taken a pounding in Iva's secret garden. Her gardens were always such a joy to her guests she reminisces, especially behind door number Seven.

In this secret garden some of the stubborn tulips and hardy flocks still return like aging actors for an encore.

Something interrupts her garden visit, a shadow flapping like wind under a large bird's wing. Iva turns slowly and stares up at the upstairs window on the left of the house. An old screen is clapping against the window's glass as if for the finale in room number Seven.

There are no hands in there now waiting to spread Iva out like a snow angel and leave his imprint. So invisible it was, Iva recalls, she had to dig in the snow to see if he'd been there at all. Ambrose Kane, a lodger, held a woman up like an offering. His tabernacle was her four-poster bed where her late husband, Cullie Spears, a country doctor, died on the most romantic night of their lives in 1944, eight years after they were wed.

Dear Cullie, she had given him two shots of brandy at his own insistence that night. He smiled as they made love for the third time. Iva unravelled herself out from under his racing heart and camphor-grilled ribs and chest. Watched his smile melt from his lips and smear the pillow with saliva. He turned a watery filmed eye upwards and winked. She was on her knees looking down at him when she announced in a low voice, "I believe I just killed the poor doctor."

On their wedding day in 1936, she'd walked down the aisle with the best of intentions with Cullie Spears and his bad heart. It was not bliss that she vowed to keep intact but a man twenty-five years her senior who needed brandy to keep him down at night and Dodd's Kidney Pills to get him going in the morning. He had the soft full face of a much younger man. Under rimless glasses slept a stillness in Cullie's dark eyes that comes to a man mapping out his own impending death.

He wore expensive suits and vests with the gold chain of his pocket watch crawling down his chest like a string of fire. She watched each night as he peeled out of these garments like an onion and asked for a hot water bottle.

It pleased her that he loved cats. His brown and black spotted cat, Migraine, rode along with him on his house calls.

He called her Iva instead of the dreadful name Ivadoile, imposed on her by her teacher mother and her strict accountant father, who worked for Dominion Coal Company. Cullie made several visits to the General Store where Iva worked as a bookkeeper. She looked up from her ledger and met his gaze. He appeared to be looking at her in the same manner he would examine a rash, carefully, observantly, with an urge to scratch her soft skin and take her away in flakes under his nails.

He nodded and smiled before asking her out. They travelled around the twisted turns and glens of Cape Breton in his Ford Coupe before stopping beside the Swallow River.

He proposed under a scorching sun with Migraine stretched out on the back seat in a heat-induced sleep. They were both sunburned before Iva agreed to his request. He could offer no prospect of her ever becoming a mother due to a malady which he explained to her by its Latin name. This didn't bother Iva. She preferred cats to children.

And besides, Cullie offered her a seven bedroom home near the Atlantic Ocean, where the mischievous ebb tides flowed in and out of their dreams like a sensual melody. These moods forced the young bride to time the tides, to keep her hand warm and ready to count his frail ribs. It was the least she could sacrifice for a man who softened her name and gently sliced open her skin to remove her splinters.

When they met, Cullie was a mild-mannered widower who sized up a woman the way a man would size up a horse. His hands were gentle as he stroked each limb, stopping in the troubled spots to make an observation.

"You broke a bone in your knee some time ago," he said on their wedding night.

"Yes," she answered as he felt her ankles, not bothering to tell him she'd fallen out of a tree when she was twelve. It seemed futile to go back to her childhood at this stage of her life.

He had fallen asleep full of brandy and pills. The next morning he told her that he dreamt she was a broken woman. They made love that afternoon for the first time after the kidney pills took hold and he shooed Migraine out the back door. Iva looked up at the two posts at the bottom of their bed. She was sure they were mahogany.

TWO

SPRING OF 2007 looms its lusty scent in the air of Iva's kitchen. The aroma of new grass is sweet and tempting, slicing into her senses. The lilac bushes poke their purple heads in the window like peeping toms, spraying a deep perfume on the ledge as if something indecent was about to happen in the sedated village of Port Murdock, two miles north of McRae's Point where she was born.

Iva smiles as she pours a cup of tea and removes an old cedar box from the kitchen shelf. She has rummaged through its contents many times and come face to face with the dead. The lid whines as she flips it open and takes out a photograph of her mother and father.

She can almost feel their hot breath on her fingers, see their chests swell in their Sunday finest. Her father is tall and poised. He stands behind her mother who is sitting in a wingback chair. One hand rests on her shoulder. Her father is dark skinned, compared to her mother's pale complexion, and handsome in the way all men in suits presume they are. He is clean shaven with a shadow of a moustache beginning to ferment over a full mouth that has tasted its sour share of "I do."

The feather in her mother's hat stands as straight and pointed as a lightning rod that defies to be struck down.

Iva can see her own reflection in her father's portrait, the full mouth, long legs, and icy glare in his eyes. Her mother's blond hair is all that has rooted Iva to her mother's branch of the family tree.

"Ivadoile," she knows it is her mother's Sunday voice. "Don't be stalling up there in your room and have us late for church!" Her mother always threw her voice up the stairs on Sunday mornings. Heaved it up like an ice pick.

Iva is ten and is dressed in a white cotton pinafore over a navy dress. Her mother waits at the bottom of the stairs with a white ribbon to tie in her hair. Her long blond ringlets bounce down the stairs waiting to be lynched. She always hated ribbons in her hair. White ribbons lying on her head like splattered bird shit, her mother in feathered hats, and her balding father making their way up the aisle of the church, Sunday after Sunday. She did not look to the right or left for fear people would know what she was thinking.

By the age of eleven, she had put an end to her mother's ribbon ritual by chopping off her hair and blaming it on a boy in her class. Said he tangled her hair with gum and only a pair of scissors could get it out. Her mother was mortified as she sized down a hat of hers to fit her daughter's head. Iva was more angry as her mother placed the hat on her head, after adorning it with a brown feather.

Iva tires of this picture and tucks it back in the box. The next photo she holds is of her mother taken in New England where she was born. She is standing by the school where she taught for a year or two.

She is dressed in a long skirt and a blouse buttoned up to her chin like a hangman's noose. Her blond bun is shackled in hairpins to her head. You cannot tell that her eyes are grey-blue. What she is looking at is anything but amusing. Her square chin looks as if it owed its width to a schoolyard brawl of rowdy boys.

Iva chuckles at the thought of the school rules set for teachers she'd just read in a 1915 magazine her mother kept in an old trunk.

You may not smoke cigarettes, cigars, or pipe or chew tobacco or take snuff.

You may not ride in a carriage or automobile with any man unless he is your father or brother.

You must not loiter downtown in any of the ice cream stores.

You may not dress in bright colors.

You must wear at least two petticoats.

Your dress must not be any shorter than two inches above the ankles.

Iva puts the picture back in the cedar box and closes the lid with a smile on her lips. Growing up, she often thought about her parents' courtship and their first intimate kiss.

She questioned them about their courtship and was always scolded, like a cat about to unravel a ball of wool, while her parents stood red faced, unable to look at each other, as if their daughter was closing in on a secret too close for comfort. She longed to know about the secret life of her parents, about what went on under their heavy garments.

She lay in bed at night and imagined her father lifting her mother's skirt over her knees. Did her mother wonder if he was about to stroke her with a piece of chalk to mark the spots that he could erase or come back to on a whim? Did he need to map out a direction as to which part of his cold wife he could go to for comfort without her indifference interrupting the moment?

They had met when her mother and her mother's cousin, Opal, came to Cape Breton for a summer visit. Iva wondered, too, how these two people could have conceived a child together. They barely spoke between meals.

"Pass the butter please, Rory."

"Your buns are not up to snuff today, Nettie," scolded Rory with his butter knife held in the air like a sword belonging to King Arthur.

Nettie sat stiff backed in her chair and snarled.

"They are your mother's buns, Rory McLaughlin. I used the recipe from her old cookbook."

Two days later as the crows pecked under the kitchen window on the sodden McLaughlin buns, her father moved into the spare bedroom down the hall. Her mother sat at the table and stabbed at the roast pork in front of her.

By the time the cold pork reached Iva's plate, she had made up her mind. She would never have children. She could never subject them to cold pork and grandparents handy with knives.

Iva's first love came out from behind a wild bush when she was eleven. Full of fleas and burrs, the cat nestled up to her and purred mournfully at her heels. She named the cat Rose in honour of the wild bush and gave it a warm bath in lice powder. The male cat thrived on the child's gentle touch and thick bowls of cream for a year.

"A rose by any other name is not a rose in this case," said her angry father, stretching out the cat as if it were a rope, to check its gender. Iva refused to change the cat's name to Tom as her father insisted. Rose hissed at her father and clawed at his hand before escaping, leaving a deep gash on his thick sweaty hand.

Iva heard her father's boiling voice leaking out from behind the kitchen door as she scooped up the cat. "I warn you, Nettie, that child doesn't think or behave like a girl."

Rose's disappearance a day later caused Iva great alarm. She found her cat in the back clearing beneath a thorny briar. Rose's green eyes were plucked out, taken neatly by nature's jewel thieves, the crows. The wound to the throat left an open seam between the yellow fur. A dried trail of blood ran down the cat's belly like a crude zipper. Iva looked down at the two front paws crossed in some form of sadistic ritual.

"This is my father's way of having my cat repent for having bloomed as a Rose," thought Iva as she knelt over her dead pet. She firmly believed he had done the deed.

At the supper table that evening, she put a space between her father and death, hoping it would catch up to him as quickly as it did for Rose. But she was not quite sure what to do with the pain of waiting, of watching his eyes dart from the window to his plate, so she would not see in them the inward commotion of the violent act. She swallowed each mouthful slowly as the food choked down her anger, let it sneak into her heart and wait for the moment to get her revenge.

After Rose's death, her father avoided her as usual, along with her mother who had taken up silence like a hobby ever since he left her bedroom. She didn't bother to tell them that she had taken a shovel and buried her cat under the briar before the wild animals would get Rose. They never inquired about the missing cat that she had buried on Black Friday, nor the promise she made at the dinner table to name every cat she'd ever own "Rose."

Rose Number Two was black and sassy, bold and clever, an old female who appeared like a reaper on the garden fence in 1930. The cat kept a yellow and green eye on the pretty girl approaching with a bowl of cream in her hand.

Iva loves this picture. She is remembering without having to take it out of the box.

SHE IS HOLDING the cat in her arms against a sky that scatters its clouds out like dust balls. Iva is standing in an open field with her plain skirt ballooned out, a warm breeze between her legs. The cat's head is nestled under her chin as if it expected drops of rain to upset their day. The picture taker is her mother's cousin from Boston, a spinster librarian in her thirties with the long formal face of one who never made it to the altar in satin and lace. She was not a homely woman, but the kind that was forced to turn to muscle to provide men with other parts of her body to admire.

Opal knew early in youth that she would never be as pretty as her blond cousin Nettie with her soft muscles and defiant chin that could steer a man to the altar.

Opal darted through the clearings and fields like a pacer during her summer visits to Port Murdock. She would rest her lean thighs and full breasts against trees and fences with her Brownie Box Camera in hand. She wore dark coloured dresses and round straw hats as if her head would melt down over her shoulders like butter if the sun were to shine on it. Her last visit ended in 1930, the year the picture of Rose Number Two and Iva was taken.

Call it black magic, call it revenge, but Iva instinctively knew what was going to take place as she crept quietly into the barn. She watched her father enter in his white shirt, dark pants, and suspenders. Sunday morning's sermon drenched into the fibres of disobedience. He was followed a few minutes later by cousin Opal in a black dress that clung to her like a bad mood. Empty handed, she had no intention of leaving a photo of this scene.

Iva's mother, dressed in her grey pleated dress, was attending a church meeting. Iva could hear the hushed voices between muffled giggles of her father and Opal in the loft. She climbed the ladder slowly with Rose under her arm like a blanket, and hid up on a low beam. Opal lay on her side, stark naked in the hay bin. Her dark braid trailing down her pale back like a streak of mud, her muscled shoulders and arms covered in freckles. Her father was stripped to the waist with his suspenders dangling as if he were a horse with a loose saddle. He tried to shimmy out of his trousers as cousin Opal laughed at his antics.

It is strange how people's personalities change when they are naked. Her father called cousin Opal, "My naughty darling."

Cousin Opal purred in his ear, "Come to me my pussy-cat. Here puss, puss!"

Their bodies folded together like soggy toast. Rose began to loosen herself from Iva's grip as her father began to rise on his shaky knees. This was Rose Number Two's cue. She noticed the barn swallow circle above the lovers. The cat leapt from the beam and landed on her father's back. The screams that followed were of sheer terror.

"It's the devil, I know it. We must repent, Rory, repent!"

"Shut your goddamned mouth!" her father ordered Opal in a frosty voice. Rose jumped out of the bin and down the loft, her tail outstretched. Iva, with all the confusion and panic in the hay bin, made a getaway as sleek as the cat.

Iva was in the pantry peeling potatoes when she saw cousin Opal come out through the barn door (straw-flecked) and look both ways as if she were about to cross a busy street.

At the dinner table, in a change of clothes, Opal announced that she would be leaving for the States the next morning. Something urgent needed her full attention was her explanation for her sudden departure from Port Murdock, as she sat staring at the flowers she murdered for the table as though they were a wreath laid out for a corpse. Rory McLaughlin spoke not a word at the dinner table. Nettie gave Opal a rather stern looking over, but made no comment. She had caught the silence between her husband and her cousin. Iva cornered Opal in the kitchen and insisted she take a picture of her and puss-puss before she left.

Cousin Opal trembled then mumbled that she was allergic to cats.

"No you aren't, cousin Opal. You love cats. I can prove it." Iva's laughter was brazen. "Here, darling naughty puss-puss," she quipped as she picked up Rose and inched the grinning cat towards Opal with its claws out.

The cousin leaned against the cupboards for balance and took a deep breath as she fled the kitchen to get her camera to record her last picture of the evil child and her crazy cat.

Iva's father drove cousin Opal to the train station in the morning. It rained as hard as silver bullets on the hood of the car. Iva and her mother gave blurry waves through the kitchen window to cousin Opal, who shrank out of sight under a rainproof hat before the engine started. Iva thought she saw a blade of fire in her mother's eyes as she turned. It wasn't that her mother disliked her cousin, although Opal's Methodist sermons drove her mother to rattle her pantry dishes so hard against the shelves of her Presbyterian beliefs that a full set of dishes was already maimed before Opal left for Boston.

Her father returned from the train station as silent as he'd left and went to his room. Rory McLaughlin stayed behind the closed door for hours before he came out and went into the barn.

Tucked under her sheet later that night, Iva added a mental scrawl to her never to do list. Steer clear of organized religions and their impact on fine bone china and free will!

In the fall, she watched her father walk down the front steps of their house carrying a heavy suitcase. He never once turned around to see if he was being followed. Her father's image grew smaller and smaller on the landscape of her life as he proceeded down the long lane, balancing the rectangular remnants of his own life from hand to hand. He looked like a man walking into the setting sun.

In a rocking chair by the kitchen window, her mother marked the going away of her husband by carefully knitting a heavy wool garment. It was brown. She didn't look up at Iva, who crossed the kitchen and looked down at the wool dropping to the floor.

"He is gone," she said in a flat voice. "He won't be back," as if she had just swatted a bee that buzzed between each knit and purl. Her pale face looked starched. Small crystals of sweat formed at the edge of her hairline and went no further. "He left us the car," she mumbled as if he had left behind a cold.

Her grey-blue eyes lay dry in their sockets like two stones in an abandoned wishing well. She watched her mother's lips curl into formation a word she had never heard spoken in the McLaughlin house. Sealed her mouth shut like two wet spoons.

"I'll not have you asking me any questions about your father, Ivadoile. Do you understand?" Nettie McLaughlin never mentioned his name again.

Iva blinked at the dark wool, at the form of a man's sweater curled on her mother's lap like a dead beaver, and whispered under her breath, "I will never learn to knit."

Her mother put the unfinished knitting in a basket and busied herself with her teaching outfit for school the next day. The drab looking grey pleated dress dangled on a hanger in her hand. It looked as if it had been hung for manslaughter.

A letter from cousin Opal addressed to Iva arrived a few months later. It contained the picture of her holding Rose, and a brief note. Said she hoped that Iva and her mother were doing well. She'd added that she was praying for them daily. Her words ran in and out of the lines as if written with a broken hand. Iva burnt the letter over an open flame to melt Opal's blessings out of it.

There was no mention of her father who was sending a money order from an address in Boston every month. He never returned to Port Murdock.

In 1934, Dr. Cullie Spears pronounced Nettie McLaughlin dead from natural causes. It was spring. She was washing dishes in the pantry when she collapsed while Iva was at work in the General Store. Iva looked down at her mother's creased face. Even in death it looked as if it had been kicked by a grudge that rendered a severe penalty on it that only her grave could erase.

Nettie McLaughlin's face looked much older than the forty-two years of natural causes that pulled death's mask down over her square chin. She lay there with her legs sprawled in total defiance of death's final insult on the living, the inability to be found in a decent position. Her skirt, several inches above her waist revealed red lace underwear that she kept hidden in a locked trunk.

Her mother never did see her father again. Whomever she spoke to (if anyone) about the once tall handsome adulterer who fathered their only child, and why he up and walked out, no one would ever know.

Iva never did tell her mother about the day she followed her father into the barn, but she knew her mother suspected something was going on behind her back.

Iva and her mother sat in the back seat of the church after her father left. They slipped out quietly before the other members of the congregation. Nettie McLaughlin took no pity or questions. She laced the minister's words to the rim of her soul with a hard stitch. "Thou shalt not commit adultery!"

Had she any last temptations before she died? Iva kept these questions in her own mind. Did she do a pirouette around the pantry in her lace underwear, plan a trip and catch a husband that she never divorced in the act, slip a few pieces of bone china in her luggage to do battle with? She was suspicious of Opal when she never did return for a visit.

What had she planned on this day in lace underwear that had never before been revealed? She had let her hair down. Its limp blond strands were plastered up against the cupboard like mop strings, a convoy of hairpins resembling Daddy Longlegs were lined up on the window ledge.

Iva swept up the broken blue platter from under her feet. It was a wedding gift to her parents from cousin Opal. The platter looked as if it had expired before her mother died. It lay shattered and spread across the floor with its sharp edges pointed in every direction.

THREE

MARGARET LAMAE'S HANDS appear suddenly in the doorway. "She's never learned to knock, this woman," Iva mumbles under her breath, "just flutters at the door like a fish out of water."

"Is anyone home?" Her voice is raspy.

Iva refuses to answer for a moment to make Margaret call out again even though her voice annoys her.

"Where else would I be, Margaret, out on a date? I'm surprised you're not."

Margaret moves her cane slowly across the kitchen floor as she follows Iva's voice by the window.

"I brought you some tea biscuits to warm up," Margaret adds politely. Her small knotted hands place them on the cupboard in full view of Iva who sniffs at them as if they were mouldy. She's ignored her remark about a date.

Iva has to be careful. Margaret is as crafty as she is, the old bugger. Iva can feel Margaret's intentions slide like a blade of grass along her thigh. Margaret watches as Iva examines the biscuits like a hound dog. She has not relinquished her old ways. She will lead her nose where her eyes are beginning to fail. She has the urge to tell Iva that her glasses are for her eyes not her nose, where they are forever hanging.

This is Margaret's invitation to get the kettle going to make tea before they both forget that the warm biscuits are what they have in common, something that connects them to the past, to the inn where Margaret worked as a cook for years. They don't give a damn about the moon landing or who in the hell Ed Sullivan brought into their homes every Sunday night, when a blade of grass will do. Women are as handy with grass as they are with knives.

An air of misery settles in Margaret LaMae as she stares at Iva, at the woman whom she felt she begged for a job many years back, when Iva turned the grand old house into the Tides Inn in the '40s.

Margaret, at twenty, stood on the veranda a good ten minutes before Herself (as she secretly referred to Iva) opened the door and asked what her business was at the inn.

A marmalade cat toyed at Iva's open-toed sandals as if they were mouse holes. Ivadoile Spears was wearing a pale cotton dress. She kept tugging at her collar as if it were full of fleas before she invited Margaret in to what appeared to be a small parlour turned into an office, and questioned her as if she were a spy. She agreed to give her a three-week tryout. Maragaret believed she would have less of a challenge in New York looking for a job. She'd watched Iva then as she does now, crawling through her mind with that glare of hers. Be careful, Margaret, this woman knows what you are thinking. She knows, the old fool, that you both have a deep past, the same tastes for fine cooking, and a secret.

Iva slides the half-full kettle on the front burner and fumbles for the jam in the cupboard.

"Feels like we're in for some rain," Margaret's voice crawls up Iva's spine like a buzzing wasp as she pours the boiling water into the teapot.

"Says who, Margaret?"

"My old bones, for one. I use my cane for the third leg before it rains," she explains while Iva sets the table for their tea. "I can't stay too long. I thought I heard thunder in the distance."

"Thunder won't hurt you, Margaret. Did they not teach you that in school? It's the lightning that's the killer."

They face each other at the table as they sip from the fine bone china cups Iva has set out. The tea biscuits are delicious, they melt on your tongue like butter. They always do, but Iva does not say a word. She never does. She never cared much for lavishing her staff with glittering compliments. It would have spoiled everything, made people believe they were too valuable, too irreplaceable. They had to be kept on their toes at all times. She decided on turning the old house into the Tides Inn out of pragmatism, not for the handing out of compliments. Ivadoile Spears suffered no fools.

Iva does not mention that, at her age, Margaret LaMae is still a handsome woman, fine-boned and delicate like a favourite cup, eyes as soft and brown as a doe's hide. She could have done something with her life instead of lagging behind and getting trapped into taking care of her old folks.

And what has Margaret gotten out of it? Iva wonders. She should have taken off to the States like her sisters did. She went to work and church and knitted socks for the poor.

Iva can't imagine having to look after old stale parents splitting at the seams, spilling organs that would never function properly again. And making demands to ghosts at all hours of the day and night.

She would never have looked after the McLaughlins, as she refers to them now, as though they were a liability all her life. She can barely remember what her father looked like. He'd sent her a letter after her mother's death with an awkward invitation to come and visit with him. He mentioned that he had something he wanted to tell her. She fed the letter to a flame and didn't reply. He sent another letter, but she never bothered to open it. She threw it into her trunk and slammed down the lid.

Her father's face is always clouded by his nakedness, by his deep rotating rhythm into a woman who preached hard religion in the pantry with her mother, while he filled the hay bin with soft straw for a bout of adultery.

She remembers what sprayed from her father and hit Opal's visible flesh and coasted like spilled milk down her lean sprawled thighs before the cat struck.

Later in the kitchen, her father watched Iva in the pantry as she dropped the naked potatoes into a bowl of water. He had changed shirts and wore a fully buttoned vest as he braced himself into a chair. Iva looked past the vest and the shirt and the man wearing them and concentrated on his back. Was it red raw?

How long had the blood run before it stopped? How deep were the gashes that caused him to bolt upright with his penis erect, still swaying like a rusty scythe. Did all men do this on slow Sunday afternoons while their daughters peeled potatoes for dinner?

Something cracked in his face when Iva looked him square in the eye as she dropped a potato into the bowl, something fragile as a wave rippled over by a change of wind. His lips parted and his cheeks spread unevenly above his quivering chin. He raised his hand to hide the tremble. A shadow formed over his mouth, over what could have been mistaken for a smile. He did smile at times, Iva remembers. He brought them to the surface when her mother informed him that her cousin Opal was coming for a visit.

He smiled at Iva when her report cards were filled with the letter A. He had affirmed himself with the scarlet letter, long before Iva had picked up the novel to read its true meaning.

Iva looked around the kitchen to see if the cat was in sight. She watched through the kitchen window as Rose stretched out on the fence for a nap, her head nestled comfortably on her bloody paws. She would keep an eye on Rose to make sure she was close to her at all times.

Opal, in a clean white dress, stood in the corner of the room like a coat rack. She had let her hair down. It clung to her back with the motion of an unwrinkled wave as she went outside and robbed a hodgepodge of flowers from their stems for the dinner table. Opal and her father exchanged very few words.

Iva does not offer to fill Margaret's cup the second time around. She is tired of her own thoughts now. She never liked women who uprooted flowers or spit their opinions out like chewed straw while the weakest part of them wept between their legs because they didn't or couldn't say "No" fast enough. She does not think this way about Margaret. Poor virginal Margaret is, after all, her verbal vehicle to the past. The most she's done for a man was make a pair of socks for his feet and smile between them. Men had never travelled with bouquets to her door.

Iva watches as Margaret's small frame walks slowly down the lane, indenting her cane into the road with each step as if she were trying to turn over the earth.

Everything about Margaret was always exact. Iva's silent thoughts are generous. Her gravy was flawless, her biscuits and pies golden, and her roasts always tempting. There was nothing that she couldn't turn into something golden and delicious. She is one of the few people who comes for a short visit with something golden in one hand.

"I'll have no caretakers impose their disinfectants and pots of soup on me, no nurses checking out my state of mind. I will dry out as flat as a run-down toad before they'll cart me out of here." This is her weekly conversation to Margaret, a warning, as if someone has put Margaret up to keeping an eye on her.

Margaret is out of sight now, tapping her way to her home a quarter-mile down the road. Early fall is an unfinished colouring book in Port Murdock. Soft yellows, fading greens, and smudges of orange, colour the road home.

She is on her way to an empty house through the fallen leaves that lie upon the ground like torn pages under her feet. There is one ghost that remains as Margaret enters her house, is always there when she returns with a blush to her cheeks. Not all ghosts are as demanding as Ivadoile Spears believes them to be. She'd dissolved her father and mother from her view long before their death.

Iva turns from the kitchen window and clears the cups from the table to the sink. She shakes her head as if to sift out her memory, to shake something loose that would give her a reason for distrusting Margaret LaMae. There is something about Margaret's demure approach that leaves Iva sore in parts like a rabbit waiting on its demise with a snare tightening around its neck.

The cedar box is still on the ledge as she picks it up to place it back on the shelf. From under the open lid, he stares up at her, smiling. And she smiles back at Bowzer as if he were sitting here in her kitchen waiting to be served a cup of tea. But of course he is not, she reminds herself. He is dead like all the others in the box.

Bowzer, he went by no other name, arrived at the Tides Inn shortly after its initial opening. It was 1948. He drove up the lane in an old green Chevrolet. The car shone in the sleeting early fall rain and shook when it came to a sudden halt and spit into the air a tail of black smoke. A flurry of feathers rose from the back seat.

He ran from the car in two leaps to the entrance and adjusted his bow tie before ringing the bell. He was very formal in his beige suit and red bow tie when Iva answered the door to her first lodger, an American salesman from

New England who sold fine suit cloth along the eastern seaboard.

Iva looked down at the five-foot-four soggy stranger and smiled inwardly. His grey-red hair, dyed a brassy orange, gave his head the appearance of a wet citrus fruit. A flat nose spread above his thin lips. His large green eyes drooped at the lids as though he constantly lived in the rain. From his pointed ears, raindrops dripped on the mat. He reached out a wet hand to Iva and spoke in a bootleg English accent.

"Bowzer, Mademoiselle, I noticed your sign at the gate."

Iva smiled. She had a sudden urge to take him in and offer him a bowl of cream.

"I do not travel alone," added Bowzer, "my friend travels with me. She takes up very little space and will be fed by me alone."

Iva had not seen a woman in the car when it drove up. She envisioned his old mother asleep in the back seat, worn out from her long trip in the battered Chevrolet.

"Bring her in!" said Iva. "There is plenty of room."

"Much obliged. There's not every place that will take the old gal," cried Bowzer. Before Iva could say another word, he ran towards the car and opened the back door and rushed in with a bird cage that housed the old gal named Humphrey.

The parrot looked at Iva from under her wet crown and spoke in a clear concise New England accent, "Goddamn rain. Goddamn Canadian rain."

Iva escorted her guest to a first floor room after Bowzer apologized for Humphrey's outburst. He blamed it on the weather. He claimed that Humphrey was friendlier with the sun above her crown.

Iva stood outside the door for a few minutes after Bowzer closed the door and bid her a good day. She could hear Bowzer and Humphrey engaged in a whining seesaw of voices.

"She's a nice lady, Humphrey, keep it down!" Bowzer scolded.

"Nice lady, nice lady. Sun above the crown. Keep it down, keep it down!" Humphrey repeated.

Iva put her hand to her mouth to stifle a laugh. Down the hall she could see Margaret LaMae and her inn caretaker, Bertie, in a hushed conversation. She could make out the word asylum as she rounded the corner to register her first guests. They would be staying for seven nights and one day.

At the dinner table that evening, Bowzer asked permission to have Humphrey's cage and stand placed to the side by the window, where he could keep an eye on the old gal.

"She gets rather obnoxious if I am not in sight," Bowzer explained.

Margaret circled around the cage as if it contained a gorilla as she served dinner to Iva and her guest.

"You will have to forgive Margaret. She is not used to talking birds here in Cape Breton," Iva announced sarcastically.

Iva and Bowzer chatted freely like old friends. Iva learned that Humphrey, an African grey parrot, was given to him in exchange for a payment for a few yards of burlap.

"The poor chap was in dire straits," Bowzer went on. "We made a deal. I got the beak and he got the burlap. The old gal has been with me for years. She was quite young; she's just like my child."

Iva laughed as she listened to the story. Margaret entered the dining room with a freshly baked apple pie and circled the parrot. Humphrey's beady eyes followed Margaret's movements. Her mouth widened as if in a great yawn before she yelled.

"Forgive Margaret. Forgive Margaret! Not used to talking birds, talking birds."

Margaret's face paled as she mumbled, "Jesus, Jesus, it's possessed," and she dropped the pie in the middle of the bowl of potatoes and fled to the kitchen out of breath. She could hear the bird growling like a small dog behind the closed door.

"Dear loving Jesus," Margaret pleaded, "get me through this day unharmed."

FOUR

A FLICKER OF sunlight leaks over the leaves and melts under a bank of clouds, a last kiss of energy before the leaves fall to a new season. The rain is not far off. Iva checks the veranda to see if Old Rose has returned. The cat does not like the rain. She is accustomed to the tricks of Mother Nature, to the kind that interfere with her killings. Iva can make out Rose's shadow coming up the path to the kitchen door where she is standing. The cat races between Iva's legs and scurries to her feeding bowl.

Iva closes the cedar box and places it back on the shelf. She has a picture of Humphrey in the box but does not want to look at it at the moment. The parrot died three days after her master in 1970, poor gal. She had finally run out of words.

The kitchen is getting cooler as Iva wraps herself in another sweater. She can hear the ticking of the old clock in the hall. She waits for the gong to strike but suddenly remembers that it has not been ticking for quite some time. She sees no need to have it repaired as she stands to examine its old face, the fine handicraft of the Roman numerals, the intricate details carved into the oak like lovers who timed their love oh so carefully while only Eden was watching.

Iva learned to tell the time on this clock as a young child. She learned her lessons well from a hard gong in the McLaughlin house.

It was one of the few things she brought with her when she married Cullie Spears. The other furnishings she sold along with the house to a young married couple.

Iva had Bertie move the clock into room number Seven after Bowzer arrived. He claimed it kept Humphrey counting all night and screaming, "Time to get up, time to get up!"

Room number Seven is off the main hall on the upstairs floor. Its wide windows give full permission for the round moon to wander in, keeping it white and searching until dawn. Below its windowsills, in summer, the dahlias picked up what floated down, all its joys and sorrows, its lies and deceit. What tumbled down was from failed lovers, not love itself. There is a difference Iva tells herself. The mighty dahlia would not fall for anything less.

This is the room Iva assigned to Ambrose Kane when he arrived in the cold. He brought with him a south-eastern gale in his dirty shirt. He carried no luggage. He said he was from the deep south of the United States. "Georgia," he cradled the word like a lover's name. "Sailed the waves for a living on a freighter nested at the Louisbourg harbour for a week," he explained.

"Decided to get me some land legs," said Kane. "Some folks told me about the fine cooking here at the inn. I have a few days off to taste for myself." His words whistled through a smile.

Iva stood back and inhaled the turbulent sea air off the man beside the fire. The lean six-foot-two frame could bend like a rope past his empty stomach. His dark eyes landing gentle blows where she hadn't been touched in years.

Who had ever gotten this close to her with one look? She rustled him up a late, leftover dinner when he arrived. He wrapped his large hand around the teacup like a bandage, as though everything he touched in this house had been wounded. The fork slid under his knuckles while he ate the boiled dinner.

He said very few words until the apple pie slid down his throat past the dirty shirt. He avoided table knives completely, did everything with his fork. And he asked about his room.

He followed her up the stairs and into room number Seven. She turned before closing the door and said goodnight. He lay fully dressed on the bed. His hands tucked behind his head with his eyes closed. It was his feet she remembers most. They were bare.

He lodged for six years off and on (whenever the freighter docked) under her clean sheets with his hands tucked under his head when all was said and done.

The next morning he came to the breakfast table bright and early. "There's nothing like taking in the sights of a new day under a dirty sky and a full belly," smiled Ambrose Kane. Iva greeted him warmly.

"I had a lodger here from New England for a week. He left before you arrived."

Ambrose Kane cracked a grin on his unshaven face. "I see the Yankee found you before the Confederate did," he winked at Iva from across the table.

"I have a few Yankees hanging on my own family tree," offered Iva as the kitchen door swung open.

Margaret LaMae's hand shook as she tried to steady the coffee pot. She had not been informed that a man with a dirty shirt was waiting for coffee and a feed of bacon and eggs. Iva scolded Margaret for her clumsiness. Ambrose Kane grinned at Margaret and folded his smile into a gesture of pleasure.

"Mother of God," mumbled Margaret under her breath as she headed for the kitchen with the sting of Iva's remark fresh in her craw. "I should have gotten a job in a coal mine. I've seen nothing yet but a possessed bird with a deranged owner and a man in a filthy shirt with pleasure frothing from his mouth, and Herself smiling like some queen with a tilting crown under this roof."

Ambrose Kane stayed for three days before sailing out again. Returned the second day from sightseeing in a clean wrinkled shirt and spit shiny cowboy boots. He winked at Margaret as he passed the opened kitchen window. Offered up a wave. She caught the scent of fresh spruce on his limbs and a broken twig between his smile.

He introduced himself at the dinner table as Iva sliced a leg off the turkey. She demanded that the bird be brought to the table whole for her to carve.

Ambrose Kane pushed his chair back and held out a rugged hand. Margaret placed her wet palm in his as if she'd passed him a dishrag.

He thanked her kindly for her fine cooking. Margaret looked over at Iva dismantling the turkey limb by limb. It hadn't occurred to her how adept Iva was becoming with a knife. Later Margaret made her way to the kitchen with the leftover turkey carcass that she'd use to make a pot of soup.

FIVE

IT IS PAST seven in the evening and the sky is hawk black. Lightning is scribbling like a mad child against the southern sky. No rain is falling. "A dry storm," Iva grumbles to Old Rose. "There's nothing worse than a dry storm. Always dangerous should it strike without the rain to put out the damage." The cat ignores the sound of Iva's voice and continues to eat from her bowl.

"You can cut in at any time," Iva scowls at the cat. "I'm damn well sure I'm not the only crazy old woman who is loved and courted by fur for affection. All over this bloody world there are women in love with four-legged creatures. Sleeping with them, chasing them like wayward lovers at all hours of the day or night."

The cat lifts its head from the bowl and sways over near her chair. Curls up near Iva's feet. She drops her hand on its head and strokes gently. The old cat purrs into her hand.

"So do you have a voice, my love? Yes you do."

Old Rose follows Iva down the hall to her bedroom. Rain is hitting like machine-gun bullets against the windows to her right, lashing down on the roof of the old house in spades. The windows a silvery blur behind the lace curtains. Iva is thankful for the rain that has begun to fall.

For one fleeting moment she has an urge to call Margaret, to see if she has secured her doors. Against what, she thinks, at their age. She decides against it.

"How much life is left in me to be oozed out should a young man break in?" Iva lingers on the thought. Her smile hardens. "Poor bugger, I hope he'll give me enough time to remember the feeling. Let me dirty my grave with the thought of his young hands at my throat."

She idles beside the old clock and looks towards the stairs. There is nothing up there that she has a desire to stretch her limbs for, or break her bones to get to. She hasn't been up there in a long time. "Why," she questions herself, "is there a need or a want to go climbing the stairs this night?"

Come spring, she will have someone swipe away at the ghosts. Rid her house of their cobweb limbs. Ghosts do leave them behind. She made it a point not to reveal her beliefs to Margaret and have her and Gladys (the cleaning woman) believe she was going religious in the head. She's always known the possibility of the supernatural existed since one of her guests died up there years ago. She hadn't believed in ghosts before all this happened under her roof. Died flat out in all his regalia, her guest had, because he found the peace he was looking for all his life, Margaret informed her. "All Catholics pray for a death like this," Margaret had added.

Iva will have the cleaners wash away the cobwebs until the ghost returns the following year.

She remembers hearing the old clock's gong when they moved it up the stairs and set it down on the landing. *One, two, three* it sang out on the top of the stairs like a nursery rhyme, before they moved it into room number Seven where it remained for years. She must have had it returned to the hall after Bowzer's last visit. It now stands in its original spot with the same time on its face day and night.

Ambrose Kane was oblivious to the twelve gongs the first night they made love in that same room. Iva smiles and speaks as if she were not alone.

He was thirty-six years old when the wind whistled out of his half-buttoned shirt while he stood beside the fireplace of the Tides Inn in 1949. A mixture of dirty heat and arrogance weighed down by a boiled dinner. He paid the full price for Iva's services.

Her mother, Nettie McLaughlin, may not have been so domestically available to a hungry man. Or she may have nibbled when no one was looking. What would she have done had she known how often her husband padded down the hay bin for himself and cousin Opal? She may have used her sharpest knife to slice their hunger.

Six

IVA LAYS HER head against the pillow and pulls up her quilt to just below her chin. She can hear the rain mating with the wind, intoxicating people with the rhythm of their own heart, leaking out like a drum sound under the quilt. Sometimes she will bring colours into her dark room. She played this game as a child before sleep. She always loved yellow. Spread her flowers throughout the darkness as if she were in a moonless garden and identified what lay sprouting at the tips of her fingers by their fragrance. Daisies, irises, daffodils, sunflowers, tulips, wild roses. She could not be fooled by their fragrance.

Iva recalls the yellow streak of taffeta and heavy perfume that showed up on her doorstep during the early summer of 1949. Signed herself in as Miss Esther Neulands. Came rolling in one morning in the mist, lost and blurry-eyed, and parked her new Ford two inches behind Bowzer's old Chev. Claimed she was from somewhere out west. The long drive left her wilted like a dehydrated bouquet of daffodils. She was about sixty and clinging hard to hold onto forty with her expensive creams and lotions. A slippery slope for a woman to cling to, past a certain age, Iva thought when they first met. You can't fool another woman when it comes to the feminine setbacks of the change. Creams and lotions can't fool old age. They just mock it with a certain tell-tale sign.

Iva invited her to the table for lunch. Esther slanted down the stairs from her room facing the ocean. She had changed into a red silk over-sized kimono.

Gold earrings in the shape of a reptile hung from her lobes. She sat across from Bowzer with her back to Humphrey.

Esther Neulands carried her wedding album in her hand and placed it to the left of her plate while she held her hand over the word wedding. She turned slowly and kept a watchful eye on Humphrey.

"That parrot has eyes like the man I just divorced," cried Esther. "Edgar's eyes were so close together, I swear he looked out on the world through a peephole."

A scent of sour rum swept across the table and ambushed Bowzer's nostrils. He snorted lightly before pulling a hanky from his lapel and burying his flat nose deep in its linen fibre. He looked over at Iva who seemed bemused by the woman, but he was rather glad that she stayed away from under the cork. Iva offered Esther a cup of strong coffee and rang the bell for Margaret.

She had to ring the bell twice before Margaret appeared with the coffee pot. Margaret eyed poor Esther slouched over the album, weeping. She believed the distraught woman had lost her beloved husband and was in mourning. She pulled the cup and saucer to the edge of the table and began to pour the coffee as quickly as she could to console her.

Esther Neulands drank the black coffee in loud gulps like the swill of a thirsty pig. Drops leaked down over her silk chest. She glanced over the rim of her cup at the others at the table as if seeing them for the first time. Bowzer threw a dirty look at the woman across from him, assaulting her fine silk with total disregard for its worth.

"Did I mention that the bum left me for an older woman?" Esther Neulands shouted. Bowzer smiled behind his hanky and thought to himself that her husband must have raided an old age home. Esther pounded her fist on the table. Margaret appeared swiftly with the coffee pot and refilled Esther's cup.

Humphrey, who had been quiet, let out a yell. "Left me for an older woman. Ya Ya. Left me for an older woman."

A stunned grimace appeared on Esther's round face. Her dyed blond hair swept upwards into a broken beehive. She sat for a few minutes like a clown gazing at its distorted image in a mirror, as coal black mascara streaked down her face. Her red lipstick clumped in the corner of her mouth as though she were spitting out a half-eaten red berry. Esther Neulands was a woman wrapped in a red flame of silk bursting out of control. She laughed hysterically between puffs of smoke and stared at Bowzer with an evil eye.

"Do you realize that I have not slept or had sex in quite a while?" Smoke curled from her mouth and clouded her face like an image in a dirty mirror. "My doctor suggested I find a quiet environment where I could be lulled to sleep by soft winds and sudden storms," said Esther.

Bowzer coughed up a faint, embarrassed laugh. Iva smiled. Spit flew from Ester's mouth as she spoke.

"People who are deprived of sex and people who don't pray cannot be lulled to sleep." She took another gulp of coffee. "My doctor was wrong," snapped Esther. "Women like me have to be stunned into sleep with a brick to the head or be chemically drugged into slumber."

Humphrey piped in on the conversation, "Deprived of sex. Ya Ya. Don't pray. Drugged into slumber."

Bowzer, who had never grown used to emotionally wrecked women, grabbed his bird and headed for his room. Reared by a single mother and three matronly aunts, Bowzer's affection for misty women had cooled ever since he learned his aunts had set out on a secret mission of salvation to have him collared into the ministry. He left home at an early age and kept on the move. Humphrey screamed as she was led down the hall. "Deprived of sex. Ya Ya. Deprived of sex."

Margaret came through the dining-room door just as Esther's head slumped forward.

"I see," said Bowzer, returning to the table, "that poor Esther has lulled herself to sleep under her own storm," as Margaret and Iva led Esther off to her room by the arms. Her long kimono trailed behind her like a deflated balloon.

She stayed at the inn for a week then left on a sober note with a fresh flask of coffee by her side. As she drove down the road, Iva did not expect to see her again.

SEVEN

IVA CAN HEAR the storm settle outside her bedroom window as Esther Neulands' face fades from her memory. A small wind idles on the windowsill and spins like a child's top before it runs out of steam. She can make out the blur of the half-moon through the window pane. It will be full circle in a few nights. Mother Nature's toy will come bouncing in to play tricks on Old Rose. It will find a spot and have Old Rose reach out to it with her paw and swipe at it to knock it off its moorings. She is quite amused at the antics of Old Rose. The cat swipes playfully, believing she can catch and topple the moon over at will. But it always escapes her.

Iva is glad for the darkness now that clings to her like skin. The darkness will erase the day's beginning and ending. And in her secret garden, the plump bird and its song will soon fly away until spring.

Iva takes on a light scent that has crept up along her quilt and settled itself in its folds. She is sure it is the tangy scent of the lupin. They grew everywhere in Port Murdock. Painting the side roads and ditches as purple as bruises, crawling their way under fences like fierce warriors. The farmers cursed their existence, claiming them to be a poisonous weed for their cows. Iva never grew lupins in her gardens. She always hated the way they ambushed the land, using the wind as an assailant to scatter their seeds. "What would send them into her room on this night?" They have been dead since summer and yet she is alone in a dark space surrounded by the scent of lupins.

Omens never rented any space in her head. They belong to Margaret LaMae and her saints and apparitions, something or someone drifting over from the other side with a message or plea in the form of a lupin. Margaret would believe this one for sure. She always claimed her late mother sent her messages from the beyond through the scent of boiled cabbage in the kitchen.

Once it had even happened at the inn, shortly after Margaret's mother's passing. Iva refrained from asking if it was her pot that her mother was reminding Margaret to bring back home after work, Margaret liked to bring her own cooking utensils to the inn at times.

Poor Margaret, thought Iva. She couldn't risk having her in sobs when dinner was about to be served, so she kept her remarks to herself.

Go back, Ivadoile, go back to your childhood garden! And before she can complete the thought, her hands are in mid-air. She can't control the tremor as if she has just pulled her hands from out of a snowdrift and the pain is one constant sting. She wrings them out like a soft cloth. On the tips of her fingers the fragrance is mellow and cool. The air is fresh with wild roses. She opens her hands to collect them. One or two will suffice. But they are gone as quickly as they bloomed. Only darkness survives. She tucks her shaking cold hands back under the quilt. Iva weeps silently but cannot remember why.

"Is it the scent of wild roses or the scent of blood that catches old fools off guard?" she asks the night darkness in a voice that comes from somewhere in her youth.

EIGHT

A SOFT TATTLETALE BREEZE whispers along the screen on this September morn. Old Rose is meowing at the foot of the bed. Iva rustles out from under her quilt and drops her two feet on the mat. Her toenails have folded over her skin and found a permanent home at the tip of her flesh like an overlapping piecrust. She feels no need to disturb them with a pair of scissors or a file. Women her age should not tamper with sharp objects, she reminds herself.

She moves slowly towards the kitchen and lets Old Rose out the back door before she makes her pot of tea. Iva does not see the car driving down her lane but hears the sound of doors being shut. Two strangers stand beside the car parked in front of her kitchen window. The young woman holds one hand over her forehead to shelter out the sun's glare and surveys the land around her. The man is pointing to something in the distance towards the back clearing.

Old Rose is stretched out on the fence like a floor cloth hung out to dry, her tail hanging down like a torn rag. She watches the couple climb the back steps and ring the doorbell. Iva opens the door with a cup of hot tea in her hand. The man introduces himself and his wife. Iva studies their bland faces. They are older than she thought at a distance. Jehovah Witnesses no doubt. They are plainly dressed.

The woman in a casual brown skirt and buttoned up sweater, the man in light brown dress pants and a long-sleeved beige shirt. They look straight out of a Buckwheat ad. They are rather worn looking. The man has a long chin and eyes the colour of cooked oatmeal. A dark mole has taken growth below his left ear reminding one of a sliding earmuff. The woman has the flat chest of a young girl waiting to bloom. Her long hair slides down her back like dark rain. Her eyes, which are her best feature, are a river of blue. She smiles pleasantly before she speaks.

"We hope we haven't woken you up."

"Something wakes me up every morning," Iva answers, "that's when I realize I am still alive."

The couple laugh nervously as if they were trying to avert a cross dog, to feed it something it would take as a kind gesture.

"You have a lovely piece of property here," the man offers calmly as he looks directly at the old woman in front of him.

Iva stands stone faced with steam rising from her cup of tea like a volcano about to erupt. The woman adds to the conversation, "You have a grand view of the sea."

Iva takes a quick sip of tea. She knows she is being impolite not to invite them in, but she hasn't figured out in her mind what they are looking for here at her door this hour of the morning. She is waiting for one of them to mention Jehovah or Moses and how he walked on the sea like the rising Atlantic and divided the waters, but they do not mention religion. They must think that she still takes travellers because they are not from around here. She cannot place their accents.

"Where are you from?" Iva inquires.

They both answer, "Manitoba," as if they had it rehearsed.

"What brings you here?" Iva does not take her gaze off them.

"We love the ocean," the man replies, "it's so eternal."

"Nothing lasts forever, young man. I am assuming you're looking to buy property down east and someone has directed you to my door."

"We were hoping that we could strike up a deal," says the man, his voice more demanding now that Iva has figured out the reason for their visit. This seems to annoy him because she has not given him time to tell her of their honest intentions.

"At my age there is very little to strike up in me. I don't need the money, nor do I want a change of scenery."

Old Rose jumps off the fence and runs between the woman's legs to get in the door. The woman lets out a startled cry and grabs her husband's arm for support. This amuses Iva as she looks at the woman. "It's not a tiger," she chimes with a sly grin aimed towards the woman.

"I'm not a cat lover. Cats are not my favourite animal," she sighs with a scowl. Iva has seen this scowl on another face, in another time.

"One of the reasons come-from-aways want to buy property by the water is to enhance their sex life," Iva quips in a sharp voice. Old Rose scurries to the kitchen as if she can sense Iva's anger at the woman and her dislike for cats.

The couple stand as still as altar boys caught with church wine on their lips. They are speechless, as though at her age sex should have been long forgotten like a dead relative.

"Do you see that old dilapidated barn over there?" Iva points towards the building. The man and woman turn their heads slowly. The roof of the barn is caved in, giving it the appearance of the letter V. It is ready to come crashing down at any minute.

"It had an adultery bin in it, as many barns around here have," Iva half whispers as if she is running out of breath. The woman is still holding onto the man's arm as she mumbles under her breath, "Make a run for it, Wilfred. She's as mad as a drunken hen."

They hurry down the steps hand in hand without looking back. Ivadoile watches the different shades of brown whirling, darting, drifting further away from her like awkward dancers stumbling off a dance floor.

In the garden Iva can hear the plump bird singing. Its voice is lighter this morning. Perhaps it is saving its strength for its long trip south. Old Rose comes out of the kitchen and twirls at Iva's feet. She picks up the cat and snuggles it in her arms.

"I do believe my father was wearing brown when he made his getaway," she purrs into Old Rose's ear. The cat turns and licks her face as though she were a soft hungry kitten.

NINE

IVA CLOSES THE door and walks back to the kitchen to pour another cup of tea. There was something about that bland couple that looked familiar to her, she tells herself with each sip, especially that cat-hating woman.

The west side of the old barn catches her eye as she sits at the table. It looks like an old silver jewellery box in the morning sun, with its cover falling in. The dancing ballerina is caught somewhere under the collapse. She will never again hear the music, the poor nameless dancer. She is trapped under the fall with her small feet aching to rise one more time to prance on the floorboards with her lover. Perhaps the barn mice gathered as her audience.

Iva reminds herself to call the construction company to bulldoze the barn. A few men from the city have been here already to warn her of its deterioration and the danger of flying debris. They were dressed in suits as they surveyed the barn at a distance. Iva laughed as she watched them decked out in hard hats like official beehives.

"It's beyond repair," said the foreman of the crew as he explained the situation to Iva in her driveway, and she answered the man as quickly as he spoke.

"So am I, young man. Do you see anything on me that could be repaired?" The men smiled to themselves and looked towards the barn.

"I don't think the barn is of any use to you these days," said the foreman. He wrote something down in his notebook. The two others walked towards the car. Iva's mind raced as she looked at the pleasant-faced man in the official beehive. He had a decent look about him, almost innocent in his nervous manner. She could not picture him naked in a hay bin. Where would he place the hard hat? He reminded her of Cullie with his round soft face, his white hand scribbling on a sheet of yellow paper that would make his visit official. He passed her a card with the name and phone number of a construction company.

Iva did not tell the young foreman that she enjoyed watching the barn's demise. She looked for new signs daily, new cracks in its spine to twist and turn it out of shape. Once she had thought of putting a match to the barn but it was too close to the house. Its fiery tongues could reach out and lick at the shingles of her inn if the wind turned direction. Decay would settle the score she had with this barn. She could watch its skin crumble every morning like a corpse in an open grave. The barn where she had seen her father and Opal had been demolished by its new owners and replaced with a smaller workshop. But this barn is the one the music came from, deep down in Ambrose

Kane's lungs. She will not allow her mouth to speak its beautiful words, its slow rhythm. The silhouette image of him and the woman in his arms twirling across the old floorboards as the hay dust filtered their embrace and sealed them into a dusty dome. She never did see the face of the dancer before the woman limped out the back door.

Ambrose Kane whistled his way out of the barn like a rooster at early dawn. He did not see Iva in the shade of the giant maple as he walked towards the kitchen door.

It is hard to know if they are dead or alive, or has she been watching the wrong grave for decay? She has no name to identify the dancer with and, if she did, what could she do to her now? What is the worst name she could saddle her with, especially if she were demented and feeble and spoon fed with soft mush these days? An old woman who could piss herself from the force of a smile is what could be left of the ballerina now. She should have followed her and confronted her when it happened so many years ago.

Iva pulls down the cedar box and rummages through the old pictures. There is one of her with Bowzer and Humphrey perched on his shoulder. They are standing in a field of dandelions with the ocean in the background. Dear Bowzer is smiling like a beauty queen with his arm around Iva. How she loved his visits. She confided in him as she did in no other, and he confided in her. They were soul mates of the mind. It is not often a woman can get a man to agree on everything with her. She knew intellectually that he could not cross barriers without sinking into a reef that she would pull him out of with a gentle tug. He catered to life from one room at a time, a man layered in cloth that he sold by the yard. Perhaps he was a prophet (she smiles) in off-white linen that she could rely on for sentimental responses. He knew her view of religion, he was safe with her.

He spoke very few words to some of the other guests, but took delight in criticizing them to Humphrey behind closed doors.

"Beware of that Confederate, Iva," he warned her over the rim of his wine glass. "He can't be trusted. Damn Confederates, they often mistake the bed for the altar." Iva smiled. They shared the same logic for love.

Humphrey is staring directly into the camera as if it were a loaded gun about to be fired at any minute. She cannot remember who took the picture. Perhaps it was Ambrose Kane himself before he took up barn dancing. He fancied himself quite a snapper behind the lens.

A picture of a couple is tucked inside a yellowed frayed envelope. The letter is addressed to Iva. She studies the picture as Old Rose curls up at her feet.

"Well, I'll be darned," Iva sighs as she stares into the face of Esther Neulands and her new husband, Lud something-or-other. She had written to Iva to let her know they'd be down for a visit to the Tides Inn just after their wedding.

That woman at my door with her hate for cats could be Esther Neulands' granddaughter. Iva believed it could be possible, a relative of some sort, but the woman hadn't mentioned anyone she knew had ever stayed at the inn.

Esther returned to the Tides Inn two years after her first visit, a changed woman with her hair tied back like a grey knot on an old running shoe. She wore no makeup or jewellery, no reptiles hanging from her earlobes. From her dull skin, the pale light of salvation flickered off and on in her river blue eyes. Esther looked anemic to life the second time around.

All colour had bled from her cheeks. She found religion and her sixth husband under a large tent in Flin Flon, Manitoba, she announced in a flat monotone. Her new husband looked like W. C. Fields, rather round with a thick short neck that settled under his collar like a sinking foundation. A black tie protruded from under his heavy chin causing a black shadow effect. He cast a steady eye on Esther whenever she quoted from the Bible at meal time, calling out, "Amen. Amen."

Esther looked around the table as if she were looking for a sacrificial lamb, someone that her husband could test his faith on, like a magician who asks for a volunteer from the audience. *Who would like to be sawed in two and come out whole?*

Lud Tilley asked to be addressed as Reverend Tilley. "Amen. Amen," Humphrey shouted as if in chorus to the reverend.

Ambrose Kane gave Tilley a critical eye on their first meeting. Life was easier living out of someone else's purse, thought Kane. Esther watched Ambrose Kane sum up the man at her sleeve. She could sense her husband's uneasiness. Reverend Tilley kept his tongue light, stayed away from religion while the Confederate was around.

The Reverend dropped his hand between his knees and gave himself a rude scratch. Bowzer waited for Reverend Tilley to fire up, but the man remained cautious around

Ambrose Kane. Iva turned her face towards the window. Outside the day was folding like a grey blanket over the gardens. One last stem of colour trembled and was lost.

"Be not afraid," cried Reverend Tilley over a bowl of Margaret's homemade chicken soup the next day, as if by chance it may contain poison and he could dilute the poison with his faith.

"Be not afraid, not afraid, not afraid," chirped Humphrey, flapping her wings as though she knew the soup was safe and wholesome.

Bowzer turned to the reverend with an amusing glance but spoke not a word. He watched as Humphrey eyed the people, her head turning to each voice.

Reverend Tilley slurped down his soup and asked for a refill and more bread. Iva rang the bell for Margaret's services. A disgruntled Margaret whisked the empty soup bowl and bread basket off the table.

"More soup, more soup, more bread," Humphrey called out as if speaking to Margaret directly.

"That bird comes in handy," noted the reverend, turning his thick neck towards Humphrey.

Esther looked at her husband and spoke in a hushed tone. "You've had three bowls already, Lud. There are others at the table."

Reverend Tilley turned sharply and stared at his pale wife. "Pray tell woman where on the mighty slab does it say 'Thou shalt not eat'?"

Iva studied Esther's weary face. The fat man beside her was a dribbling, gorging imposter. Reverend Tilley wrote his own bible and placed Esther where his shrinking violet worked best, in his bed. Her flame for life was burnt out. Her breasts sagged and her nipples shrank like water in a dehydrated puddle. Her eyes were cast downward, as if she were watching herself turning inward, away from the world in shrinking silence.

Iva excused herself from the table and made a quick exit to the kitchen where Margaret was filling up the soup bowl with a heavy ladle. "Do not bring that bowl to the table!" Iva commanded. "I will tell that leech that the pot is empty." Margaret smiled. "Good enough. What do you expect from a pig but a grunt?" Margaret stood behind the kitchen door as Iva went back into the dining room.

"The soup pot is empty, Reverend," announced Iva in a firm and fixed voice as she took her seat at the table and looked him squarely in the eye. Esther stared down at her empty bowl and did not look up as Reverend Tilley stood abruptly and ordered his wife to leave the table with him. Esther followed closely behind like a child whisked from a birthday party before the treat bags were given out. Iva could hear him mumbling as they walked up the stairs to their room.

Esther had requested room number Four when they arrived a week earlier. She said she'd remembered it from her first visit. The childlike doll in the white wicker reminded her of a doll she once owned, she explained, while her husband sniffed the aroma of the turkey roasting in the oven.

Iva could sense what was to come as the couple entered their room at the top of the stairs as she and Bowzer exchanged glances.

Margaret entered the dining room with a Boston cream

pie with its thickly piled cream puffed up like a cloud balanced carefully in her two hands. She placed it in the centre of the table before she realized that Esther and Reverend Tilley had left the dining room. Silence followed as all eyes descended on the cloud that dropped before them. Bowzer's lips cracked into a sarcastic grin that spread across his face before he spoke.

"I hope the mighty slab doesn't fall on this pie before we indulge." Iva laughed as she looked towards the stairs. "Mighty slab, mighty slab, thou shalt not eat!" Humphrey chanted as if she had learned a new rhyme.

Margaret, unaware of the reference to Reverend Tilley, scurried off to the kitchen. She sat beside the window with a cup of hot tea before finishing up for the day. She wondered why Ambrose Kane was not present for dinner. She had made his favourite pie. It mattered not to her what went down the gullet of that wretched Reverend Tilley. She was warming up to Bowzer, the dear soul, and hoped to add a pound here and there to his slight frame. The bird she could boil in a pot every time it startled her. She figured Reverend Tilley left the table because of Iva's insistence that the soup pot was empty.

Poor Esther, thought Margaret, she made a more colourful drunk than the pitiful wife of that man. If only that dear man Angelo Pinotti had been here at this time. He could have tamed her heart into doing the right thing.

Behind door number Four, Reverend Lud Tilley—car salesman, rodeo clown, ranch hand, bible thumper—opened the buckle of his belt and made his wife turn to face him. What Esther saw when she turned her attention away from the doll was an elaborate swell of white flesh like rising soft bread dough left too long in a bowl. A crude scar ran across his belly from a knife wound. Reverend Tilley took delight in the fact that it had healed in the form of a two-headed snake. A tattoo he earned as a child from his drunken stepfather. Reverend Tilley laughed at the fear in his wife's eyes. "Come on now, Esther, I know you like playing with dolls."

Esther walked slowly towards the man she both feared and hated. He gloated as he held her delicate chin in his rough hand. A flower about to be ripped from its stem. The doll sat very still but kept her green eyes fixed on the white flabby flesh. That's all a doll can do. Watch from a distance. Esther knew that a long time ago. Reverend Tilley had trained the two-headed snake well for hateful bitches who lied to him the same way his mother did. The image of Ivadoile Spears's face cracked like a puzzle in front of him.

"A tooth for a tooth," snarled the reverend as he threw himself down heavily on top of his wife. Esther looked up from over his shoulder as the two-headed snake dropped its venom with savage bites on her breasts, her stomach, between her thighs. Only the doll heard her cries for help. Through the window Esther watched as a lonely white cloud swam over the tree tops and drowned as she followed her pain into a dark slumber.

But the doll watched as the naked and angry Reverend Tilley threw their clothes into an old suitcase. Angry men don't fold well. Esther's clothes went in first. They had been neatly hung on crocheted hangers in the armoire. He dressed in a hurry and pulled Esther from her deep slumber. She staggered from the suddenness of it all, then dressed quietly and took small steps towards the door before stopping and looking back at the doll. For a moment she thought of taking it with her, of hiding it under her coat. But a reverend's wife could not steal. She never knew the doll's name was Victoria and that she too had never been loved.

Iva watched them leave under a sepia coloured sky. The light of the day swallowed up by the dust, heaved in the air by a gust of wind. She was happy to see him leave. She knew he would not step foot on her property again.

She would not permit it and Lud Tilley had gotten the message through her eyes. The rodeo clown knew sad from happy, hate from love.

Iva tried to get Esther's attention. To get her alone for a few minutes would have been all she needed to encourage her to stay. But Esther did not rear her head even for a second as Reverend Tilley paid the bill in silence.

Bowzer was in the parlour with his nose pressed between *The Sound and the Fury*. He looked up as Iva entered the room.

"Is the bastard gone?" asked Bowzer, closing Faulkner like a prayer.

"Indeed, but I couldn't get Esther's attention. He wouldn't leave her side. He knew very well I'd say or do something to get her to leave him."

"If I had to live with it, I'd kill it in a flash!" cried Bowzer in a high, shaky voice. "We should have cornered Esther alone and told her what she was in for with that man."

"Kill it. Kill it in a flash. Bastard gone," scowled Humphrey from behind the wingback chair. Gossip was at its best between fact and fiction. Humphrey pecked like a type-writer for the sound of a word in this room full of books.

"He has her brainwashed. You saw how broken she was the first day they arrived, Bowzer."

"And he has her money, Iva. She was ripe for the picking when she went into that tent. The heart has no respect for willpower."

Iva looked out at the dusty afternoon floating over her garden. Behind her, she could hear Humphrey pecking at her cage. Cornered into her little world but loved, smothered with gossip and affection, she was luckier than many females. A flock of dusty crows flew overhead. Perhaps Esther had seen them too and wondered in which direction her freedom would land.

TEN

IVA NOTICED THE lone figure as she walked awkwardly up the lane, stopping to rest along the way. A slab of sharp wind lifted her blue skirt several inches revealing one long slim leg and the other concealed in an iron brace.

Violet Summers came out of the dust in the summer of 1954 and returned to it two months later. Her real name was Philomena O'Grady, but when she developed polio as a child of four, she began to soften things in her life. Her name was the first thing she changed. She'd arrived at the Tides Inn for a purpose she told Ivadoile when she hobbled up the steps with a light suitcase in hand and tapped gently at the door.

"I'm just off the train," explained Violet in a slight Irish lilt. "I wanted some sea air in my lungs so I headed for Nova Scotia. My parents are used to me taking off here and there without a peep. They live in Toronto and are fine with me tramping around the globe as long as I keep in touch."

Iva invited the young woman in. Violet asked if she could sit near a window to get a view of the great garden. Iva directed Violet Summers to the parlour while she checked her registration list. Bowzer turned to greet the young woman in the blue full skirt and soft sweater. He smiled as she limped to the window overlooking the garden and sat down.

"Lovely isn't it?" Violet commented as her large eyes filled up with the colours that stretched in rows towards the back field. She turned and held out her hand to Bowzer. "I'm Violet Summers and you are someone else."

Bowzer smiled at the plucky young girl. "Call me Bowzer, and this feathered female is Humphrey, my parrot. Be careful, she'll remember any secrets you let loose."

"Will she now?" The young woman gave a strong hearty laugh as she looked over at Humphrey. "Looks quite harmless to me there in her own little braced up quarters. I'm rather fond of parrots myself."

The parrot listened to the new voice in silence before repeating, "Fond of parrots myself. Fond of parrots." Violet Summers applauded Humphrey and threw her a kiss. "Aren't you the smart one, little parrot!"

Iva came into the room carrying a tea tray and sat it on a side table beside the young woman. She noticed the strange pallor of Violet Summer's skin in the light from the window. Her long rusty red hair was tied back from her face. A few loose strands seemed to grow wildly out of her neck. Physical beauty had not settled on her from the neck up. Her high cheek bones gave her face a crude chiselled look under a blemished complexion. A long sharp nose bridged like a bolt of lightning, ran down her face, and dipped partially over her top lip. Her pale blue eyes were alert, daring.

Violet's thin body coaxed life out through the fibres of her skin. She knew its graces. Even her limp would make one imagine that she was about to curtsy to you at any moment. Her long thin fingers reached out like a wing. Despite her physical affliction, she graced each room like a gentle bird pausing to rest.

Violet settled into the big chair with her cup of tea. Bowzer pulled the footstool close to her braced leg and watched as Violet swung it up slowly without looking down at her display. The leg dropped into the fabric without a sound. Violet's eyes searched the room as if it were a place she already knew. Already loved. Her muscles depended on comfort. At this point in her life, her therapy lay in sturdy fabric and warm hearts. She knew she would like it here. They had already warmed up to her.

She smiled at Bowzer who was emotionally available to women in need of company. He would not touch them, Violet knew. He was a gentle philanderer and from his cocoon this gentleness that he could render to women was open and innocent. Violet noticed Iva's curious eyes on her. Her questions sealed behind her lips.

Here was a woman who needed questions answered, Violet realized, yet Ivadoile Spears was a solitary companion to her own mind. Woman instinctively knew these things about other women. She had perfected the loneliness of her being. It lay angled in the shape of the room, the curvature of her mouth. She was suspicious of anything that got close to it. The essence of it all cornered so that one had to look outside to catch its real beauty in the hands of the wind teasing her magnificent gardens. The woman depended on the beauty around her for pleasure.

Did she walk to the inn from the train station, Iva wondered. *How old was Violet Summers? How did she afford to travel alone with her handicap? Why had she not taken a taxi to the inn?*

Violet let Iva ponder her thoughts for a while as she sized up the pretty blond lady who sat across from her, as braced in as she herself. Her ring finger was empty. Had it ever been escorted into marriage? She had to be in her thirties with the fashion her body adapted to. A long slim-fitting skirt supported by a blouse with a lace collar. A corset, no doubt, sucking into her flesh and living off her sweat. Are there any hands available to sink into the after flow when her skin is unleashed? Perhaps she had been on an outing, a doctor's visit or bank business, because she is not the type that will be harnessed in by a spinster's attire. There is more to this woman, much more than she reveals to formality. She is aware of each thread she bears.

Violet reached down and unlaced her high black shoe, removed her brace and placed it beside the footstool. She unfolded her thin stocking and curled it into a ball. A small white foot sat like a knuckled fist on the stool as she placed her good foot beside it. It was perfectly formed, a strong stem of white flesh turning pink in the flush of the afternoon sun. Violet Summers introduced herself from her deformity up. It was a game to her now. It gave her possibilities and strength. It drew attention away from her face.

What she had yet to tell Iva and Bowzer was that on these two mismatched feet she had travelled the world. Stood back in the shadows of the great mountains. She had tapped her good foot to the beat of Africa's drums, watched the newly crowned queen wave from her balcony. She was told the queen's feet were quite small. Violet had stepped lightly into other people's rivers and left her uneven footprints on distant shores. The Nile was her favourite.

And yet, when she looked down at her feet, she forgot about these places. They had not yet done what she wanted from them. And her journeys were coming to an end.

ELEVEN

IVA IS STARTLED by what sounds like thunder rolling down her lane, so close to the ground she believes she is in line for an attack. It is eight in the morning. Fog is rising and falling in the back fields to sip at the tips of the budding blooms. Old Rose is hiding under the cot in the kitchen. This is the only way Iva can tell that her hearing is still intact. She cannot coax the cat out for breakfast so she slides the bowl under the cot. Old Rose does not move.

The aloof looking morning thunders on until its shapes and voices emerge. Iva remembers now that she had called the demolition company to demolish the old barn. "Crazy woman can't tell anymore if yesterday turned over into today. A good hurricane would have sent the barn flying over Port Murdock," Iva sighs.

As the fog lifts, she can see a large boom being hoisted from the back of the truck. A young man appears on her step and taps loudly on the kitchen door. Old Rose rushes past Iva towards the stairs. "It's not World War Three for Christ's sake," Iva screams at the flying cat scrambling for cover.

The young man, in his thirties, bids her good morning with a daring grin on his tanned face. "We should have everything cleared up by the end of the day," he informs Iva. He is a good looking man with strong bones and teeth. A local no doubt, Iva believes by the sound of his accent. Perhaps the man is a returned soldier from one of those foreign countries in Asia and is willing to tear things down. Get it out of his system one way or another.

"You should stay inside," he adds, "because of flying debris."

"I wasn't planning on lowering the boom, young man. Be sure you don't topple that big maple beside the barn!" Iva warns him.

"I'll pass the word, Madam," he smiles as he walks away from the door to join the others.

Iva takes her tea into the parlour and opens up the drapes. She is assaulted by dust as she sits close to the window. There is something about the urgency of dust and rubble surrounding young men, their voices calling through it, the orders given and received through its haze, the way it sneaks into pores and makes its home in their open skin. Iva strains to hear the excitement in their voices.

"Move it more to your fucking left!"

"Move your grandmother, you stupid bastard!" a different voice cries back. Iva smiles at the dirty threats rising up to her window. This language would not have been deemed proper on the McLaughlin property unless it was used for sex in the barn, or the going away of a husband. "*Bastard!*" curled on her mother's lip that day and never left. Whenever her mother spoke after that day she always had to pass that word. She died with it on her mouth, the way her lip drooped.

Boards fly through the air like dead limbs and land with a crackling thud. The sun makes an appearance. The men appear and disappear in the swirls of debris like dancers in smoky fog.

Boom.

Boom.

Boom.

Iva can see the skeletal remains of the barn now. The men have come close to its bare bones. Silence rests in the dust as they stop for lunch. She can see them moving around the old stacked wood, removing their hard hats and leaning their sturdy backs against the trucks as they tilt their thermoses back and drink deep.

The sun is eloquent on their bare dusty arms. A couple of them remove their shirts to flex their muscles. They pour water from drinking jugs down their backs and shiver from the thrill of it running like a cool waterfall down their spines. They bend over and place both hands on the ground and suck in their stomachs as if half expecting someone to sprawl beneath them and sip from their dripping navels.

They have placed themselves in dangerous positions, these boys. Iva cannot tell from her window how old they really are at this stage in their lives. She has an urge to call out a warning to them, but restrains herself. They would look at her with pity in their eyes. She will not stand for that.

"You must not interfere with their youth," she scolds herself, "not with your squeaking voice and withering old frame." In their state of sexual anticipation they would never believe that you were even aware of their conquests or that the first time Ambrose Kane made love to you behind room number Seven, sprawled under him like that, you felt your flesh separate from your bones and your bones being flushed from you through the healthiest wound you had ever let open.

It rained that night and you opened your mouth to the possibility of a raindrop, but they would never believe that at all. They might believe that you are talking about a laxative. The young fools, they more than likely imagine they've invented this play themselves. It was never a game people excelled at back in the old days.

A few of them point to something in the heap of wood as a flock of barn swallows take flight. They have disturbed their nests, unearthed something that lay deep within its old walls for safety. There are other secrets that have been demolished, but they know nothing of this either. The invisible dancer has lost her throne. It has gone to dust like everything else. They watch as the birds fly off in uneven directions darkening the sky with streaks of fury.

The men are back to work now, hoisting the old boards like toothpicks into dumpsters. The bare-backed men have put their shirts back on. It is early summer. They still have time to deepen their skin to any shade they choose. Iva wonders if they are turning brown to attract women. Cullie Spears was white as chalk, except on the day he asked her to be his wife. He turned pink with blisters then peeled back to white. He never turned brown, because something in his pigment forbade it, he explained. Iva stayed out of the sun. She saw no need to turn as dark as her father.

Ambrose Kane wrapped his brown summer skin around the dancer's waist and held her hand gently as they twirled. He and Iva danced this way when the inn was empty, around and around the living-room floor. Iva always preferred the waltz, the grip and tremble in his arms sealed what was to follow. A song without words can always be heard by a lover.

"Damn them!" Iva's voice hurts when she growls in the empty kitchen. "Damn the ballerina and Ambrose Kane for disturbing the swallows like that just for a dance and who knows what else. There must have been swallows in the barn that day."

The men have cleared away the boards and are rolling something along the ground to pick up the rotting nails as Iva checks out the vacant space. The maple tree bloomed early this year and looks much bigger.

She can see down the lane to where the sign hung for more years than her memory can hold onto. Beside the empty space lies the path Ambrose Kane took on the last day she laid eyes on him, its lush sides tunnelled in by heavy lilacs.

The lilacs had begun to fade when he left and were dropping their petals to the ground. A purple path escorted him away. She has never crossed the mouth of that path since, just watches the activity of the seasons fall upon it and do their duty; strip it bare in winter and colour it again in spring, until summer drops in and lends her colours to the fray.

Iva turns her attention to the young man approaching

her door. She greets him with a smile as he hands her a paper to sign to verify that the job is complete. "I hope we didn't cause too much of a hassle for you, Mrs. Spears."

"What kind of a hassle were you planning, young man?" she asks. The man smiles as he leaves and thanks her.

"I'll have the boss hassle you with the bill."

"By the way, young man, did you see the swallows?" He turns to face her again.

"We scared them off, there were young ones amongst the flock. I don't think we destroyed their nest. All their eggs would have been hatched by this time."

For a brief moment Iva can see a flicker of sympathy in his eyes, the kind that he might use on his grandmother if he had destroyed something meaningful to her.

He reaches out to touch her hand as if to reassure her that the birds are safe. But she is not worrying about the swallows. She knows they will return. They always do. She has something else she wants to ask him, but she cannot remember what it is at the moment. It is too late when the question comes back into her head.

"Where in the hell am I storing all these questions?" she asks Old Rose as she comes out of hiding. Iva opens the kitchen door and stands facing the lane. The empty path is in full view. There would have been no use asking the young man if he had seen a man with lilac dust on his feet. She is glad she didn't bother him with this question.

The last of the trucks has gone, leaving only a distant hum behind them. All the young men have left Iva alone on the veranda searching the path, but there is no one to be seen in the purple distance.

TWELVE

"DO YOU REMEMBER" when you had Bertie, Lord rest his soul, put up a swing in the old barn, Ivadoile, because you didn't want children hanging from your trees like monkeys?" Margaret LaMae is slightly out of breath as she looks out at the empty space through Iva's kitchen window.

"I never did tell you this, Ivadoile, but Bertie called me over from the clothesline where I was hanging out the dishcloths and asked me to try out the swing for him."

Iva is amused at the excitement in Margaret's voice. The childlike quality it evokes as she surveys the spot where the barn once stood. Everything sounds like a fairy tale as she hops through the past.

"He wanted me to make sure it was secure before the kids came swinging on it."

"He should have swung you to the altar, Margaret. You two spent a lot of time together."

Margaret blushes deeply before she responds. "Dear no, there wasn't anything like that going on. Bertie was a gentleman."

"Gentlemen can be boring, Margaret. Women would have nothing to argue with if they were so damned perfect. I was married to one of them. He was aroused by the sound of a cricket chirping in spring. I hate crickets."

Margaret takes a deep breath. She knows Ivadoile is prying her way into something that is none of her business. She sips her tea slowly and faces her directly.

"There are worse things in life than celibacy, Ivadoile," Margaret interjects hoping she will not probe into her private life.

"Name them, Margaret!"

"You know what I mean, Ivadoile." Margaret is aware of that look of determination in Iva's eyes. She wanted an answer for everything. "At our age, Ivadoile, I see no need for this conversation. We are not likely being sought out for marriage or anything of the sort."

"Who is talking about marriage, Margaret? I'd go to the electric chair before I'd get into the destruction my parents called marriage. They should have shot each other to even the score."

Iva smiles as Margaret seeks out the peacefulness of the bright day outside the kitchen window to avoid her look. She knows that Iva has once again caught her off guard like a teacher sneaking up on a student, checking out their invisible homework. Or does she already know what the invisible words will reveal?

"You don't know what you have missed, Margaret."

"Well in that case I have nothing to compare it to, like you having been married to such a nice man as Doctor Cullie. He was never boring to his patients."

"I was not one of his patients, Margaret."

Iva gets up to let Old Rose in through the kitchen door. The cat meows and goes over to her bowl. Margaret is happy for the distraction, but annoyed at herself for even bothering to pay her a visit. But she knows she must because it is only Iva who can forgive her for the secret she carries.

Iva returns to the table with the teapot in hand and refills the cups. That look is still in her eye like a beacon searching its target. There is a deep cut in the conversation between them. Whose voice will dive in for what must be added to this visit?

Iva sits down across from Margaret and looks directly at her. "Did I ever tell you how my husband died, Margaret?"

"I know the man had a bad heart for some years. He worked too hard." Margaret removes a hanky from under her sweater cuff. The kitchen is getting too warm.

"He died after having sex, Margaret. Can you imagine how that could have been worded on a death certificate?"

Margaret swipes at her brow before saying another word. "I don't think I have heard about that being a cause of death."

"I should know, I was the one he was having it with for eight years right up to his last gulp. It's a killer alright. He died with his tongue hanging out like a stunned ram. Don't blame me, I didn't ask for it. That's probably what kills most men. There was more than one bite taken out of the apple. Adam means man in anyone's religion."

Margaret drops her cup awkwardly on the saucer and watches her tea swirl in the cup. She is not quite sure why Iva is sharing this personal information with her on this day. Margaret is baffled by this outburst.

"I believe that is your personal business, Ivadoile. One does not have to share everything." Iva ignores Margaret's comments. At her age, she'll say what she wants.

"Imagine that, Margaret, cause of death, sex. I would have had that framed and hung up on a wall like wallpaper if they'd written it up with the real reason for his death. The guests would have loved that bit of information."

Margaret is aware that she is aggravating her into a response. She cannot bellow now about a work related matter after all these years.

"Bowzer nearly fell over when I told him the story. He said I was incorrigible. He called me Mae West. So did Humphrey." Iva smiles as she imitates the parrot. "Mae West. Mae West. Incorrigible."

Margaret shakes her head as if a crazy dream had lodged in it and is stopping her from waking up. At Iva's age, she should be talking about gout or rheumatism. She ought to be put away in a nursing home for going on about things like she does. Three sweaters on in July, it's no wonder Iva is overheated, Margaret thinks to herself as she watches the smug look on Iva's face. The foolish woman is going senile. She never used language of the sort before. They say senility loosens the tongue. Before too long Iva's tongue is going to hang out like a belt if she keeps this up.

"Would you have any Tums, Ivadoile? I have a burning in

my throat." Margaret realizes she is having a bout with stress. She always lets Iva get to her.

"I never get indigestion, Margaret. It's bad for your heart. You ought to be careful. You could end up in the nursing home. They'll never get me in one," Iva continues. "They're nothing but reform schools for old people. Reform you to this. Reform you to that," Iva comments, passing a roll of unopened Tums to Margaret. "Old age is a nuisance to these people. I'd rather wash my own arse like a cat than have them do it for me."

Margaret rattles three or four Tums between her teeth as Iva continues to ramble. Her head is splitting in two, the longer Iva goes on.

"I'll say one thing for Cullie, he was better at dying than he was at sex. At least with death he completed the act."

Margaret swallows deeply and coughs as she fumbles for her cane on the back of the chair.

"I must get going, Ivadoile. I have my wash to take in from the clothesline." She lets out a sigh as she moves towards the door. "I'm feeling much better now."

Iva watches Margaret's small figure turn at the end of the lane. She resembles a small child trudging along with a stick looking for a summer puddle to dip into. The road she walks on is hard and dry as a sore thumb. Few people make their way out here anymore.

Iva calls a taxi to go into town for her groceries and things needed for wasting limbs. She lost her driver's license ten years earlier due to speeding. Nobody can say they see her face appearing in malls or churches. She keeps herself well-oiled so as not to be seen in a doctor's office jammed with people with superficial ills looking for a cure for death from some son of a bitch who fears it himself.

Margaret has disappeared from her view. She always has a reason for coming and going. Iva is the only reason she has available in her closing-down years. She is handy. It is good for her circulation, giving her a cause for an extra-long walk each week. She doesn't need her cane for anything but to swipe at cross dogs and pesky cats that try and curl at her ankles like a charm bracelet. Rose ignores her. She is used to the scent of old age. Margaret's lungs get a workout as well. She merely has to open her mouth and let the salt air rush in and disinfect any bacteria hiding in them. She believes in these remedies.

"Poor Margaret is full of indigestion and Tums," Iva confides to Old Rose. "She was always troubled by one thing or another. She will return like the swallows to claim her nest. Poor Margaret, she is the only one who has not abandoned me."

Something swells up in Iva's chest like a balloon in a turbulent sky. It is hard to let go of the sweet agony it expels through her lungs. It has a life all its own, calling out names and events, even footsteps. Her father was silent when he walked away. Yet something has put a noise under his feet this day. There is gravel crunching, pebbles being scattered about.

There was a dull thud when he dropped his suitcase to shift it to his other hand. She remembers them as if she has heard them for the first time. Ambrose Kane took the soft path. Lilac petals do not scream. His going away was silent.

Margaret is nearing her own house before she realizes that she is still holding the roll of Tums in her hand. She stuffs them into her sweater pocket hoping to stuff out Iva's foul mouth as well.

Iva is starting to sound like Gladys who died from all that smoking. But Gladys had a likeable heart. It was her lungs she darkened. Iva won't miss the Tums, she has no heart that needs repair.

Margaret's house is cool when she enters. She looks over at the stack of folded clothes she had taken in from the clothesline and ironed before she paid Iva a visit. Margaret busies herself putting away her wash. The top drawer of her dresser is where the picture is secretly hidden. Ambrose Kane smiles up at her. A perpetual smile. The picture was taken a few months before he disappeared. Margaret had to be very careful when she removed it from the trash. Noise would have betrayed her. She waited until only the wind whispered under her feet before she slipped Ambrose Kane's picture into her handbag and carried him home.

THIRTEEN

THEY ARE BOTH smiling broadly in the picture. Violet Summers and Bowzer. Wildflowers rushing up behind them like a wave. They are clowning for the pose. They never exposed their serious side of life to the camera. They lied to it with a smile. It is only now that Iva can expose the truth of it all, after their deaths.

Violet Summers was twenty-five years old when she came to the Tides Inn with her thin arms bruised and hidden away in a tunnel of long sleeves.

"I'm in remission," said Violet as she pushed up her sleeves exposing the point of entry for the needles that pricked her skin, carrying liquid hope one drop at a time. They were sitting in the parlour drinking lemonade that Margaret had made extra sweet for Violet, whom she wanted to fatten like a goose. She had been at the Tides Inn for three weeks with no intention of leaving until she was forced to leave for treatment.

"These two skinny arms are my lifelines for blood transfusions," said Violet as her smile soured with a tinge of despair. Bowzer's mouth curled as he looked away from her bony limbs. He had never learned to comfort regret with regret. He spoke not a word. It was Iva who asked the questions and got the answers.

Leukemia had been lurking through her blood for a year like a polluted river, she confessed.

"The only time I pay heed to it is when the bloody needles try to flood it out. My parents are doctors and I have received the best of care. I'm their only offspring, if you can imagine that for the Irishman." Violet laughed with an introduction of sadness in her voice. "I got tired lying around the house," she moaned. "If we lie down long enough we'll all die from some horizontal exposure to life, you know."

Bowzer stared out the back window with his empty glass in his hand. Humphrey swung back and forth on her wire swing and chanted, "We will die, we will die," like a mad crusader charging into battle unarmed.

Bowzer tapped on the parrot's cage as if to shut her up, but Violet came to her rescue. "Let her be! I think it's rather amusing that the truth comes from such an unlikely source."

Humphrey bellowed as if she had just learned a new verse, "Let her be. Let her be."

Violet laughed as she poked her finger into the cage to stroke Humphrey's crown. "Pretty girl, yes you are a pretty smart girl."

"Pretty smart girl," Humphrey repeated as if she were talking to Violet alone.

Iva watched as the young woman walked back to her chair beside the window to rest her braced foot on the stool. There was no denying her fierce determination and intelligence, but Violet's body was shrinking closer to her bones daily. Her pace had slowed. She ate less. She verbally offered what her body had already told them.

She was very fond of the net of people that had cast her in. They let her explore, expose the wounds she carried in her blood. They were, she knew, all part of the wound by now. Iva carried it in her subtle affection towards her. She was careful not to touch her. This would have been too visible in the light of day. She only touched in the dark. Bowzer coveted like a gentle bird around her with his wings spread out, and hid his tears in an empty glass. Dear Margaret, with her old soul in her young body, touched outwardly and held Violet's thin shoulders like delicate lace that needed mending.

Bowzer, who had spoken not a word, spoke up in spades in a nervous flurry. "No more doom and gloom. I won't hear of it." He tapped on his glass for attention and more lemonade. "My dear Violet," he exclaimed as he twirled around the chair and stood directly in front of her, "when I was your age my partner left me for an African lion tamer. I lay on my back and wailed for two weeks like a night owl. Whooo-whooo-whooo."

Bowzer drew a deep breath and continued. "It got me nothing but a pair of red eyes and bags to go with them. I looked like I peeled onions for a living."

Violet laughed uncontrollably. Humphrey spun in circles in her cage as if she were being attacked by a mad assailant. Margaret appeared in the doorway to see who had taken a seizure. She knew that Violet Summers was not well.

"Do you know what I did, Violet, to get back on my feet?" Bowzer asked as Violet shook her head back and forth. "I took up tap dancing." Bowzer began to prance around the room tripping over his feet as he fell to the centre of the floor like a red oak.

Violet applauded Bowzer once again. It was a performance Violet understood completely. He needed to throw life off track in order to get back on again. It wasn't easy for him. The death of his mother and then his partner, when the lion tamer turned his back. And now Violet's impending death lay sleeping in her twenty-five-year-old veins. White on red flowing into a river that left no footprints. There were just her eyes left to close for the finale. Death was just a snooze away. Iva watched Bowzer's face carefully. She knew the strain that lived behind those lids.

Iva called for dinner to be served in the parlour that evening for the three of them. Margaret gave Bowzer the once-over look and realized he was as sober as a judge. She blessed herself when she got back to the kitchen. She was overworked, she believed. She could have sworn he was under the cork.

Violet would not have to get up from her chair by the window to have dinner. The dancer could rest her two left feet. Iva opened the window to let the evening breeze escort all the day's doom and gloom out of the room. She opened the drapes fully. Colourful flowers waved themselves in. They grew like giant spiders along the walls. Iva ordered a bottle of white wine that swam its way up to the rim of the glasses through a tide of small bubbles. They held glasses high and toasted the present with a round of good cheer and left the future to linger for a time around the corners of Port Murdock.

Through the open window, Humphrey's voice rose with a greeting of "Cheers!" before settling somewhere in the secret garden.

FOURTEEN

SOMEONE ELSE NOTICED the red and white war going on in Violet Summers' blood in the beautiful summer of 1954. Noticed the uneasy current pulling her downstream. You cannot fool a river man, an open sea man. They can spot trouble with the first ripple.

Ambrose Kane watched the dark half-moons rising under her eyes, heard her breathing strained and incomplete as a broken dialogue. She sat with him in the morning on the long veranda while Iva was giving orders in the kitchen and Margaret was taking them.

They smiled as they listened to the kitchen squabbles. Words floated around the corner of the veranda and dissolved mid-air like mist. Bowzer and Humphrey left earlier to visit a couple of tailor shops in town. A few of the other guests were rock collecting along the seacoast.

"Her bark is worse than her bite," Ambrose Kane's voice whistled like a song. "She's a mighty complicated lady. Love is never too far from its complications."

"Then I gather she hasn't bitten you yet," Violet smiled back at him.

"Believe me, Miss Violet, Margaret is queen of the kitchen. She pretends to take orders in there. It will all come out in the stew. They are more like sisters than they realize just yet."

They both laughed at the tug of war between pots and pans. Ambrose Kane turned his attention to the young girl.

"What about yourself, Violet Summers? What would you like to take a swing at?"

For a moment Violet was silent. She turned to catch his side profile, its uncanny familiarity, his dark hair clouding his gaze, his ability to stare through it with his mind. They did their best thinking behind a bank of hair. She expected his next words to come back to her with an Irish brogue. It could have been her father sitting beside her at the moment. Ambrose Kane lowered his voice as most people do around the dying.

What is it they want her to hear, Violet asked herself.

She had not given up her daring. She bent over and tightened the brace on her foot.

"Margaret tells me there is a swing in that barn," Violet spoke as she looked over at the big open double doors.

Ambrose Kane turned to face Violet. "Yes there is. I can't say I tried it, but I did see it sitting there as empty as a new moon."

"I don't really want to swing," said Violet, as Margaret came around the corner with two tall glasses of iced tea. She passed a glass to Violet and tapped her on the shoulder. "Drink up, it's good for what ails you."

Ambrose Kane bid Margaret a good morning and thanked her in a long southern drawl. Margaret disappeared as quickly as she had appeared.

"I've never danced with a man, not a real dance," Violet announced over the rim of her glass. Iced tea dribbled down her chin giving her the appearance of a melting snow angel in a white cotton dress. "I've travelled everywhere I could dig my heels into on this planet. It was my parents' wish that I see the world. They never mentioned dancing."

Ambrose Kane caught the determination in her eyes, the urgent request from her soft voice.

"I believe I have a remedy for that," smiled Kane. She watched him as he stood and knelt down on one knee at her feet. "Miss Violet, will you give me the honour of dancing with you at three in the afternoon when I return from town?"

The snow angel chuckled from behind her glass. "I sure will, Mr. Kane, and I want you to keep this a secret between you and me. You will find me near the swing."

Margaret LaMae did not eavesdrop on Violet Summers and Ambrose Kane's conversation on her way to the shed. She just listened. She was the fly on the wall in all this innocence, caught in a web of life and death. She did not eavesdrop on Violet Summers' first and last dance. Margaret LaMae respected secrets, kept them locked away like delicious secret ingredients in her mother's family recipes.

Yards of white summer clouds floated over the barn. A flock of seagulls soared beneath the clouds as if they were positioned to escort them out towards the sea. Ambrose Kane carefully lifted Violet Summers two or three inches off the floor. Her thin bones struggled under her skin to stay in place, to keep her dress from sliding along her spine like silk on a hanger. Slowly, she dropped her good foot down to hear it tap to the beat of the song that came from the deep south. Tap, tap, she believed she heard it say. *Tap, tap, you are dancing. Your feet have learned to dance.* Violet watched the dust gather and swirl, watched as it floated from around their feet, up past their knees, their shoulders, creeping like a white vine going higher and higher until they were ghost dancers in each other's arms. Through the dust, Violet could make out the outline of the empty swing. It moved slightly like an open hand extended to her.

They were not aware of the eyes that watched from a distance through the green leaves of the maple tree through the half-open door. They were not aware that Ivadoile Spears kept note of a song she would never name again. Ambrose Kane dropped Violet gently to the floor. He watched as she limped towards the back door of the barn for a breath of fresh air. She insisted on doing it on her own.

Violet slipped into a deep shade on the west side of the barn and braced her spine up against the cool shingles. She removed her brace and stretched out her feet. They looked perfect to her now. She felt nothing, not even a throb. Two blue jays, perched on a branch of a nearby tree, looked down at the tiny figure. They were silent as they flew off in different directions. Old Rose came around the corner of the barn and curled up beside Violet's bare feet. She purred as she listened to the dancing rhythm in each foot.

FIFTEEN

I VA GIVES HERSELF permission to offer up an epitaph to the lives of the people she plucks from the box on this winter day. Memories leak from her head like an un-seamed tap.

She never did get to see her father's headstone. She imagines it rising higher than any of the other stone markers in a cemetery in Boston. He was a man who would want to be noticed in death as well as in life, even after all these years.

Iva imagines his tombstone leaning over like a drunk, its engraving eroded by the elements. His name covered in moss like someone unshaven. Boned in foreign turf, he had presumably become an American citizen before his death so that his dust settled under Ole Glory. Her mother was a Canadian citizen when they married. Her headstone is rather plain with very little engraved on it; her name, dates of birth and death to indicate that she had lived and died. That was it. There is no reason in between life for Netti

McLaughlin. Her parents merely dug a hole for each other and traded graves.

They are dead so long now Iva can't assemble them or remember them as ever being whole, or having voices that startled or made demands on each other and on her.

She cannot recall which one of them sliced the life out of her beloved Rose. She cannot place if the stern sepia faces ever belonged to them. If the serious eyes looking back at her ever looked in the same direction at once. They never agreed on anything. She cannot imagine herself ever liking these people, except that their early absence from her life gave her silence. Silence shall be their epitaph.

Dear Bowzer talked about having a boulder for a headstone. "Can you imagine it, Iva?" he joked on his last visit with her in 1970. "On that boulder I want an inscription that reads 'I have landed hard.'" His death was a shock to Iva. He didn't mention a heart condition. He was rather aloof around most of the guests except for those he liked personally, with his best dialogue coming from the mouth of his beloved Humphrey, who died days later when she had nothing left to say. She was buried with Bowzer.

Bowzer had mailed Iva a blue linen scarf with the initial *I* embroidered on it along with a red feather from Humphrey. Iva may have suspected then that he would not be returning to Port Murdock, but this is a blur to her now. Her head is cloudy about such things.

If she'd had the choice, she would have buried Bowzer in her secret garden under a large stone with a parrot carved deep in its side and turned it into a bird feeder. Saint Bowzer of Port Murdock, he would have loved this resting place.

She does not know where Angelo Pinotti is buried. He was a mystery to her from the beginning, a brilliant mystery until they found him in all his regalia. Perhaps she will offer him what he loved best here at the Tides Inn, his red roses.

Poor Esther Neulands, she is not quite sure what one can substitute for the pain in her eyes. And then it comes to her, how much she loved the doll Victoria. She will offer to her the doll's shoes to match her red kimono. To Gladys she will offer a smoky cloud, where her voice comes through a cloud of smoke like a horse's hoof. To Bertie, her gardener, she will offer a handful of seeds and let him choose the colours. This he could do like no other.

There are exceptions. She smiles when she remembers the mystery celebrity guest, whom at first glance she believed to be a hobo that Margaret had let in out of pity. For Mr. Kalabash there will always be music to tremble beneath the earth.

She will not tamper with Ambrose Kane's life. It is not finished. He wrote to her often when he had to leave Port Murdock to sail the lakes. She is still waiting for a word to come concealed in a white envelope turned yellow with time. A phone call to say the least, he could respect her with a quick phone call for old times' sake. But she had taken the "sake" out of her old times herself.

"Perhaps," she rambles, "his voice will not be recognizable after all these years." And with the other party-liner's listening in, there is very little she would offer him in the way of a conversation. She forgets at times that she has a private line these days.

But his voice and his presence are clear in her mind at this moment. "Does he remember the quilt?" She could not find it for a long time after he left. The one with the daisies squared off in their own little patches, so real looking she believes they must have been plucked from the field and put on her bed that very day. He surely must remember that they are her favourite of all wildflowers.

He always placed them beside her with their lean stems drinking up the cool water from the bottom of the jug. Oh how those flowers were thirsty after their summer birth. And while she watched them drink, Ambrose Kane sliced into her like he would a watermelon and dropped his seeds all over the daisies.

"Was that the time he called me bronco? Perhaps it was," she shrugs. She can remember him laughing with her chin cupped in his hands as though he was about to put a muzzle on her.

"You're a real bronco, Miss Ivadoile, but a very pretty one." She had never told him how much she hated her name. It sounded different coming from his mouth. His accent made it sound melodic, not like a dog one would drag along on a leash when her parents called out to her.

"You're a real liar, Mr. Kane, but it suits your mouth. Be careful, I will take from it only what suits me at the moment!" Iva sang a smile to him and sipped it back with a frown.

Had she said that to him in anger? She would never have spoken to Cullie Spears in this manner. Poor Cullie, he would never address her as a bronco. Between Cullie's kidney pills and his shot of brandy, he was interested only in ailments he could tame, not broncos.

Iva cannot remember the last time she went to visit Cullie's grave. It is a rather large stone, shaped for some reason like the Eiffel Tower of all things. There was something else that caught her eye when it was erected. They had spelled her name incorrectly, left out an I. It may have been someone's way of letting her know that they wanted her left out completely. She didn't attend church services with him except to marry and bury the poor man. Dear Cullie, what could she do for him now but give him back her I on his stone to complete his epitaph?

Violet Summers' ashes are settled somewhere in Wexford, Ireland. It is hard to say if this is what she requested, or if it was a choice made by grieving parents to bury a loved one where she was conceived. Grief is all about beginnings and endings for some people. The in-between is eliminated, too many drafts left open to close out a young life such as hers.

She was fond of Violet, a fondness that settled on her like a heavy quilt on a cold bed until she began to warm up all over. Violet was too strong willed, a clever match for her to the end. She had made a connection that had yet caught Iva's attention. Iva's life. She had been in Ambrose Kane's embrace and he left it firmly planted in her feet.

Iva imagines Violet rising from her grave (she was never one to settle in one place for too long) to roam the coastline of Ireland, her thin hand braced against her forehead, one clear footprint followed by the other that danced, her blue skirt wild with wind, searching out Cape Breton's distant shores. "Violet Summers, I'll give to you a flame," smiles Iva, "to light your way."

Violet's parents came to get her a week or so after the parlour dinner and flew her back to Toronto. She died two weeks later. Iva ponders over the young girl's memory, her admiration for Violet Summers.

There was something in Violet Summers' spirit that refused to burn out. She reminded Iva of herself. Even the greedy flame of death did not scorch her. She pranced around it, even smiled at it while driving down the lane as she formed a silent sentence on her lips.

"Thank you," her lips whispered. Ambrose Kane looked towards the barn when the car drove out of sight. The sentence was meant for him. He hummed the song in silence and hoped that she had heard it as they drove through the gate.

Cousin Opal died shortly after her father, died from some obscure bone disease. Iva heard about it in the Post Office from someone whom Opal kept in contact with by the written hand.

"You have my condolences, Ivadoile, on the death of your cousin," offered the woman.

"You can have them back," Iva quipped as she walked away briskly. Behind her back she could hear a letter being sliced open, followed by a thick smear of silence. Iva is not going to give much thought to Opal's epitaph because she really doesn't care to dwell on death anymore today. A light snow has begun to fall and close the path.

Iva can feel something else closing in on her. Something she does not care to give thought to, but her thoughts pay her no mind and march themselves along the lane and up close to the kitchen step. They have the nerve to leave their footprints in the freshly fallen snow.

At one point, she tells them to get going like the advice one would give a child on their way home before dark. But they are stubborn and balk at the door. One of them has vacant eyes and is asking her for answers she will not give.

"Ivadoile, why did you send me away?"

She is eye to eye with Ambrose Kane looking into his bewildered eyes, his question hitting her like an ice pick. He has brought a posse of ghosts with him. Iva's eyes are paining beneath her brow. They feel like bruises that will take a long time to heal. When she looks beyond the door, the sun is shining on the freshly fallen snow, but there is no sign of Ambrose Kane or the others. She can keep her answer for another time, another season.

Everything is out of season in her mind. The secret garden is pleated in rows of colour as Iva stands at the kitchen door while melting winter in her head. The plump bird is singing on the arm of the sightless cherub. It is early summer. She checks her memory to give herself the go ahead to break into seasons, it is shortly after she heard the news of Violet Summers' death. The lilac bushes are heavy with blooms and the westerly wind is scurrying their scent up the lane and feeding each room with lilac fragrances through the mouth of the open windows.

There now, she has turned the seasons around like the hands of an old clock and the ghosts are rushing up to her door to receive their gifts. They are greedy and sly as they each demand their epitaph.

"Why can't the dead keep to themselves?" Iva hears the

sound of her own voice as the snow begins to drift onto the floor. Winter has brought her back to her senses, runs between her legs like a cold hand.

Old Rose is meowing at her empty bowl after being let in the kitchen door. Iva makes her way to the cupboard for her food and turns to face the cat with its saucer eyes concentrating on the can of cat food in her hand.

A trail of dainty imprints of soft snow petals form a procession to her back door. A small puddle circles around her feet where the petals have begun to melt from the cat's paws. Old Rose is impatient. She is greedy for what is right-fully her gift as she moves closer to Iva and rubs her back up against her legs to hurry her along. They are in a tug of war now. One has the gift, the other has the hunger. Iva is impatient as she hisses at the cat.

"Have patience, Miss Rose, or you'll be eating snow for the rest of the winter!" Iva warns the cat.

Old Rose moves toward the empty bowl and licks her right paw and holds it in mid-air. Iva can see the paw print, the four indents under the nails, and the thicker indent in the middle of the paw. She moves slowly towards the bowl and empties the contents from the can with a thick spoon. Old Rose looks up at her before she laps into the bowl. Her eyes are curious and her tongue curls like the tongue in an old leather shoe. Iva runs her hand gently over the cat's feeding head. She can feel the cat's warmth fill her hand like a warm mitten.

SIXTEEN

THERE IS SOMETHING that Ivadoile Spears wants to set back to its original form before she croaks: her secret garden. This is what she tells Margaret when she makes her first spring visit following the long winter.

Margaret looks over the rim of her stained cup at Iva. She noticed the stain at the bottom of the cup before Iva poured the tea. She never could wash dishes properly, but now Margaret believes that this could be a sign that Iva is getting dimmer in the head, going on like she is about a garden that stretched on forever years ago. It hasn't been attended to for so long neither one of them can remember the last time its soil was turned. And cleanliness is next to Godliness. This would not put a dent in Iva's dim head, Margaret can well attest, because God was a mere stain on Iva's life to begin with, as far as her religious beliefs were concerned.

"It will cost you a small fortune, Ivadoile. They won't pick up a shovel for less than fifty dollars an hour today. It's not like when we were young, people believed in work back then. People like dear Bertie are no longer with us."

"To hell with money, I can't take it with me. I have too much of it. I might as well look at something of beauty growing out of the ground before I'm planted in the sod like a root myself," Iva replied.

"You could have someone clean up the front garden beside the parlour windows, the one with the cherub in it. Some hardy perennials still make an appearance after all these years in the cherub garden," Margaret adds.

It's as far as you can see from your window at this time of your life, Margaret thinks without saying it out loud. She is careful in what she says to Iva at any time. Her body is getting frail and her mind is beginning to wander, but her tongue still swings like an axe.

Iva pauses before she gets up and walks towards the cupboard. She returns with a plate of crackers and cheese that she places beside Margaret's tea biscuits.

"You know yourself, Margaret, how well-loved my gardens were by my guests. Especially Violet Summers and Bowzer and that Italian man. They loved my secret garden."

Margaret lowers her head and concentrates on the tea stain at the bottom of the cup. She convinces herself that Iva is going back in her head for sure, as the old people used to believe.

"It's your money, you can do as you wish."

Iva catches the concerned look on Margaret's face.

"You think I'm going batty, don't you, with all this talk of gardens and money at my age."

"It is none of my business, Ivadoile. It is your property."

"Then what concerns you? Your face is twisting like someone having a stroke."

"Oh dear, I was thinking about that young woman, Violet Summers. She was such a dear soul. And that Mr. Bowzer and that bird of his, he sure did give me a terrible fright the first time I heard him speak."

"Humphrey was like his child," Iva's voice has mellowed. The mention of Bowzer's name is a tranquilizer for her. "She travelled everywhere with him, even to his grave. He made sure to add that in his will. 'Wherever I go I want Humphrey with me.'" Ivadoile continues, "They are noted for their intelligence, those African grey parrots. They make wonderful and very affectionate companions. Some people say they are like having a five-year-old child."

Margaret tried to imagine how a bird could be put to rest in a Catholic graveyard. Years ago you'd have to sneak in the dark and dig a small hole and pluck the bird in the way you'd place a carcass in a pot for soup. There was no telling what they'd do across the border to comply with someone's wishes. Their graveyards could be full of reptiles and dogs and cats curled up at the foot of a corpse for all she knew. But she was happy that Bowzer could have what he desired.

Iva is looking past Margaret and out the kitchen window. Crumbs form a small mound and slide down the front of her sweater. Stripes of white porcelain appear between her blue-veined fingers as if she is holding the rib cage of a tiny bird in her hands.

Iva is taking inventory of the most famous garden she had ever visited, the Tuileries Gardens in Paris, designed by some queen for the royals to prance about in the 1800s in their wigs and tights. Was it in the '50s or the '60s that she had gone to Paris? No, it had to be after Bowzer's death or she would have invited him along, she corrects herself mentally.

She had planned on other things to see and bring back from her trip. The Moulin Rouge was on her list. Prints of Toulouse-Lautrec's paintings, her favourite of the artist would make their way back to Port Murdock.

But she had seen something that amused her equally, an older couple on a bench near the gardenia gardens in the Tuileries. They resembled a painting of Lautrec's in motion. Iva smiles at the memory of it. Others passed the couple without as much as a glance their way. Perhaps it was their age that amused her the most. The woman was seventy or more and the man was somewhat older, wrapped in each other's arms like dirty sheets. One sagging breast hung out of the embrace like a stained broken seam. The woman's hair was dyed jet black. Her red lipstick ran up under her nose, giving her the appearance of a heavy nose bleed. The man wore a dark toupee that slid back and forth on his head like a hand waving at dusk. His head was misshapen by a hollow dent above his right ear. They were oblivious to people passing by.

When they looked up, they noticed Iva watching them and they smiled toothless grins her way. They were not the thread of bourgeois Paris; they were its colour, its poetry in motion, a ragged bouquet of forgotten lovers who were grateful for the smile Iva offered up to them.

The man reached into his jacket pocket and took out two rolls wrapped in a brown paper bag. He and his lover sat side by side chewing slowly on the rolls. In no time, they had an audience of pigeons. They chuckled as the birds bowed at their feet and collected what was left of their embrace.

SEVENTEEN

ANGELO PINOTTI ARRIVED at the Tides Inn in the bloom of summer, 1968. The first request from the slightly built man, who spoke softly from under a meticulously groomed moustache, was for three red roses to be placed on his bedside table daily. He insisted that he pay extra for this eccentric request.

Margaret brought up the freshly cut roses one morning after cleaning the kitchen. She knocked quietly at the door of Angelo Pinotti's room but got no response. The door opened slightly as she called out to him in a quiet voice. Stepping inside she was taken aback by the order of the room. Three or four hairbrushes were lined up in perfect order on the dresser along with a silver comb and cufflinks. They were placed in a line as if they were about to race each other over the edge of the dresser. Beside them lay a small covered book with its title concealed. His clothes were hung neatly in the armoire with its door slightly ajar. Shirts hung close together with their starched collars and cuffs, so stiff they looked as if they were about to march out on their own. Four or five pairs of dark trousers hung beside them as smooth as marble. Other garments were concealed in black plastic bags. His highly polished leather shoes were arranged in perfect symmetry at the bottom of the bed.

Margaret surveyed the room a few more minutes before placing the roses on the table beside the bed and removing the three from the previous day.

She kept the day old roses in the pantry while she worked. They were too fresh looking to discard.

She was surprised to see that the bed was made up perfectly as if it hadn't been slept in, although Gladys the cleaning lady had not made her rounds to the top floor. Margaret walked towards the flaring lace curtains of the open window as quietly as a moth when she heard voices.

Angelo Pinotti was strolling through the garden with his fine dark hair blowing around like dust shadowing a thin pointed face and an ill-shaped goatee. His face had a deep redness to it as if he'd been shamed by something his soul would render no mortal absolution towards. He paused beside the broken cherub with his hands behind his back and looked into its face as if he had asked it a question and was waiting patiently for the reply. Several smaller cherubs were set back amongst the gardens towards the back fields.

Ivadoile appeared behind the man as he turned slowly and greeted her with a polite nod of his head.

"A rather gentle morning," said Angelo Pinotti to the woman his friend had cautioned him about.

Iva smiled and agreed with the man. "It's always like this

with a north-westerly wind."

Angelo Pinotti turned again to face the cherub. "The Creator is a great weatherman." His face was solemn as he looked at Iva.

"I'm not into religion," she answered quickly, as if the man had brought up a terminal disease. "I'm an eternal atheist. Rain or shine, Mother Nature has the last laugh on us all."

"Ah, but you are in the wind, Madam, and it gives you cause for either serenity or turbulence. Mother Nature has been eternal much longer than the rest of us. It is up to you to make the ultimate choice. Even an atheist has to carry an umbrella when it rains."

"I have never been afraid of rain, Mr. Pinotti,"

Angelo Pinotti observed the clever woman at his side with an air of sympathy as he studied her drawn face outlined by a shadow of morning glories. There was a frequent eclipse of discontent in her eyes.

Iva studied Angelo Pinotti's face. An intelligent man will always study a woman carefully. They will start with the eyes and make their assumptions later, she thought.

Iva surveyed her garden as far back as the naked eye could see, as she turned her gaze from Angelo Pinotti. She was happy that she'd gotten Bertie to clear several paths for people to stroll along throughout its pathways. There was no telling how many flowers now grew in this maze with its magnificent gazebo in the centre of the garden.

"Pictures of my gardens are all around the world," she'd mentioned to Angelo Pinotti the night before at dinner. "Many of my former guests have sent along pictures they have taken of the gardens to me."

Angelo Pinotti smiled. "I was fortunate enough to have a friend send some of them along to me. Beauty is a great commodity. It brought me here."

Margaret bit into her bottom lip as she served and listened to Iva going on as if all the work had been done by her alone around the place. As Angelo Pinotti had seen in the photos and now up close for himself, if the truth were told, she could do nothing but give orders for the physical labour required here at the inn. And Bertie had little help in keeping everything in such great shape. He had to plead with her for a few extra hands in the gardens.

Margaret continued to watch Angelo Pinotti and Iva in the garden. She overheard the man say he was from Montreal and then he changed the subject. He offered nothing more about his personal life and Iva did not question him. Margaret guessed that he was probably in his sixties, a retired professional no doubt, with his fancy clothes and shoes.

Who else could afford such attire? The cleaning lady, Gladys, believed he was probably hiding out from the mafia but Margaret shrugged this off with a smile.

"One of their big mob bosses," Gladys observed from reading crime novels. She maintained that the FBI got most of their information from reading these books. "The mob bosses are always neat and clean cause they don't do the shootings themselves," Gladys offered. "Never a drop of blood spilled on the big boss when you can pay someone with a good aim to do the dirty work. Probably grabbed somebody else's friggin name and ran for cover. We could all be shot between the eyes before sunset."

Angelo Pinotti reached out to touch the broken hand of

the cherub. "A flaw in the cement," said Iva, observing him. "But I liked the face, that's why I didn't bother having it replaced."

"A possible flaw in the angel," offered Angelo Pinotti as he looked up at Iva. "It has been known to happen," he smiled.

Iva turned up her nose at the thought of angels being at play in her garden. Cherubs she could take, they weren't fully grown and turned into angels and would always remain winged children. Margaret related this story to her for some reason she couldn't recall at the moment. The thought of it reminded her of a fairy tale, a magical place where winged children ruled and smashed into each other as they flew about scattering their broken parts at will. For once, she wished she had paid closer attention to Margaret. Fairy tales and winged children imposed an innocent delinquent upheaval in her gardens.

Iva studied her guest with great intensity as he looked down at the cherub. Why did he request red roses each day? Perhaps he was grieving a lost love. The troubled heart seems to carry a seed for roses. Especially for men. Impossible, thought Iva, to read the eyes of a man who fills them at this moment with the hand of a broken cherub.

Angelo Pinotti seemed rather amused as he looked down at the ornament. A muscle in his neck twitched as he ran a cool long hand up to interrupt it from interfering with his leisure.

If his conscience led Angelo Pinotti to God and angels that was his business. Iva would not get caught up and spun around Eden by an Italian with Angelo for a first name. Never. Every man is entitled to his charms and the space between his fantasies, Iva trusts, but she will not throw religion into the mix.

Angelo Pinotti was smart and cautious. He walked softly between women and cherubs. He smiled as he caught the look on Iva's face.

"I have seen that look before, Madam. I truly apologize for my intrusiveness. I do not preach religion."

Iva cooked up a slight grin. "I stopped believing at an early age, Mr. Pinotti. I can't visibly remember what my parents looked like, nor do I wish to on any given day. I'd had too many nights without lullabies." She sighed deeply, "I had one good husband and one bad lover. The first one death called for, and the other called attention to himself. I believe the only difference between love and lust is that one of them requires you to take your clothes off."

Angelo Pinotti bowed his head. His body wasted no emotions. He realized that one or two conversations with this woman would not even begin to touch her wounds. She was like an out of control fire looking for a place to strike. Her emotional and academic knowledge had never met hand to hand. He cast his eyes slowly on the face of the cherub once again, at its beautiful sightless eyes looking upward as if sensing the direction of the wind by touch, out of love for all that touched it. One fat hand posed in mid-air, the other limp at the end of its chubby arm, as though it had been mangled like a wounded naked child of war, sightless, seeking its direction in a life unmapped, yet aware of its surrounding beauty and the bird that comes to sing.

EIGHTEEN

"HE LOVES ME…He loves me not." The disrobed daisy falls between Iva's hands and drops at her feet. "Did he love me or did he not?" Iva can't remember if the *love me* or *love me not* petal was the last to fall as she looks down at the ground. The *love me* and *love me not* petals swirl and leave with the passing breeze.

The sun is darkening like dried blood. The waves wash the shoreline with tattered cloths of foam. Lovers drift to the back seat of their cars, as if the sea itself had something to do with their hormones swelling out of hand, and the back seat came with its own relief system. Iva wonders if young girls still use daisies as a form of *He loves me…He loves me not* delusions. Such a primitive thing it is to ask a daisy about the love in your life at ninety-two. It's like asking a wasp if it intends to sting you. What do the young people of this generation know about love? They go around half naked looking for what they think they are missing out on.

You are missing nothing but the other half of your clothes, you poor fools, she wants to call out in warning but she knows they would pay her no heed.

Iva shakes her head and mumbles to herself as she watches another car drive down towards the water.

She never bothered the daisies when Ambrose Kane came into her life. Perhaps it was his feet that she fell in love with the first time they graced her white sheets, without a hill of corns or bunions to interfere with their beauty, just invisible footsteps that she liked to stroke. She would pretend that she had been at his side along these imaginary paths. When she wiggled his toes, it meant they had waded through a stream. When she massaged his ankles, they had run barefoot through the forest. When she pressed hard on the soles of his feet, they had climbed up a mountain. He had a ruggedness to him like Leonard Cohen, who could bruise a woman's soul with a dandelion.

Or was it his closed eyes and the way his hands clasped under his head and sank into her pillows, tucking himself into his own flesh, that deepened her heart?

They were walking in a light rain. She and Ambrose Kane were both bareheaded as they strolled along the back road near the inn. It was early fall of 1949. Orange leaves brushed up against Ambrose Kane's skin as they walked. He refused to wear a jacket. Felt his flesh needed a drop of rain to keep it lubricated. Iva wore her all-weather coat. It was blue.

He stopped and picked up orange leaves from the path and placed them in her hair, Hawaiian style. A gust of wind shook them loose and hid the leaves between the trees. Iva was excited by it all, the light rain, the flying leaves, the bare-armed man beside the blue-wrapped woman with a growing desire to throw him into a bush and shelter him with her coat while he stripped her bare and shared the raindrops with her. *Was this love*, she thought, *or a descent into madness?*

She was a successful thirty-two year old businesswoman and a hump in the woods was not on her list of things to do. She will…She won't. She had not killed a daisy in a long time.

"You don't look your age," said a young guest to her at dinner the night before. This reinforced her love life.

"Neither does my bread pudding," she smiled as the young man, a pimple or two out of his teens, swallowed hard to choke down his embarrassment.

Humphrey growled, "Don't look your age! Don't look your age!" The thought of daisies and age seems rather juvenile to her, at her age now.

Nature has always fascinated her. It is always ready to offer perspective lovers a nest on its hidden paths, against its trees. There is an open invitation in the air. The birds sing its praises. "Do it! Do it!" Then they fly off with your secret under their wings.

A memory of Cullie flashed like a shadow through the trees. The branches looked like they had been buttered with sunlight as they swayed, conscious of their own sound, as raindrops dripped one by one from their limbs.

This is not something Cullie Spears would have tried out in the wild. The fear of being caught naked by one of his patients would have been too stressful for him. He'd have kicked out under a tree in this weeping forest and died from embarrassment beneath the branches.

Nineteen

MARGARET LAMAE GIVES the soup pot an extra good scrubbing and stands back to admire the shine. She can still light things up, make them sparkle. She places the pot on the back step to let it dry out completely. The sun has broken through the haze of light drizzle and glides against the pot in crippled streaks.

Margaret sings her way to the big pantry off the kitchen where she drops the lid of the pot on the edge of the cupboard. Singing soothes a woman's soul, fills out its dents, dilutes the conscience, she tells herself. Margaret has to tame her conscience at moments like this. "Their souls are full of vinegar," she recalls her grandmother's saying about people who did what she was about to do. She waited for Iva to leave for hours so she could get it done. Swiping comes naturally to her now. It will be easy today.

She is an expert at folding a sheet into flat corners, sizing it down to look like a napkin and then plunking it into the clean soup pot. Margaret stares out the back window towards the path where she watched Iva and Ambrose Kane drift into the back woods earlier. Iva in the lead like a hound looking for the kill and Ambrose Kane following at her heels, unarmed. Margaret will be gone before they return for the evening. There is only one guest to serve for dinner. She can leave early.

Margaret moves slowly up the back stairs to room number Seven with the key tucked in her apron pocket and a paper bag in her hand. From the hall window, she can see Bertie turning over the soil in the front garden. His head is turned away from her. If he should look up she will wave to him as if all is right with the world. He would be mystified if he knew what Margaret is up to in Ivadoile Spears' room, swiping to her heart's content.

And it is her heart that wants the content and comfort of Ambrose Kane. The sheets that he sleeps on, his aftershave lotion. She took a whole bottle in her last hoist, then sprinkled the pillow slips from another hoist. Something else catches her eye this day, a nightdress belonging to Iva that she has seen on the line a few times. Ambrose Kane had no doubt lifted it from Iva's pale-as-pie-dough body like a second skin. She must look like a ghost in it, Margaret imagines. Perhaps it is the searching that thrills him, the peeling away at a ghost. The rattle of her bones beneath him.

Margaret smiles at the thought of the nightdress now belonging to her. How she will shroud her slim dark body with this plain white cloth and hope for a pair of hands to remove it. She would give Ambrose Kane a hard time, let him peel it away as she twirled and fashioned herself into a dark moving muscle. Make her skin smile for him.

There are no frills or lace on the nightdress. Three buttons run down its yoke like bumps on a map giving you directions to some hidden treasure. She scorns herself for weeping at the heartache this cloth brings out in her. This permanent ache she has to steal for and let beat beneath three buttons alone in the night. At once she tucks it back neatly into the pile of garments in the wicker basket only to retrieve it again, on second thought, and place it in the paper bag with the sheet and another bottle of aftershave lotion. She listens for footsteps before making her escape as she closes the door quietly and goes down to the pantry.

Voices gather in the parlour, men's voices, strong and alert, discussing the world at large from the newspapers under their noses. Soup pots are too small for these businessmen from out west to take an interest in. The evening clerk is telling them something about the weather.

Margaret takes in the pot from the step and deposits her stash and ties down the lid to the side handles. Placing the pot carefully into her shopping bag, she is off for the night.

The sun shines stronger on thieves. Or does she imagine this as she scurries along the road? Margaret is in a hurry to get going. She realizes she has taken the path that Iva and Ambrose Kane had taken earlier. This path will take her longer to get to the main road, but she is in no hurry now. She is safe among the trees.

Their leaves stretch out a golden welcome mat for her. Her steps are light and airy. A slight breeze brushes at her hair. She tucks it into a scroll at the back of her head with a clip. She is in no hurry to get past this quiet. Her mother will be watching for her at the kitchen window. She is always there, like a plant on the ledge with her fading red hair, stale and unruly, pulled back against the back of her neck like tangled rusty wire.

Mrs. Parsons is afraid of combs, they all have teeth. She is afraid of water, it drowns people.

It has been like this for a while now. Her mother's fear of combs and water. This dark fear came with the death of Margaret's father from a heart attack.

Her two older sisters disappeared to the sights and sounds of New York after their father's death. They send Christmas money in their cards, but never return to see how it is spent.

Get something nice for Mama and yourself from Old Saint Nick!

Perhaps New York needed them in her neon lights, in her crowded streets as their husbands escorted them here and there with combs in their purses that do not bite. Margaret spit out the thought of it along the road.

Their brother's name was never spoken in their home after the war. Someone opened the windows and doors and his name disappeared on the back of the wind. What is left of Margaret's pilot twin brother are hidden pictures. Sometimes Margaret will take them out just to see a handsome smile in the house once again. She is standing beside him arm-in-arm looking more like lovers than twin siblings. Handsome paper smiles fall at her feet and for a moment in time she imagines him walking through the gate in full uniform. She would never have believed then that a man like him could die in a cloud.

Margaret is grateful to her neighbours for keeping an eye on her mother while she works. They would have to rely on charity if she didn't work. She would have to stay at home like a second apron as she refers to herself, if there were nobody around to do such a kind favour for her.

The air is cooling. Margaret wraps her old coat closer to her as the shopping bag sways against her leg. She checks to see if the lid is still secure on the pot. She smiles at the thought of Iva believing that she prefers to use her own pot for cooking stews and soup. She could bring a bucksaw to slice the homemade bread she makes three to four times a week or so for the inn. The fool would be too daft to know the difference. She just pretends that she knows what the sharpest things in life are and what they are capable of doing.

Ambrose Kane's back rises as Iva's two pale arms wrap his flesh in a bow, a tight lover's knot, they are part of the earth that trembles beneath them. They have caused it all, they believe, but will be sober from love in the near future. Outwitted and outdone since neither one of them has ever found a home for their own emotional salvation. Margaret recognizes their voices, giddy and wild, leaking out from under the branches of an old apple tree.

They startle her into silence. She remains still, fearing another step will expose her as a snoop, a busybody. She has an urge to run, to turn back towards the inn and take the road home, but her limbs disobey her. They will not move. She watches as Ambrose Kane's body descends over Iva's, an avalanche of muscle and flesh in slow motion. The bow loosens around his back as one arm drifts slowly to the ground. Iva's blue coat, spread out at her side, catches her limp hand. The other hand comes undone and slides off his back out of sight. The sound that comes from Iva's throat has the secret beauty of danger and control as it shivers back down into her lungs and exhales.

Margaret forces her feet to move slowly, backwards. She is colder now as she turns forward and keeps walking back towards the inn. Her mind is cold. She is in a hurry to go nowhere and takes a shortcut near the inn that takes her out to the main road. There are other noises to escort her home, but she does not bother to identify them. The shopping bag feels like a dead weight in her bare hand.

The land is turning into soft silhouettes all around her. Falling leaves shower her in gold. Her feet scuff at them as if they were stones being thrown down from the trees. The wind hurts her as it makes a laughing sound in her lungs. There is no more room in Margaret's body for any more pain as she stumbles towards her house with her head lowered to keep her balance.

Later, Margaret slips the nightdress over her head in slow motion. She stands barefoot and still in the middle of her bedroom wearing another woman's stolen garment. The cool cotton pools at her feet like a hem that's come undone. It is three or four inches too long for her. A dim nightlight casts a dull glow across the room. Margaret presents herself to the old mirror. She cannot identify herself as she stares at her own image. Her sudden beauty surprises her. How long has it been present? Much more so since Ambrose Kane came to the Tides Inn. She has let her hair down and it hides the redness that starts at her neck and is crawling along her jawline. You are right, Margaret, even shame has its own colour.

Whose voice is speaking to her? Sister Bernadette's voice. Margaret is in her grade seven class studying catechism when she asks someone for help on a question.

"Why is it a sin to let someone touch you?" Margaret whispers innocently to a classmate. But her question is intercepted by Sister Bernadette and she is ordered to face the class. This is her penance for cheating. "Shame on you, Margaret, you should know what touching can lead to!" Sister Bernadette's face looks as if she were speaking from within a flame.

But Margaret puts her shame out when the image of Ambrose Kane's rising back is touchable. So close she can count the knots on his spine with one touch. She is happy he has a long back to count on.

The lonely wet night sings outside her window. It has started to rain again. She listens for other noises, perhaps her mother is listening outside the door. Nothing but silence moves in the room.

She walks over to bolt her bedroom door. Click. She smiles. A different smile, a premeditated smile is always dangerous. She moves to the center of the room beside her bed and turns down the spread and top sheet before she undresses. She sprinkles a few drops of Ambrose Kane's aftershave lotion along the goose feather pillows. Hail, hail, the goose is dead.

The nightdress covers her feet like a scattering of feathers when it slides down. She steps out slowly. Margaret has only one song to escort her feet into dance, the lonely wind song outside her window. She cannot turn her radio on for fear of disturbing her mother. She picks up the nightdress and lets it hang like a shroud around her dark nakedness. Margaret moves it easily around her small frame. Up and down her breasts it glides as if it had a direction of its own, its own hands to guide it, someone to break its yoke and make her spill. It is between her thighs now, this cotton turned shroud, and this is where the song grows lonelier outside her window and drags itself out on a one-pitch note before the dance has barely begun.

Margaret wants to dance forever, or move, or touch, or keep in motion with the smell of him on her flesh, but it doesn't matter anymore at this moment because the song has died.

She leaves the dance floor and tucks herself indecently under her sheet. She is naked. She straddles a pillow over her with a scent of his after shave lotion seeping into her senses. Desire is the ingredient of the night. What does Ambrose Kane use before he claws his whiskers with a blade? Iva hates whiskers. She heard her tell him so.

"It is whiskers or me, what will it be?" She will never know the answer to this, because she will never ask. Margaret is too shy to tell him how much she admires them. She would allow them to travel intimately with her, use them as a scrubbing brush on her skin if he so wished.

She cradles the pillow in both arms and rocks it mournfully like a sick baby. It is always more real to go to the innocent. Was Ambrose Kane as innocent as she believed? What part of him required the most loving?

Margaret sinks her face in the warmth of the pillow and waits. But the night waits back and offers nothing more. No answers to her questions. It has shifted into silence as if it has fallen into its own sleep. Nothing stirs. Not a leaf in motion on the run from its own demise. Even the rain has stopped falling. The stars in the dark sky are spread out on their own, offering only little buds of light, like children carrying small flames at twilight to find their way home.

TWENTY

IVADOILE SPEARS HAS always saved paper like juicy bits of gossip. Paper does not confuse her. It is steady in her hand like an old lined face she can trace as well as her own. She stares at the date on the 1953 calendar, at the blue circle around July 7, like a fading moon ring. It is her circle, there is no question about it. She rounded everything out. She's a circle specialist, her grade-school teacher told her so one day. After all these years she can recall the smell of rum on the teacher's breath.

On the cover of the calendar, a small pensive looking child stands beside a shallow pond stirring with a crooked stick. Scattered images lie on top of the flat water as if the child is trying to stir herself into pieces.

Iva gave her full attention to circles. They remembered things for her, urgencies, bill payments, hair appointments. Dates when Ambrose Kane returned from the sea and the lakes and straggled up to the back door, a present tucked somewhere or other in his wrinkled clothes. She was given permission to search every inch of him. No wrinkle was forbidden to enter. In the folds of his left shirtsleeve, she found the gold watch. Its hands outstretched to the exact time of his arrival. Four o'clock in the afternoon.

MARGARET LAMAE WATCHED the wrinkle-search from the pantry. How smoothly he wrapped the watch on Iva's wrist while Margaret stirred a pot of clam chowder up to her own empty wrist. A full-sized clam rose to the top of the pot. Margaret hauled it from the pot and sliced it in two with a vengeance. She could hear Iva and Ambrose Kane engaged in a heavy conversation as they headed up the back stairs to Iva's room. They were discussing clams of all things. "Clams and sex," Margaret sneered while avoiding the proximity of the paper divinity in the pantry. "Wouldn't that be a sight for sore eyes combination on the menu." The nerve of that woman, she thought, as she stirred the clam chowder.

Margaret looked up at the calendar she tacked on the pantry wall above the main counter. The Sacred Heart of Jesus was trimmed in thorns. His eyes followed Margaret from the pot to the knife. When she turned and looked up again, Jesus cast a reverend stare at her. The squares that contained the numbers were large enough for her to write in the supper menu.

"Clam chowder, salmon/white sauce, garden vegetables, apple delight a la crème" (her own invention).

"It's still not a ring, and I have this strange feeling that there never will be one," Margaret heard herself whisper to the man whose paper eyes were still watching her every move. Had she been a superstitious woman, she could have sworn Jesus winked down at her as though to assure that her day or night would come. Her own circle would be complete.

IVA SMILES AS her hand circles the number seven. She remembers that day well. That time in her life when her wrist was numbered in gold. But something is getting in her way now. Perhaps it is time itself. Had this been the day he asked her to be his bride or was it the time he'd asked to be her lover forever? Two questions from the same man can be confusing on the same day. Did he want a bride or a lover?

Ambrose Kane dropped pieces of his personal life on her sheets in a rhapsody of sighs. Sex made a good confession. A marine in the war, he claimed this title when he stopped talking about clams. He lived with his mother after the war, and she longed for grandchildren while she could still remember them. His father died from a bad batch of corn whiskey. He had a brother on the lam and a sister who walked out of their back door and straight into a swollen river. Rivers can take care of a broken heart. A full moon located her in time for Ambrose to fish her out. He'd dropped his own breath deep into her lungs before she spit it back at him and climbed the bank. She married a millionaire in Mississippi a few years later, remained child-less and avoided rivers.

Iva remembers lying on her sheet with one foot touching the floor after this conversation. She did not answer either of his questions. She felt a flush of river water between her toes. It was cool. An image of his sister came to Iva. A woman she never met. A river temptress, bloated between life and death, with an urge to spit from a pair of clean lungs, but how much of the river had stayed in her? Women always keep a bit of leverage on pain. Her own mother kept broken china.

She'd gotten out of bed and dressed for dinner while Ambrose Kane slept peacefully. His sturdy hands enveloped under his head. She had no desire to disturb him. She looked down at the man who was capable of saving women from swollen rivers. She had an answer for him as she bent down and kissed his bare foot before she left room number Seven. She had given her answer a lot of thought.

Margaret LaMae heard one set of footsteps on the back stairs as Iva came down to dinner. She knew Ambrose Kane would not be down and that she would have to place his food in the warm oven for later.

Sometimes he ate in the kitchen while Margaret cleaned up. She secretly wished that he would come down before she left for the day. He always had a story or two to tell about people he'd met and places he'd been. He was her atlas to the outside world. Her departure.

Ivadoile stuck a spoon in the whipped cream and swallowed slowly before going into the dining room without leaving a word for Margaret to digest in the pantry. Without a sigh of satisfaction or displeasure, Iva hit the swinging door like a bouncer and disappeared into the dining room. She had changed into a bare-armed dress to show off the gold watch.

Margaret looked up at the calendar while waiting for Iva to ring the bell for supper. She printed BLOOD PUDDING in bold letters in the square of the calendar for dinner the following day. The paper Jesus watched Margaret at work and for one brief moment Margaret imagined a drop of blood from His thorns spill over the blood pudding. She blessed herself quickly as the shrill of the dinner bell rang out from the dining room.

TWENTY-ONE

I VA PAID PARTICULAR attention to Margaret's sanctimonious customs with fresh loaves of homemade bread. The way she indented a cross on each end before the initial slicing took place and the trouble she took to bless each and every loaf. The swift silver dent, the mark of the cross rising out from the tip of the knife under the warm crust. For some reason this fascinated Iva.

Margaret's eyes were always wet after this ceremony as if she'd just carved into a pet lamb to feed the hungry.

"It's a sign of respect for the body and blood of Christ," Margaret explained to the watchful Iva.

Iva smiled, "You Catholics use a lot of knives. Is the respect in the blade or the handle?"

Margaret turned her back so Iva couldn't see her sneer. What could she expect her to comprehend? She's never prayed or left a footprint in the church dust for years. The good Lord would need a search party to find her kind in a church. She didn't have the decency to bend a knee on her husband's grave, even on his anniversary, to thank him for the one mortal moment of pleasure he'd given her here on heaven's green earth.

Margaret could not understand what poor Ambrose Kane saw in her. She was pretty enough. It was puzzling what men could be drawn into by a woman.

Love is indeed blind, but Margaret doubted that in Ivadoile Spears' case. Iva saw everything that touched her. Felt them out before advancing like a sergeant with his platoon. She was always armed. She had that look in her eye that warned you that she might be carrying a loaded pistol hidden somewhere under her clothes. Explodable Ivadoile Spears. Ambrose Kane could have had more pleasure jumping into a snowdrift and becoming snow blind. Margaret could never see Ambrose Kane, as polite as he was, as the marrying type of man.

Margaret heard Iva rattling some dishes behind her but did not turn to see what she was up to at the moment. A loud crash made Margaret grab the edge of the cupboard for safety just as Bowzer and Humphrey entered through the kitchen door.

Bowzer looked down at the splattered mess surrounding Iva's feet and shook his head.

"Cooking up a storm again, I see," said Bowzer, as a cloud of white alarm rose from the kitchen floor.

"Cooking up a storm," Humphrey repeated as Iva screamed at Margaret to get the broom.

"I was trying my hand at bread making," Iva sputtered through the flour that assaulted her nostrils. "I can't do everything around here."

"It looks like you were trying your feet on bread making," laughed Bowzer in a joking manner.

Margaret pounded the rolling pin like a steam roller over her pie dough. She could feel the hair on her neck stand at attention.

The nerve of that woman to imply that she was needed in this kitchen to make bread was pure insanity. She was as capable as a wasp around food. Margaret dropped the rolling pin and reached for the broom.

"I'll take care of it," Margaret suggested in a voice that told Iva to leave the kitchen duties to her. Iva and Bowzer left the kitchen and went out to the garden with tall glasses of lemonade in hand.

Iva regained composure in her garden. Standing beside Bowzer, she was inches taller than he was, with her shoulders pulled back in a strong stance like an archer. Margaret watched them from the pantry window as the pie shells baked in the oven. The afternoon sun cast a lazy yellow eye over their heads and warmed their words, tamed by friendship that had taken hold for a few years now. The bird had no doubt contributed to this, thought Margaret as she watched its cage dangle from Bowzer's wrist like a large charm bracelet.

Bowzer opened the cage door as Humphrey aired out her wings and swooped five or six feet in the air before landing on the broken hand of the cherub. Humphrey looked around as if she were lost in the jungle surrounded by so many flowers. Margaret could hear Bowzer cheer and applaud as if the bloody thing had performed a miracle. The poor bird appeared alarmed at the attention coming its way. It hobbled meekly back into its wired world and folded in two like a wallet. Humphrey appeared to tremble violently. It had been caged for so long that freedom became a burden.

Margaret turned her attention to Rose as she sniffed at the remnants of the flour mixture under the kitchen table. She turned from it the way she would turn from gunpowder and walked towards the pantry. Rose circled around Margaret's ankles with her back hunched and her tail whipping the air. Margaret felt the heat of its fur warm her skin like an old mitt with fresh fire in its fibres. When she looked down, the cat looked up. They seemed to understand what each other was thinking. Margaret smiled at the cat.

"I know, Rose, she'll never be a cook," Margaret winked at the cat as she took the damp mop and went over the spot under the table once again, before it got a good scrubbing. Little balls of flour curled on the mop. The idea of Iva with her hands in a bread bowl puzzled Margaret. What was she trying to prove? She hated cooking and baking of any sort, yet she was too proud to ask for help. Ivadoile Spears in a bread bowl, no, no, there had to be something else behind this, something sharper in her mind.

Gladys appeared with a bucket and scrubbing brush in hand along with a can of paste wax. She swore as she surveyed the floor as if she had been summoned to a fire to clean up the remains of white ashes.

TWENTY-TWO

A T NINETY-TWO, anything can be imagined out of proportion. Old age is a prerequisite for deeper confusion, a bog where all flowers are sent to fade from view. Iva believes that Ambrose Kane is purely an invention at the tip of her fingers. But she is not holding flowers now, flowers never wept in her hands or flooded them with a creamy part of him that she washed away with mild soaps and scented lotions while he lingered, where? Between her fingers or in the V of her thumb and forefinger?

At times, in her mind, he appears to her out of nowhere in her father's apparel, starched white shirts and black suspenders, but Ambrose Kane's face is always much kinder. Softer, like Cullie's. Smiling into the wind, he sometimes sails up to her back door naked as a stripped daisy. It is always summer. She lets his smile in first. His flesh can wait. There is barn straw in his hair. Why had the wind not disturbed it, hidden it from view? She must be a certifiable fool this deep into her subconscious. The world is full of fools waiting to be plucked from life's limbs and squared off into rooms built for people who've run out of the present. They surround people in these rooms with remnants from the past to pacify them. They might as well slap up a picture of the vicious dog that once bit you and label it life.

It happened to Margaret's mother. Ran so far from the present she had to be planted in one of the rooms in some hospital or other before she died. Margaret missed work for a few days getting her mother settled.

There is something else she believes happened around this time. Or was it later? She'd opened the door wider and Ambrose Kane followed his smile in. They were alone in the kitchen when he scooped her up like Old Rose and brought her upstairs. They had not received word yet of Violet Summers' death.

The cat followed them upstairs and meowed at the closed door. Ambrose Kane threw a slipper at the door. Or was it a shoe? Perhaps it was neither, only a sound that Iva borrowed from some time, some place, where sounds hurt less. But the touch was real. Starting at the base of her spine, or was it from the base of her neck, he'd trace her like a road map with one hand. And where was the other? This is where it all came to an end, his final touch at the tip of her spine. She had not let him travel every intimate trail of her this day. She had other plans for him.

"You are not to come back to this place ever again!" She eyed him like a gunslinger in a dual. She watched his every move. The look in his eyes, blank, as the words in his mouth gasped for information. They were still connected physically, the bridge of flesh and bone swaying on its last pulse when she ordered him to be quiet before she called him a cheater, a bastardly two-timer. He raised his hand to protest. He looked at Iva, at the madness in her eyes that was leaking down her cheeks as her lips puckered up for a venom spit.

The cat stopped meowing and raced down the back stairs. A condemned man and a frightened cat are usually silent under a woman's rant.

He left without luggage, just as he'd arrived. No, she is wrong. There was something in Ambrose Kane's hand when he walked out the bedroom door and down the front stairs. Something golden in colour.

He'd bent down and picked up the clip from her hair that had fallen to the floor. Ambrose Kane left with a gold clip indented in his fist like a thistle. He left behind a few spots of blood too, footsteps apart.

Men walk away from your life in different directions. Ambrose Kane chose the path with the drooping purple lilacs. She'd watched it all from the upstairs window with the sun brushing a violent loose flame against her bare breast. He never looked back, Ambrose Kane, not once, to see that Rose was following closely at his heels with a look of panic in her eyes.

Twenty-Three

SOMETHING THEATRICAL LIVES in the lonely heart. There were two new performances Iva acquired in her life after Ambrose Kane's departure. Watching and waiting behind the curtains, her hand ghostly white and trembling against the heavy drapes, opening and closing them as if on cue by something urgent in the lead actor's voice.

She stood at opened doors and stared, watching for signs of his approach with an apology tucked inside a wrinkle. How could he possibly unravel a word off his tongue? What would she have said if he had bounced in and asked her to search his wrinkles for his loneliness?

Margaret watched along with her and waited. "Bitch" braced behind her teeth like a bitter pill every time she had to face Iva. She hated the fact that the words "bitch" and "body of Christ" shared the same tongue when she went to communion on Sundays.

She hated, too, looking at Iva or having to engage in conversation with her, but Margaret was grateful for one thing. She no longer had to fill up the soup pot with anything from Iva's room. She had everything she needed but the pleasure of fixing fine meals for him or the accidental brush against him when she put Ambrose Kane's plate down before him. This was something she looked forward to whenever he was around.

Roast beef gave her a longer brace against him. She would fill his plate with extra and rest her hand against his arm for support. He always smiled up at her, her future delusion, and offered to carry the plate himself the next time.

She never let him know that she'd fallen in love with him between roast beef and gravy trips to the table. But she felt he knew, had known for some time.

He was always patient with her, the way he would be to a child or an old woman needing something that love could only hand out from a distance. There is a long distance from the hand to the heart. She missed his smile the most. It was always moist, that smile of Ambrose Kane's, as if it lived for rain.

Iva was in better cheer when Bowzer and Humphrey were around. Margaret made it a point to eavesdrop on their conversations when possible.

"I always said you can't fully trust a Confederate, Iva," Bowzer's word floated along the veranda. Humphrey, in her cage nearby, echoed Bowzer's words. "History not wrong. Not wrong."

Iva puffed a faint form of laughter, "I should have been

more careful. I'm not usually taken off guard like this, but to see him red handed in the barn dancing with another woman was the straw that broke the camel's back."

"The man just wanted to rattle his chain on both ends, Iva. You were too good for the wrinkled son of a bitch."

"Wrinkled son of a bitch, son of a bitch," Humphrey bellowed with her little eyes focused on a passing crow.

Margaret made her way back to the kitchen. Her breathing came in deep sighs as she reached for a chair near the window. In her garden view, three or four red dahlias swung back and forth like children bucking heads. She took a deep breath as her hand rose to stifle a sob. So this was why the bloody fool had disposed of Ambrose Kane.

"No, no, Ivadoile," Margaret whispered to herself, "there was straw, but nothing to break the camel's back. The man did nothing but a kind and loving favour for that poor dying Violet Summers."

A week later Margaret heard the thud of broken glass as Iva threw Ambrose Kane's picture in the trash can. Margaret watched as Iva put the lid back on the can, stopped, and looked back at what she had just done, as if something had changed in her mind. She turned and walked away toward the gardens.

Margaret had to be careful of noise when she went to get the photo. Noise is what Iva listened for now, sudden footsteps, something appearing from behind a drape, a shadow that moved like a man, her name being summoned through a breeze. A gentle tap at her bedroom door.

Margaret made sure Iva was a good distance away in the garden when she pulled Ambrose Kane's picture from the bin. The broken glass hailed to the bottom of the can when she picked up the picture and stuffed it under her apron. In the pantry, she wrapped it in a dishcloth and stuffed it in her purse and then reminded Bertie to empty the trash cans for the dump in the back of his truck.

Iva would not have a chance to change her mind at this point. Margaret ran her hand along the edge of her purse and smiled as Bertie drove off to the dump. Ambrose Kane's smile was hers forever.

TWENTY-FOUR

RELIGIOUS PEOPLE ARE more adaptable to God's plan of plucking you off the face of the earth when your number is up. Even now, after all these years, observing the sun-bleached graves of those whom she loved and hated, one thing still comes to mind for Ivadoile Spears. The colours of death, that rainbow that hangs its arch for you to walk under and disappear into an eternity that slyly called out your name and number when you least expected it. A very Catholic thought, Iva reckons, one that Margaret would bear witness to on her knees.

Cullie was as naked as a newborn when he died. His death was as colourless as rain falling into an old barrel.

Her mother's red lace underwear both amused and confused her then as now, the idea of Nettie McLaughlin in such apparel leaves one to wonder. She never wore red. No red sweaters or dresses, not even a hanky with a red rose on it comes to Iva's memory. Where did the red underwear come from? Was it a gift from someone?

She mentioned it again to Cullie after her mother's death but the man was too pragmatic or dull to draw any conclusions.

"They were not the cause of death, Iva, we must let the dead rest."

"How can a woman rest in red underwear, in life or in death?" Iva asked herself.

Perhaps her father had sent them to her mother in some form of mockery to celebrate her celibacy. She had never seen another man in her mother's company since her father left. He was capable of it, Iva believed, recalling sample memories of him from her childhood.

The way he stood beside the dining-room table holding an orange from the glass fruit bowl. It was Christmas Eve. He cupped his hand firmly around the fruit and squeezed, then put it back in the bowl and picked up another. Squeeze. Squeeze.

Iva watched from the wingback chair beside the fireplace. She was six years old. The fire trotted up the chimney like a slow horse before bursting into a violent groan. The Christmas tree stood in the far corner as if hiding from the sparks. Her father braced the tree with two pieces of wood nailed to its trunk in the form of the letter *X*. A red satin tree skirt, sent from a relative in the States, covered the wood. Dull icicles hung from the branches like dried out soup bones. Large striped glass balls clung to the branch tips in a merry radiance as if they were faces in a barroom scene. Standing back at a distance, her mother took in the scale of the tree.

"The width is out of balance for its height," she said, as if speaking to someone in the tree. Iva turned as her father bit deeply into the unpeeled orange. He looked as if he was eating a ball of fire, but he didn't reply to his wife's remark. Her mother backed away further, scaling the tree size and height from different angles with her hands. As Iva sees them now, there is her father in his dark sweater molesting oranges while her frustrated mother attacked the symmetry of it all, as the unbalance of life itself hung before her in make-believe icicles.

Under the out of balance tree, a doll named Victoria lay in a white rectangular box, waiting to be loved.

Surrounded by fire and ice, Nettie McLaughlin opened one Christmas gift from her husband. Tradition allowed one peek in the McLaughlin house, one chance at delight. One bow to be undone and then cast to the fires of the season of joy. Iva watched her mother's mouth, breathless with anger, as she looked down at her gift. The legs of the woollen bloomers were tied in a knot. They were blue, as if they had suffocated before being opened and dropped to the floor like a dead goose.

Juice gathered on her father's chin like streaks of melting frost. He crossed the floor with his hands behind his back and stood in front of Iva. His right hand made a semicircle as he dropped a box into her lap. He spoke not a word. A whimpering cry like that of a weak lamb rose from under the cover. Iva stared down at the crying doll with its eyes closed in its pale face. She lifted it up from the box and stood it in the light of the fire. On a small brooch, pinned on the white pinafore, the name Victoria could be read by the flame. Iva held the stiff body of Victoria in both hands. It surrendered to her movements. Its little red shoes shuffled along the arm of the chair.

She made her bow to a make-believe audience. When it bent over, it began to wail again. She moved it along like a slow train on the arm of the chair towards the edge. Her intent was to drop her off accidentally. She had asked the magical man in red for a cat. Iva watched her mother watching her. There was still leftover anger on her mouth.

She pulled Victoria back from the edge and placed her back in the box. Her mother's eyes moved slowly from Iva to the small present on the branch of the tree. Iva walked slowly to pluck it from the branch. Her father sat beside the fireplace with his pipe to his lip. She placed the gift in his hand as he nodded to her.

He tore into the paper with the urgency of a hungry rat. Bits of white paper sprinkled his slippers like wet snow. He opened the pipe tobacco and filled his pipe. The sweet aroma of the tobacco made her father smell like a baking fruitcake. Iva watched as he sat engulfed in a haze of smoke. Her mother disappeared into the kitchen as Iva walked past her father's chair with the doll in the box. He sat motionless, his face muted by the smoke dancing in the energy of the flames rising on the hearth like a smouldering beast cast from the spit and waiting to be pricked with a fork to make sure he was cooked. His head dropped forward as he surrendered to a deep smoky slumber on that silent and holy night.

TWENTY-FIVE

THERE IS A secret written in the lines of Margaret LaMae's brow. She closes its pages when she frowns. But it is beginning to leak out and run down the bridge of her nose when Iva gets her in a vulnerable spot. The mention of hell usually loosens Margaret's brow. There is more fear than fire in this small word, as if heaven had dropped down a cinder to keep sins from flaring up.

She is talking wildly about Angelo Pinotti, in Iva's kitchen, about the dear man who carried a dead weight on his slight shoulders when he arrived at the Tides Inn.

Iva listens, not for any new gossip about the man who turned out to be an ex-priest, but how Margaret floated him directly into paradise off of Iva's white sheets, with a prayer and a screech from room number Three.

"Priests age faster than ordinary men," Margaret exhales over a cup of tea. "They carry two souls, not only their own, but that of their God."

"Shouldn't that give them an advantage?" Iva frowns as she listens to the thrill in Margaret's voice.

"Oh no, the poor man must have feared that his soul was crushed when he left the priesthood."

"Which of the two souls would that be, Margaret?"

"That is not for me to judge, once a priest always a priest, I'd say."

"Do you suppose then that the man's soul went straight to heaven or did it land in a holding cell?"

Margaret's voice trembles at Iva's question.

"He was a good man, Ivadoile. Men have different reasons for leaving things in their lives. You should know this."

Iva squirms in her chair. Margaret is fighting back with her *men have different reasons for leaving* theory. She is referring to Ambrose Kane and letting her know it. Iva moves to silence the singing kettle whose long spout is jarring at her nerves like Pinocchio belting out a dull hymn.

"A man is a man, Margaret, in or out of the cloth. There is nothing complicated about him, just more to unravel from the cloth," Iva retorts, removing her hand from the handle of the kettle.

"But there was something special, Ivadoile, about this one. I know you liked him."

"He was intelligent, I'll give him that for starters. He left the priesthood and became a psychiatrist. Two professions man does not necessarily have to excel at. They merely place themselves in the arena of the mind and soul, and who has come face to face with these blind assumptions, other than the mad and the gullible, to challenge them? Happiness is not an exact science and it's about time these people stopped taking credit for it."

Margaret opens her mouth to say something but stops.

"You bet he was smart, Margaret. He left the priesthood to get paid for all the confessions he heard without pay."

Iva smiles as she leaves the silence of the kitchen.

"We must not judge others, Ivadoile. Belief itself is blind."

Iva snickers at the remark. "I've been colour blind for a long time then, because there is very little people will make me believe about these assumptions, no matter what colour they die in."

Margaret closes her eyes to the sounds and steam around her and offers up a silent prayer for Angelo Pinotti.

Oh my Jesus, forgive us our sins and lead us not into temptation but deliver us from evil. Amen.

Margaret liked the man the first time she met him back in 1968. There was something out of the ordinary about Angelo Pinotti. He walked with a gaiety about him. Everything he touched stood still. Even Rose, at his cuffs, bowed her head and glared at the shine on his shoes as if she were observing two clumps of dark ice. He had luxury for life and within it he fashioned his limbs to kneel in expensive wear, then stood erect wrinkle free. She remembers too, how his hands folded like a dove's wings over his food. Everything had to be prepared without salt for Angelo Pinotti. Margaret added special ingredients to enhance the taste, a sprinkle of cinnamon, a dash of pepper, a squirt of lemon. Angelo Pinotti asked her politely if it would be a burden to have her prepare his meals separately.

At times, he asked if she would have her meals with him when Iva was gone to the village. Margaret heartily agreed to the man of the roses, whose delicate health, she felt, had been placed in her hands for some spiritual reason. She loved the sound of his voice. He spoke softly as they sat at the kitchen table where he preferred to sit and watch the giant wildflowers.

He asked about her life in Port Murdock.

"Have you ever travelled, Margaret?"

"Not too far from the island. I believe my footsteps were not destined for the big city like my sisters' were. They left for New York and never returned. We had an aunt who lived there. My twin brother died in the war."

"Your twin, you say. It's a big adjustment to lose a part of oneself. You have my sympathy. I suppose you spend much of your time here working at the inn."

"If I didn't, Mr. Pinotti, people would starve waiting for Ivadoile Spears to feed them. She tried to boil eggs once."

"And?"

"They exploded. It took me a week to get the smell out of the kitchen."

Margaret watches a smile travel along Mr. Pinotti's mouth.

"She was an only child," Margaret continued, "I think they used to let her peel potatoes. She's not very domestic. She can't sew or knit or make a pie to save her soul. She'd no doubt sew the button to her thumb, the poor woman. Her father left when she was young and never returned. Her mother was a teacher. They gave her an office job back then, separated women could not teach in the Catholic or

Protestant schools here."

"She doesn't look that poor, Margaret, but I'm glad you do all the cooking."

"Indeed not, she was married to a doctor for eight years. I trust he was a good cook."

"I trust you are her right hand," smiled Angelo Pinotti.

"I certainly am, but she knows well enough to leave the kitchen to me."

"Have you ever thought about leaving to get a taste of the outside world?"

"Once or twice, I wondered what the big cities were like, but I didn't put any effort into my thoughts."

"I know several people who would love to have you work for them in the big city. In Montreal, you would be famous for your skills. And the language would be no problem for you."

"That is very kind of you, but I am bolted to this place for some reason. I looked after my folks for as long as I could. The wanderlust leaves after that work is done. And you, Mr. Pinotti, what do you do to keep yourself busy?"

"I help people out whenever I can to try and sort out their troubles."

"My dear man, I could get you work here at the inn."

They both heard Iva's voice as Margaret was clearing the table and Angelo Pinotti went out the back door to the garden for a light walk.

Margaret marvelled at the idea that he requested three red roses to be placed on his bedside table on a daily basis.

In the heat of Iva's kitchen, several years later, Margaret's sentimental memory rises to meet her and she is in Angelo

Pinotti's room on that fateful morning. She retreats for a moment to let her mind take in the whole scene before she enters the room. Gladys, the cleaning lady, was off with some malady that day.

She is at Angelo Pinotti's door with her hand wrapped around the roses, holding them as tightly as a nervous flower girl at the back of the church. This was unusual for him because he was always up with the sun and strolled through the gardens before he settled down for his hot oatmeal.

Margaret tapped gently at the door. Three knocks and one call later, she turned the knob slowly. The door opened with a small breeze rising at her ankles then swimming up under the hem of her skirt. She remembers this because the breeze was cool when it passed her garters and collapsed with a whistle. She barely called out his name before she screamed. "Jesus, Mary, and Joseph, call a live priest!"

Angelo Pinotti had made up his bed and lay directly in the centre of it with his head resting on two propped-up pillows. He dressed himself for death in his full priestly attire. His black biretta perched on his head resembled a three-winged bird resting against the white pillows and his pale face peeked out from under thick brows like grey porridge that lay under a splatter of sour milk.

A slice of a smile had left his teeth partially visible and crawling out over his bottom lip as if he had spit out some grave mortal sin he wished to have absolved before death. Lace trimmed the long white linen alb that flowed down to his black socks and shiny shoes. A white cincture (a fashionable black cord) was tied around his slim waist. Over his alb, a green sleeveless chasuble ran like a smooth patch of fresh wet grass on the still body of Angelo Pinotti. A green stole (the symbol of a priest) was wrapped around his neck and covered at the folds by his two cold hands clasped firmly around a black rosary. Its gold cross dangled against his bluing thumbnail as if the ear of the crucified Christ listened intently to the last storm under a seal of still flesh.

Iva watches a tear roll down Margaret's cheek. She always weeps when she mentions Angelo Pinotti. It was Margaret who called her own parish priest (who knew Pinotti by reputation) to the inn, along with the local doctor, that day and cleared up the mystery.

Iva is interrupted by Margaret's sobs. "I knew he was one of a kind the day we met." Iva listens without interrupting her. "Such kindness in his eyes, it wasn't until he died that I understood his request for three roses." Iva raises her cup to her lips and sips slowly and watches the slow embrace of agony settle in Margaret's face.

"They represented the Trinity, the Father, the Son, and the Holy Ghost," Margaret whispers before making the sign of the cross with a shaky hand as if this trinity of men would appear at the table and demand to be fed.

Iva has heard all this before about the brilliant Pinotti who entered the seminary at sixteen (no wonder he escaped) and left after a few years in the priesthood to study medicine.

Oh indeed, Iva thinks to herself, *leave it to the well off to sneak three more in the inn without paying for them.*

Iva is finished her tea before Margaret takes a break from talking and sobbing and decides to cast her weary bones to the wind on her walk home. Iva watches as Margaret reaches the opening where the gate once greeted her guests with its strong iron limbs curled into the letter S inside a large round circle. She seems to have paused to check something out in the distance with her small frame upright and stiff in the contour of fear or aggression, suffering holding onto her like a bad cold as she stands still. Iva can see nothing or no one moving along the road. The sky has lowered its clouds over the trees. Perhaps Margaret is wondering if she can make it home before the rain falls. She begins to move slowly towards the left of the gate. Her long navy coat, a hand me down from one of her New York sisters, opens at the flaps giving the wind the freedom of a lover, stroking her in sudden wild flutters. Her body sways back and forth. She swings her cane lightly in the air then dips it into the ground.

A flight of leaves rain down from a nearby tree and interrupt the drama. She pulls her coat around her and crosses her arms over her chest. Iva watches as the dark bundle of the childlike woman she has known longer than anyone else in her life disappears like a shadow out of sight.

Iva felt something bump around inside of her. What? Old Rose is behind her in a running frenzy, sliding into walls. What could she be thinking about Margaret that she hadn't thought already?

Had life closed the door in Margaret's face? Yes.

Why in the hell didn't she make her move out of here like her sisters had done years before? Who knows?

Why hadn't she gotten herself married? Even the home-liest women in the village got to boast about the flatirons and His and Her pillowcases they'd received as wedding gifts.

Why hadn't she looked for love like everyone else? The search is not really your own in these matters.

Unless. Unless the way she smiled at Ambrose Kane left a smear on her heart. He liked her well enough to leave her alone. Her innocence charmed him. He'd often mentioned to Iva how much she reminded him of his sister. But Margaret stayed away from rivers. She contained her sorrow on dry land.

Sorry, Margaret, the river beat you to it, but wet women are pitiful, especially the ones you have to pump air into.

Margaret wasn't in the barn that day because she was in the kitchen when Iva entered the house. No, Margaret, you are not the ballerina. Iva is aware of this.

What else did Margaret stay away from? She had never asked one question about Ambrose Kane after he left. There had to be more to it. Iva's mind pays more attention to what was never asked. Women in love with the wrong men are betrayed by hints. They drop them everywhere like broken china, the poor fools.

When would he return or where had he gone? Margaret never bothered to ask. Or was she being polite, not wanting to interfere with Iva's business. Perhaps it was best that she didn't ask. Iva herself could not answer this question. How much of the truth would have come out then, without a name or a face to identify the dancing feet in the barn?

TWENTY-SIX

THE SHADOW OF James Francis Kalabash appeared in 1965, between a pleat of sunshine and a purple cloud, as Margaret folded the last of the dry linen napkins at the clothesline.

"A woman's work is never done," she heard a voice behind her say as she turned and stood face to face with a man who carried only a brown shopping bag under his arm.

"James Francis Kalabash, Ma'am. I'd offer you a hand but I may need two of them for a few more years yet."

Margaret smiled at the good humoured soul who was, no doubt, in need of a meal and a hot cup of tea.

"I'll be with you in a moment, Mr. Kalabash. I have to have these napkins ready for the evening meal."

Margaret was relieved that Iva was off to Halifax for a few days. She had warned the staff not to be too friendly to hobos.

"Hobos are like friendly pigeons," Iva scowled. "Give

them a few crumbs and you'll never get rid of them."

Bertie watched the scene from the back garden. Margaret waved to assure him she could handle the situation as she glanced over at the bedraggled stranger.

Margaret folded the last napkin and smiled at the man whom she sensed was not looking for a handout. His long uncombed hair appeared to be attached to a small brimmed hat. (She was sure it was a wig by the coarseness of it.) Thick glasses magnified his beady little eyes like round cookies with indented raisins in the middle. His face was unshaven. A rim of grey whiskers formed a horseshoe appearance along his jawline.

"My name is Margaret," she smiled at the friendly Mr. Kalabash as she picked up the laundry basket and walked towards the veranda.

"A lovely name, Margaret. It was my mother's name. You, dear lady, may call me Jimmy."

Margaret turned to tell the man that she would whip something up for him, but he was already at the kitchen door ahead of her with his hand on the latch.

"After you, Margaret, if you please!"

"Thank you, Mr. Kalabash."

"Remember for you, it's Jimmy."

He stood in the opened door as Margaret made her way to the kitchen to get the iron ready to press the linen napkins.

"Entrée, dear Margaret, there is enough room for you and my schnozzola in this doorway."

Margaret pretended not to notice the man's rather large nose as she slid past him and walked straight to the closet to set up the ironing board.

Mr. Kalabash appeared right at home as he rocked in the chair beside the large kitchen window.

"I'll not be too long at this, Mr.…Jimmy. I'll have the tea on in jig time."

Something or someone caught Mr. Kalabash's attention beside the window as he kept a steady raisin eye towards the central garden.

"Lovely place you have here," said Mr. Kalabash, turning towards Margaret. "I'm sure you get lots of people staying here for a visit."

"Oh, it's not mine, but I've worked here so long it feels like home at times. It belongs to Ivadoile Spears, who is away for a few days."

"I've gathered from your tone of voice, Margaret, you've not been away from here for any length of time." Margaret glanced over at the man in the chair. His face was serious and his two raisin eyes were as still as two moles on the face of a corpse.

Their conversation was interrupted by a loud noise coming down the back stairs. Gladys, the cleaning lady, dropped the scrubbing bucket down the stairwell and was sloshing her way into the kitchen swearing profusely. She stopped dead silent in her tracks when she spotted Mr. Kalabash in the rocking chair. Rose bolted for the back door and bunted the screen with her head to get out. She swayed like someone under a liquid influence before eyeing the mat and folding into slumber in a fetal position.

Mr. Kalabash smiled as he stood up to greet Gladys. Her open mouth formed a crooked curve as she stared at the stranger with water dripping from her shoes.

Margaret, fearful of what Gladys might say, volunteered to help her dry up the water. She suggested Gladys get into dry shoes while she got things settled for the cleanup.

"I see that I may have arrived during a monsoon, dear Margaret," Mr. Kalabash addressed in a jovial manner as Gladys backed out the kitchen door still swearing.

Margaret, still at the ironing board, jumped back when smoke rose from one of the linen napkins. She had forgotten to stand the iron upright when Gladys entered the kitchen.

Mr. Kalabash, sensing the dilemma, suggested to Margaret that he should register in the place before he would need an ark to get out of the kitchen.

Margaret apologized and asked him to follow her through the dining room and down the hall to the office where the receptionist swallowed her chewing gum and stumbled up from her chair while tipping it over. Mr. Kalabash paid in advance for a week's stay in room number Three. He smiled as he looked around the lovely parlour as Margaret gave him a tour of the place.

"A piano," exclaimed Jimmy as his little eyes flashed like fireflies. "I've been known to tickle the ivories for a laugh now and again."

"We will be dining at five," said Margaret as he thanked her once again for her kindness and walked up the stairs with a glint in his eyes and his shopping bag under his arm. He carried a suitcase that he had left on the front step.

Gladys, still swearing over the spilled bucket, turned to face Margaret when she entered the room.

"What in the name of Christ did the cat drag in? I hope

you get rid of him before the other one gets back or you may be leaving with Jimmy and his bag yourself."

"I did no such thing. Mr. Kalabash paid in full for a whole week's stay."

"What with, a gun?" cried Gladys.

"You are too distrustful of people, Gladys. He is a good soul. I could tell by the look in his eyes. He is a very kind man."

"I swear to fuck, Margaret, you'd let Al Capone in through the kitchen window. For one thing, I'm not cleaning his room alone. You're coming with me, cause if he jumps out from behind the curtains with a knife, you can offer to make him a cup of tea while I boot it out of the room."

Margaret tried to wrestle her nerves down with a hot cup of tea before dinner. She was accustomed to Gladys and her loud outbursts, but even Gladys had a soft spot should Iva attack the poor man. It would be Iva she'd have to deal with in a day or so. Gladys was right about that encounter.

Margaret looked around the large kitchen. In every creak and corner lay little parcels of energy that belonged to her after working here for twenty-four years. The ruffled edges on the lace runners that the pantry shelves wore, winter and summer, were hers. The yellow wallpaper with its red tulips in a synchronized dance had been chosen by her for the kitchen and pantry walls.

The rag rugs under her feet on the pantry floor came from her own hands. She hand primed and painted the kitchen chairs and cupboards to her own fancy.

She dare not count the meals she prepared and served or the delicate desserts like sculptures she'd created, fancied them up so that many guests said it was a sin to take a knife to them. And of course, there were the special guests that she had grown fond of over the years.

She was relieved that Bowzer and Humphrey were here. Bowzer could always talk Iva into some form of sensibility. Despite the cheerfulness she had wrapped herself in here at the Tides Inn, there was always Iva to cast a cloud over her rainbow.

Ivadoile Spears understood the theory of hurting people. She balanced people with a look, an internal sizing down of one's ability, one's worth rotating in her eyeballs. Few people escaped her direct glare or made it out fast enough to blink away the pain, not even the man who dared to love her.

The memory of Ambrose Kane starts where? Margaret sits at the table a while longer, held down by the slight gait of his feet. They seemed to dance wherever he went, through the gardens, up the stairs, along the veranda, when he emerged from under the apple trees. That is where he danced best. And let us not forget barn floors, Ambrose Kane, where you picked up your deepest wound before leaving town. How often did you dance after that last waltz?

Once she remembered staring at Ambrose Kane's feet and wondered if they were scarred. Were there wounds that he covered up before he set foot in the Tides Inn? There was a bachelor calmness and composure about the man that could and did lead the paranoid, like Ivadoile Spears, away from the dance floor forever. Perhaps this is what keeps them sane and single.

TWENTY-SEVEN

THIS IS A fact that makes Margaret smile. Nobody ever told Ivadoile Spears about the spills that occurred in her inn when she was away. Not a drop of water was ever mentioned. She was presented no damages to inspect or grumble about when she returned to the Tides Inn. Nobody cared to ask her about her three or four day getaways. They always ended too soon. But there was no way to keep James Francis Kalabash a secret as she stood in the parlour doorway with her eyes glued to his hunched over back as he rattled the keys on her piano and broke into song. The others had figured out whose company they were in.

"I know who you are," squealed Gladys, almost apologizing for her foul mouth when she dropped the scrubbing bucket on the stairs. "If you do, then please keep it for you!" winked Mr. Kalabash.

Joining in on the chorus were Bowzer, Humphrey, Gladys, Bertie, and Margaret with her lips on the rim of a glass of iced tea, when she spotted Iva standing in the doorway with a glare in her eyes that could break a bull's neck.

She stood there as straight as an arrow in a pale blue dress and matching sweater. Old Rose scoffed at her heels, twisting and turning until she positioned her head between Iva's two ankles and looked out at the musical scene in fear. The toes of Iva's pumps were perfectly synchronized as if they'd been glued to the floor.

Ivadoile Spears was at the moment a woman approaching fifty-two years of age. She was going through the change and nature, in the last few months, had pulled her jowls down too close to her chin for any cosmetic cover ups to hide. Crow's feet around her eyes made her world look smaller. Women with crow's feet are not taken too seriously, or so she believed. By the standards of the moral fashion of the time, women over fifty were over the hill and knock-kneed out of the love loop. She was revolving into another phase, like the moon, and Iva expected to round out and grow plump and then full size before being frazzled down to a comma.

Iva began to squint often as if in an effort to distract the crow's feet from getting any closer. Her once velvet skin looked more crimped. She wore only a slight blush and a pale shade of pink lipstick to outline the declining contours of feminine advantages.

A day or two before she left, Margaret had brought up to her room freshly ironed garments and placed them on her bed to pack. From her powder room came a deep sigh. A word or two were inaudible, but Margaret knew that the conversation was one Iva was having with herself, speaking to her naked body in front of the full-length mirror. Margaret dared not move a muscle. From her stand point, she could see Iva's reflection in the mirror.

Her breasts were cupped in her hands as if she were judging the weight of two stones. There at her waist, her two hands swam towards each other like two snakes about to collide. She had put on five or ten extra pounds and sensing this, a smirk like a blister clung to her lip. The crime of unwanted flesh hung on her buttocks. She turned slightly to survey the baggage, the soft and dimpled skin like rising pancakes over a fire.

White as snake spit. She took extra care when she massaged her thighs with some kind of lavender lotion, stopping now and again to stretch her legs out full to let the dew of the lavender seep into her flesh. One by one, each limb dangled in air, angled so that each long pale foot found its own image in the mirror and twinkled its toes.

Ivadoile Spears was relieved that both her husband and her lover had not required her to breed for them. Cullie's reason was medical while Ambrose Kane's was intentional. She'd found out shortly before Cullie died that she was unable to conceive.

Iva drowned some of the lotion in her belly button with the soft stroke of her hand and watched as it wept quietly down her pale, barren body.

TWENTY-EIGHT

WHEN JAMES FRANCIS Kalabash turned and met the glare that caused such gloom around his singing posse, he bowed politely to Iva while continuing to play the piano. She eyed Mr. Kalabash with disdain. The only voice that sang was Humphrey's.

"Inka Dinka Doo," belted the bird out over the gloom. Iva turned on her heels and cut a sharp turn down the hall, followed closely by Rose, before anyone could make the introduction to the piano man. Bowzer followed behind Iva as Humphrey kept repeating the same line from the song, "Inka Dinka Doo."

The dialogue between Iva and Bowzer was muffled by the melodic strings of a Bach overture playing in the background in the sun porch. Margaret listened intently at the closed door, but could only make out a word here and there.

Bowzer's voice dipped into a rasp, a tiredness that Margaret picked up on in the last few months. He was semi-retired at the Tides Inn, staying for months at a time before returning to New England. Iva kept the room solely for Bowzer. It was never given to another guest while he was away. It was his room. He had by now designed the drapes and bedspread and had smuggled a rug across the border.

"Canadian rugs," said Bowzer, "come with loose edges."

Gladys was not required to pick up after him. The room was as immaculate as a church. He painted the walls from the palette of Picasso. His room was always dark to Gladys, who referred to it as rusty looking with its crazy colours and tasselled cushions hanging like fur balls.

Bowzer no longer dyed his hair a brash red. Parted in a line in the middle of his head, two thin wisps of salt and pepper hair slid down the sides of his head like the pages of an old open book.

A few consonants had been kicked out of his accent, as well, by the locals when he went out. Gladys was the first to mention that he arrived at the inn in a "kor" and now drove around Cape Breton in a "car."

"Iva," pleaded Bowzer in a voice dampened by frustration as he followed her to the sun porch, "this man...celebrity... from...you...know...I...believe me. This... the real...fool you."

There was a long pause as Bach circled the four walls like a temptress before Iva's voice cut in.

"I...don't...pope.... Who...let...the inn...scare guests...? This...happens...gone a...days...out...control...bar...banter."

Margaret turned and made her way to the kitchen to get dinner started. In the parlour, the singing was in high gear. Humphrey swirled in her cage, singing off key. Margaret could hear Jimmy's voice as he continued to play at the piano.

"I would have gone further only for this block of wood,"
Loud laughter and applause followed.

Margaret began rattling pots and pans. She dropped a pot
cover on the floor and watched it roll like a wheel under the
kitchen table. She didn't expect Iva to return a day earlier
than planned. How smooth the evening would have gone had
she been away for one more night. Margaret had planned on
staying on to be entertained by her friend Jimmy. She hadn't
had this much fun at work since the arrival of Ambrose Kane
at the inn.

Mr. Kalabash was the most interesting guest to come along
in years. He unleashed laughter between the walls. She
cannot remember the last time everyone gathered together
for a song at the piano.

Ambrose Kane played a song or two for Iva, but not while
others were present. These were things exchanged by lovers,
secret melodies meant to twine the heart strings into a
tangled web when the music stopped, and it did. Kane let his
fingers whisper along the keys like a slow draft. Margaret had
seen their shadow one evening as she walked down the lane.
They were knitted so close together, you couldn't slip a note
between them. She stood in the warm summer breeze and
watched what belonged to someone else. A scene like this can
hurt a woman when it is too close, too dangerous a weight
on the imagination.

What was in the hurt was ugly and cruel. She had no
choice but to stomp down the summer grass, let her feet do
the killing in its green splendour, surely there was something
under her feet that death could collect from Ivadoile Spears
for having it all.

Margaret heard the swinging door open as Iva entered the kitchen. Her face looked masked and pale. She had probably lost this round to Bowzer. He had grown very fond of Margaret over the years, loved what she could do for his palate with food. Margaret was safe with Bowzer and she held all that safety in a pot. She had grown to love him as a dear friend.

"I'll be having my dinner in my room," Iva mumbled. "And don't forget to add extra ice to my tea!"

"That will not be a problem, Ivadoile," Margaret answered with a half-baked grin, with one eye on the Ice Queen.

Later, she paused outside of Iva's room with the dinner tray in hand before she knocked. She could hear the lonely strains of Bach escaping from under the door. Margaret looked down at the iced tea. A cube of ice floated slowly to the bottom before crawling along the side of the glass to settle in beside the others.

Jimmy was entertaining guests at the dinner table when Margaret entered the dining room with dessert. He had taken off his hat and glasses and smiled at everyone. He was asking the other guests about their lives, their own interests. What part of the country they had travelled from to get to Cape Breton.

He praised Margaret's cooking and the beauty of the place and invited Margaret to sit at the table and join the others.

He was naming the flowers that Margaret had arranged for the centrepiece with great delight. He was clever at keeping attention away from himself.

Merriment ran high. Humphrey sang low. Above their heads, Ivadoile Spears stood at the open door of her room and listened to it all with a cube of ice between her teeth.

TWENTY-NINE

THERE ARE OTHER things that Margaret can gain leverage from in Iva's Tides Inn. Not only did her culinary skills bring guests back again and again, but she had met Ambrose Kane in the hallway downstairs as he left the inn in 1954 and never returned. He thanked her kindly, kissed her sweetly, left a drop of blood in her right hand and asked her to convey his thanks and appreciation to all the staff he had grown quite fond of over the years.

"I don't believe I will be returning," he shook his head as he spoke. "You can pull some women from a river and they'll just spit in your face. That woman upstairs is ready for a trench. She is a warrior unto herself."

"What has she done now?" Margaret trembled slightly and wondered if Ambrose Kane was quoting from some old poet. Her hands locked in a sweaty embrace, she had not expected this sudden departure. As she looked into his face, she realized he was serious.

It is hard to look into a face that you know you may never see again. Like looking at a corpse and trying to remember where the smile once lived. Where the dimples flashed. How the eyes twinkled. Where the frowns lay hidden. This is what Margaret looked for, sought out in the dying moments she stood in front of Ambrose Kane.

Margaret fed herself on this emotional information for years. She is the holder of the scared words. They have not reached anyone else's ears. She is sly when Ambrose Kane's name is mentioned. Secretive.

What she remembers of him at this moment, when she recreates this conversation after all these years, are the wrinkles. She still can't imagine Iva being taken up with a crumpled man, fussy like she was about things having to be in order. But to find a man in a wrinkle was better than not finding him at all. It had to be his defiance that got her tail in a spin. She had met her match and he was the one who put out the flame for good.

Margaret will get the colours wrong. Were his eyes sky blue or sea blue, or perhaps greenish? She likes to keep guessing at these things. It brings him into focus, sets him in motion. She imagines his hand reaching out for a dish, feels his arm wrap gently around her shoulders with gratitude for an extra special meal. He touched her with thanks. She did the rest of the touching for him, untouchable, touchable Margaret. Were these venial or mortal sins? She questions herself.

More likely mortal, since they were planned and executed by none other than herself, she knows this for sure. She'd planned all those touches with great care like a secret recipe.

She has been planning mentally for some time now, how to rid her soul of this inquisition in the confessional.

Bless me, Father, for I have stayed in a state of sin for many years. I loved a man for years who never loved me. It kept me from the altar and motherhood because my heart never desired to be with anyone else. I couldn't lie to someone and pretend to love my groom at His altar, and go on pining for a love that would never be mine. This would have been too grave a sin in my eyes to bear children under a patchwork quilt of deceit.

Father, I am an old woman and you are a young man, so I pray that I am not boring you to death with such a wound on my soul that may never be healed. But old women come to you with the same piercing to their hearts as the young women feel. This man that I love was in love with another woman (a Presbyterian) who never believed in God. I know that the churches have herded us all together these days, Father, but she still gets on my nerves the way she goes on about the Catholics. I swear to the Almighty that I never said one word to her face about the Presbyterians, although I wanted to say plenty about her.

She threw her poor man out of her life like an old shoe and has walked on the path of misery ever since. She misjudged his actions. The dear man was innocent. I have proof of this and have never told her so, because it was my way of having one over her all these years, I suppose. Yet there are many times when I feel great pity for her. I do visit once a week with her and we talk about old times. But his name is never mentioned. I know that I am waiting for the right time to spring this in her ear, but I feel guilty at times for what I did to her over the years. No, no, Father, I did not grab the man we both loved and lure him to my sheets. Rather, I took from her what was not mine, things

*that a woman needs to get in the mood, Father. I pretended
that I was her on those nights. I stole love, if that is possible,
and set up the whole scene in my head. She never knew about
these things, Father, I was quite good at it. Yet it was my
hands, not my head, that hoisted the things away. One of her
nightdresses, sheets and pillow slips that he slept on, a bottle of
his aftershave lotion. That's all I took from her. It was only
things that a woman needs to make love work for them,
Father, not money or cars. I've never had a license for anything
in my life. I come to you on bended knees, not for pity, but for
some assurance that the good Lord understands the wear and
tear on a woman's broken heart.*

Margaret poured herself a cup of tea and sat at the kitchen
window. Things would be so much smoother, she tells
herself, had she known that Angelo Pinotti was a priest. He
was such an easy going man, so comfortable when he engaged
in conversations with people. He would have advised her on
what to do about her personal situation. Maybe even absolve
her of her sins. Once a priest, always a priest, that's for sure.
And knowing Iva himself, he would already know which way
the wind blew in her direction. "Your sins, Margaret, are as
light as a warm breeze wrapped in a rose," he may have said.
He would have known the cross one had to bear in putting up
with a woman of Iva's nature all these years.

Margaret, at her advancing age, has no choice now, she
reckons, and has to confess this secret sooner than later.
She will bend her knees and spit the truth from her tongue
and drop it quietly into the ear of the young priest in the
confessional, through the darkness that clings to her soul like
plaque.

THIRTY

I VA WAITED FOR spring, in 2007, with her head in the clouds. She always believed that the birds carried a visual map of the elements. The changes required for her to drift out of winter when the birds returned. She watched from her kitchen window for a formation of barn swallows in their forked feathered symmetry, with their perfect harmonies, their lungs filled with southern air, dropping melodies over her gardens now beginning their dilation into wild blooms.

She worried that the swallows would bypass her since the old barn had been torn down. She was wrong. They settled their mud and straw nests in the eaves of her sun porch. The swallows did not take inventory on the condition of the Tides Inn. The peeling paint hanging like open blisters, the rot formation biting into the once sturdy pillars. Its malnourished splinters falling to the ground like dead twigs.

The birds settled in comfortably and laid their eggs. Inside their hideaway, it was dark and warm and far enough away from the slim light of spring. An intimate, salty draft whistled low along the eaves and claimed no visible signs of procreation.

Iva listened for the songs under her eaves. She sat in the sun porch with her cup of tea and waited for buds to appear on trees and patches of green to cover the fields, and sap to run down tree trunks like the runny noses of small children.

Spring brought people out into empty fields and onto the muddy country roads to look around at the things they hadn't seen for months. The top of fence poles, the roofs of houses, the tombstones that shed their white winter coats and exposed their old grey identities like a purple script. In their new spring attire, the feminine scarecrows offered up their frills like cancan dancers.

Ambrose Kane loved spring. He loved the way it made him love, made him move into a woman like a delicious secret into an ear. Opened his mouth to give his lungs a treat and closed it again. He swallowed hard when he was in love. Only his smile was soft and Iva smiled at the thought of it. She wrapped her hands around her cup of lukewarm tea as she chuckled to herself. If he were beside her at this moment, she wondered what she could offer him, a cup of tea, an aching knee joint, a patch of varicose veins, especially the one that spread out like an olive branch, to mull over. She would have to offer him something to feel.

A strange word "spring," spring in, spring out. No matter how hard Iva took it in, washed in its beauty, its newness, something old lingered.

It is hard for her to imagine what would be on Ambrose

Kane's mind after all these years. Had he married? Did he ever father a child after claiming that children would never run down his path? His own siblings had fallen too many times due to their parents' bad marriage. How much did she really know about him in the six years they shared? Was he still among the living?

He'd unfolded an album once and his family stared out at Iva from full sepia poses, a string of bronzed ghosts in a spring field.

Ambrose's arm around his mother's shoulder, clinging to her in some form of biological mercy to motherhood, he understood that much. Did he really love anyone? Lilacs hung low and sleepy below the streaky afternoon sky as the Kanes wavered in their domestic wilderness.

The mother was Sunday groomed in a gingham dress and plain bolero, her handsome face direct and longing for something more than sweet, heavy lilacs and Sunday sermons, a conspiracy against women who were prettier than their religion. His sister straggled at the end of the line as though she had withdrawn from a game suddenly because she was the last to be chosen. Too tall, too short, too clumsy, too damn good for bats and balls and skipping ropes in the mud. She was secretive and beautiful, in a flowing skirt and short-sleeved sweater, with eyes that could rip open a man's mind just to see what spilled out. Enough beauty could open anything, while the river waited. His father leaned against a flagpole with his shoulders slumped. He was clearly and absolutely drunk, in a cheap wrinkled suit. He was much shorter than his sons. Above his head, the Confederate flag carried on a tug of war with the wind. Ambrose Kane's younger brother held one foot against the flagpole. He was brutally handsome with a lonesome crease in the corner of his eyes from something or someone he had stared at far too long.

Iva remembers thinking how socially decayed they looked in their hard handsomeness, except for Ambrose Kane, who smiled as if he were greeting a stranger or himself for the first time.

A SPARK OF maternal instinct had ignited in Iva when she was twenty-five years of age. It was 1941.

She'd never considered herself mother material. She had gone to Glace Bay shopping on a Saturday while Dr. Cullie was called to the General Hospital on an emergency. Commercial Street was filled with mothers and babies tucked in prams crossing her path. Small hands clung to pram handle bars. Some of the children were mere toddlers themselves who had lost the riding privileges in the pram when they stood on their own two feet. Old men sat on park benches. Shaded their eyes from the sun under fedoras and caps. Their faces solemn as they watched the parade of young mothers and children pass by without husbands and fathers beside them. Most of the young men had already left for overseas, formed parades on European soil. The faces of strangers' children somehow reminded them of their own, they wrote in their letters home.

Iva noticed a small boy, four or five years of age, not old enough yet to be self-conscious of the sailor suit that his mother had dressed him in to take him to a matinee. He skipped merrily towards the wide doors of the grand lady of Union Street, the Savoy Theatre.

A wisp of the boy's blond curls edged the square collar of his suit as his dimpled hands tugged on the brass door handles. A doorman, dressed in a red uniform, with greying hair and a wide handlebar moustache opened the door to the great lobby, looked down at the boy with his prominent gold tooth flashing.

The child jumped back and ran towards his mother. Kept his pensive blue eyes on the "red man." The smell of fresh popcorn filtered through the big doors and out along the sidewalk. Its addictive aroma swept past the boy and his mother and made its way up to Senator's Corner. People stopped to inhale the lust of afternoon treats.

Iva smiled at the clever antics of the child as he inched his mother closer to the ticket booth. He stood behind her skirt and pushed her slowly along like a mechanical toy. They had come to see *Popeye the Sailor*, but first they had to get past the "red man" and get their hands on the popcorn. The boy scolded his mother for being too slow. For all he knew, Popeye could be in the lobby behind the big machine popping up the corn and all that would be missed if they didn't hurry. There was urgency in his beautiful face that Iva wanted to relieve.

Perhaps if they were not strangers to her, she could hold the boy in her arms. Kiss the cherub face. She was in a kissing mood at this moment. Assure him that what he wanted, waited for him. She would not down talk him like his mother did. The child was too smart for that. He already knew who he had to watch out for. He was much smarter than the woman who dressed him up to meet his hero in a sailor suit once he got past the "red man." He was much too close to the thrill now to let it all go in a panic. What lurked behind the brass door handles would not stop him.

Iva had seen that look in her own face when she thought she was running out of heroes. She knew what the child knew and had felt an urgent need to love him for it.

Thirty-One

THE THOUGHT OF the Tides Inn being haunted seemed heroic to Ivadoile Spears. It gave the place a new charm, an ambience, an added attraction for Margaret and Gladys, who felt needed even more now, in 1974. Catering to ghosts as well as guests required a certain stoic presence to contend with their sightings, as long as they kept it out of their dialogue amongst the guests.

Iva had only one misgiving about the whole thing. Should she agree with Gladys and Margaret and their reports of footsteps on the stairs and slamming doors in empty rooms, she would have to confirm that she believed in ghosts. She labelled it instead under "the change" and shook her head. They were getting older like herself and every natural sound turned into a dramatic presence.

Iva laughed when Margaret told her that a shadow followed her all around the kitchen for a whole week.

"I didn't believe in ghosts when I was five, Margaret, and

at fifty-eight years of age, I'm afraid all my ghosts have gone to pasture."

"You are missing out on things that improve life, Ivadoile. I believe the dead try to connect with the living for a purpose. Perhaps there are things in their lives that they left unfinished."

"That's called regret, Margaret," Iva scowled.

"There is always something that will put a curl in a pig's tail," cried Gladys, cutting in on the conversation while crossing the kitchen floor with a wet mop she was about to sling over the clothesline.

Iva rolled her eyes as Gladys slammed the screen door as she went out with the wet mop. To reason with Gladys would be like arguing with a bobcat. Iva was well aware of the woman's wayward personality. She was ill informed, obnoxious, and foul mouthed, but despite her diminutive stature and brown teeth from chain smoking, she was a hard working employee for years at the inn and would work as many hours as required.

Margaret was slicing up a roast when Iva appeared in the pantry with a look on her face like someone who had just walked on a rusty spike.

"I won't have you or Gladys repeating such ludicrous stories to guests," Iva bellowed. "The idea of the dead returning and creeping up the stairs and slamming doors is mad. You two will empty the place out. Perhaps it was Richard Nixon hiding out from the Watergate affair," Iva interjected sarcastically. "He probably wishes he was dead and buried at this time. Get Gladys to check out the attic!"

Margaret looked down as she continued to slice the roast. "I don't know about Gladys, but I know what I heard and what I saw, Ivadoile."

Margaret's voice was set with an edge that Iva was not accustomed to hearing, tempered with a twist of spite and conviction.

"Ghosts, if there are such things, would find Europe or Asia or Africa much more exciting, Margaret," exclaimed Iva. "There would be a lot more of history's bones to rattle there. What in the hell would they want to see here in Cape Breton?"

Margaret slammed the knife down on the cutting board and eyed the startled Ivadoile.

"It is not a matter of seeing. I believe they want to settle something that was left unfinished. It could be Mr. Bowzer. It could be poor Esther Neulands or that dear Violet Summers or perhaps Angelo Pinotti. They may want to finish something that they left in limbo here on earth. I know I saw something walk up the stairs and turn out of sight. And it wasn't one of our present guests. Maybe it was—"

"They may want to cart you and Gladys off, Margaret, think about it!" Iva snapped. "Are you sure they weren't wearing white coats?"

Margaret turned her back to the roast. She kept Ambrose Kane's name close to her tongue. She had never spoken of him to Iva for fear of mentioning the one and only letter she'd received. She had her job to protect.

Margaret could see Iva from the corner of her eye, sitting at the kitchen table with a glass of wine in her hand. Old Rose kept her eyes on the swirling wine.

It was odd that Margaret mentioned Esther Neulands, Iva puzzled. She'd had a dream about her a week or so ago, dressed to kill and three sheets to the wind. Esther came stumbling out of the fog over the edge of the cliff and stood there in total defiance of the wind and rain that battered her as it would a marooned row boat.

She kept calling someone's name and it wasn't until she stumbled closer to the inn and fell in the mud that Iva could make out the name "Victoria."

Poor Bowzer was rather upset when he read Esther's obituary in the paper on a trip out west, a year or so after Esther's visit at the inn with that redneck who claimed to be a reverend.

"Thank heavens," wrote Bowzer. "Her obituary stated that she was a world traveller and a widow. Not a bastardly husband was mentioned. Apparently she died in a home in Winnipeg."

Iva noticed that Margaret's face was a potluck of contradictions. She appeared to be praying or complaining under her breath. The sound of the mop handle hitting up against the porch rattled Margaret, as she flew out the screen door. Iva watched as Margaret removed the mop from the line and swung it over the fence like a drunken sailor.

The afternoon sun braided a path up the stairs as Iva made her way to the landing. She paused and looked out over the grounds through the long window at the top of the stairs.

Iva could see Margaret and Gladys as they stood in a haze of smoke on the back veranda. It's a wonder Margaret could stand it, herself a non-smoker, getting roasted daily by that smoking machine. Gladys rolled her own tobacco between her fingers like a bullet. Gladys's hand flew in the air as she spoke as though she were directing traffic at some violent scene. She never stopped smoking or talking.

Iva never permitted smoking in the inn for guests or staff, except for one. She allowed Ambrose Kane to smoke after they made love. She never really knew if it was to celebrate the occasion or to get the taste of her out of his mouth.

The door to room Four was slightly ajar as Iva pushed it open. A slight chill swept across the room and gathered at her ankles. She checked the windows. All the screens were tightly secured. The sea was flat below the cliffs. It looked empty and lonely as if it had discarded all its cargo and now wished for a turbulence to energize it, give it a reason to growl again over the land.

Iva turned and stared into the spruce green eyes of Victoria. She tried to remember if she had ever sung one lullaby in the doll's ear. The doll was much lighter than she remembered as she flipped her over. She no longer cried or made a sound. Her shabby little dress clung like a Kleenex in her hand. She'd never cared much for dolls. They always looked dead to her, staring straight ahead like a stunned sheep with that perpetual smile carved like a tattoo on their mouths.

Esther Neulands loved Victoria. She'd mentioned it to Iva on more than one occasion. She wanted room number Four because of the beautiful doll she'd seen in the room. She'd said something or other about the doll that reminded her of her childhood.

"If I didn't know the age of the doll, I'd swear it was new,"

Esther's voice shrilled like a six-year-old's. Childhood seemed too far back for Ivadoile Spears. A place she'd never cared for or reached out to with women. How the doll ended up in the Tides Inn was a fluke. Someone had packed it in a box marked, "Fragile. Handle with care!" She shared very little with her women guests. She had always preferred talking to the men.

Iva cannot remember where her mother had purchased the doll. She didn't dare mention Santa Claus to her, since Iva was a child who only believed in what she could see for herself. She had no sightings of Santa Claus or the Easter Bunny or the bloody Tooth Fairy in Port Murdock that she could remember. And now Gladys and Margaret were seeing and hearing ghosts at the inn. The prophets of madness or imagination had taken hold between the walls and escorted themselves at will out of her sight.

Iva placed Victoria back in the wicker chair. She hadn't paid much attention before to the perfectly heart-shaped face, the dimpled hands and knees that concealed little cracks in her make believe flesh. One of her shoes had fallen off, but she didn't bother to put it back on. It wasn't until she turned to close the door that she noticed Victoria's eyes were closed as if she were in a deep sleep with her little shoe close to her bare foot.

THIRTY-TWO

IVA LAY IN a bubble of mischievous laughter before midnight, a light-hearted burst like a wheeze filtering through her soft quilt. Sometimes it is the laughter of others she hears—Margaret's nervous refrain, Gladys's gravel-pitched voice hooting over the misfortunes of the well-to-do. Sometimes she imagines Bowzer's voice pausing to enlighten a story he was telling. He never liked to waste words.

"Could you see me," shouted Bowzer, "collared around the neck like an Irish wolfhound and frothing from behind the pulpit at the vices of my flock! That is what my spinster aunts wanted for me since I was born out of wedlock." His face exploded with indignation.

"To cure me of my illegitimacy, they tried to bind me to religion. My poor mother was frantic. She had no voice against these virginal tyrants. I was sitting at the kitchen table, at sixteen, eating cornflakes when they dropped their bomb. I crunched like a mad cow but they wouldn't let up. It should be no surprise to you, Iva, what one night of passion can do. I became a man of the cloth all right, but not what the old aunts had planned."

Iva smiles when she thinks of what he might have had to say about the inn being haunted, if he were not on the "other side" as Margaret refers to death's eternal real estate, heaven.

"Dear Bowzer," Iva comments out loud, "I've been informed that my inn has ghosts. And that one of them could be yourself in dire need to straighten out something you may have left unfinished in this world."

The gongs of the old clock interrupt Iva's dialogue as they slice through the darkness. They are long and echoing gongs, announcing the eleventh hour of the night. She makes a mental note to have Bertie tone down the sound. Some of her guests always retired early for the evening. She is the only person who sleeps on the first floor of the inn now. Down the hall from her, Bowzer's room is empty. His voice stilled for over four years. His room is off limits to guests. An old cage belonging to Humphrey was made into a flower pot. The clinging vine lies whispering along the floor now that it has outgrown the cage.

Iva walks slowly to his bedroom and unlocks the door and walks in as if Bowzer was waiting for her visit. She lights the candle on the holder near the door frame. Its high deep coral walls come alive under fire and spread to the elegance of the room. Despite his absence over the years, the room remains energized as a lover's grasp. The handsome sea-blue bedspread and matching drapes level off to an appropriate length along the floor. The fringes dipping along the wood like bangs of small children leaning over to watch the journey of an ant.

His Picasso prints, in their golden wooden frames, line the walls. The eyes of Picasso's self-portrait appear to watch her every move. She never liked this painting of Picasso. The man looks mad, as if he enjoyed painting himself as a decaying corpse. A marble statue of David stands on a small table in the corner.

There is no doubt that the King, with his biblical tone and stature, had been carefully edited by Michelangelo. Men who look this good should always be naked, Iva smiles. A man with the hands of grace and fortitude like Michelangelo's made few mistakes.

A picture of her and Bowzer with Humphrey perched on his shoulder stands on the bedside table in a gold frame. Humphrey's head is turned towards David, as if she were waiting for him to speak. Iva and Bowzer share a laugh, their faces filled with the greed of contentment. They passed it on to each other like a game of tag.

There is another picture that Iva doesn't remember seeing on her last visit to his room. It is of Bowzer and Violet Summers in one of the back fields. They are sitting close together as though ambushed by the wildflowers surrounding them. Bowzer has his arm around Violet's waist as if to anchor her down from the wind. She is so thin, her arms look like stripped stocks. Violet is holding a bunch of windblown flowers in one hand.

In another photo Margaret and Gladys are sitting on the back veranda. A cigarette dangles from Gladys's mouth and the smoke curls up over part of her face. Her eyes are small and vulgar. She appears to have been caught off guard by the lens and is none too pleased. Margaret sits demure and beautiful, her dark hair unfolding and eloping down her back. She is smiling shyly. She, too, seems taken by surprise. It had to be Gladys who set up this gallery when dusting the room, thought Iva. Something else catches her eye, poking out from under the drapes. A delicate red feather. There is no mistaking who this belonged to. Iva picks it up and puts it in her pocket.

The rug beneath Iva's feet is trimmed in coral with a blue-green inset that always reminded her of a rather large fish tank. The bed and windows are wearing their summer attire. Bowzer's season of death. He changed the drapes and bedspreads every season.

"You have to live in colour and let colour live in you," explained Bowzer to Iva during his blue season after he had stayed at the inn a few years.

It is rather fitting, Iva believes, that the drapes and bedspread should not be changed now. That he be remembered as a fresh artful breeze that floated through the inn and hung up his colours for all to see. He had stopped eating cornflakes at an early age and developed an appetite for the geniuses he had not, or would not, ever meet. He sat for hours looking up at the distorted self-image of Picasso.

Iva makes her way across the dimly lit room and stands before the portrait. She stands like a woman waiting for a late bus that will take her to no place in particular. Perhaps to let the miles fill in the emptiness; women do it all the time, try to fill in their time in motion. Where is there to go from all this?

She had never cared for the self-portrait, but the word that comes to mind now, as she grins slightly, is "ghostly."

Iva moves closer to the small brass inscription attached to the middle of the frame and reads it slowly.

"Everyone wants to understand art. Why don't we try to understand the song of a bird? Why do we love the night, the flowers, everything around us...."

She pauses before blowing out the candle and looks around the room once again. She is not sure if this was Picasso's quote (perhaps more than not it was) or something Bowzer had written. She is still not sure whose ghost is speaking.

Thirty-Three

N O MORE WAS said about ghosts in Iva's presence except by Gladys, who within earshot yelled out, "Some people wouldn't recognize a ghost if it came up and bit them on the arse." She was in the pantry conversing with Margaret. Iva could hear Margaret trying to hush Gladys into a whisper, but Gladys, after a cough-ridden sleep, was raspy voiced and intolerant.

"I seen and heard my share of them, let me tell ya. Even at wakes, I heard the dead talk out loud. For some reason, they like to ramble on about politics and grudges."

Iva cringes as she leaves the kitchen and walks along the veranda to the gardens. Rose scurries from the rail and comes up to her feet and sniffs at her shoes with her damp nose.

It is early July and the gardens are fuming with dew. The grass opens wide in the back field like a dividing sea of green. Something rises from the green and is carried upward and down towards the liquid sea. It glides slowly like a wish in a shooting star, down over the cliff.

Iva, as if she is a poet, stands in an idyllic atmosphere for the muses to harvest and ripen. From where she stands, Port Murdock is in a seductive mood, poetic almost, with its green running hills and blue rotating sky collecting clouds from its edges. Birds flitter in and out of the clouds as if in a game of hide and seek.

It's what's in between that Iva ponders. She was never one for poetry, never took a liking to it. Things were summed up too quickly. She preferred the long drawn out chase of the novel where the heroine suffers it out to the end. She always preferred blood on the last page.

Lately she has found herself stalling in the pages of Ovid and Plath and the likes, tasting secretly like a child in a candy store stealing a forbidden lick. Perhaps it is her age, when women start dropping their baggage, she thinks after a quick analysis. She is cutting back on things: sugar, coffee, arguments, and words. Why words? She hasn't a reasonable explanation for this because the poetry came as an emotional bargain for her. She wasn't expecting to like it.

Her parents read poetry, a good enough reason for her to dislike it. Her father split the pages of Poe open with a macabre glint in his eye. His hand trembling as it did on Opal's visible flesh, in and out, disappearing and re-appearing. There was a noise in that hand, a wind drift like a mad shuffling of pages. And then he knelt with the words spilling through his hand, the bastard, the coward. He wasted everything he touched.

Her mother read for aggravation. The love poems of Yeats and Keats and a gathering of spine-twisted volumes she dug out of a trunk after her husband left. She never saw a shadow of him ever again. There was nothing good to remember—no rhythm, no rhyme.

Nettie McLaughlin may have wondered if life was ever served in this manner. Rhapsodies and sunsets and bird droppings forming clusters like wildflowers for urgent lovers. Everything has purpose and beauty for the newly in love, that time in your life when hormones replace reality.

What kind of images were the poets exposed to while the rest of the world stood back and waited for the prophets of sentiment to eulogize their sorrow? Nettie McLaughlin had enough. She gathered the poets by the armful and dropped them in an old cast-iron drum and marinated them in kerosene. Fourteen-year-old Ivadoile watched from her bedroom window. The flames rose taller than her mother in a crackling moaning torment of loss. The smoke turned a greyish black after the words had died together, in one smouldering heap they lay at her feet.

Her mother's soot-filled face looked up towards Iva's window. She saw the glare of her white teeth set back in her black face.

Nettie McLaughlin stood like a ragged puppet, strings loosened with limbs about to fold after its performance was complete. And all the while, behind the glare of the white teeth, her mother was laughing hysterically.

THIRTY-FOUR

THERE ARE A few blades of grass beginning to peep out where the old barn once stood. Balance space against structure, time against memory, and this patch of land looks too small for the grand barn that housed large stalls and hay bins filling both sides of the loft. Iva finds it impossible to believe, from an old painting of the barn in her sun porch, that it ever existed, if anything at all had ever taken place where she believes it had, but vividly remembers the barn swallows.

Iva is standing directly where the middle of the barn stood, where her love life ended with a song, and the swallows hid their songs high in the rafters. Songs can live for a long time between the walls. A wounded heart tapping to one more beat still lives. It's all in the echo, she says. The scientists have proof of its accuracy. Anything can be trapped and released again except for the ballerina. She will never dance again.

A new green life is sprouting, moulding itself to fit in. It is here where things will be hidden, footsteps will be unheard, butterflies will inspect, berries will flourish, a new barn may rise again, and young lovers will taste for the first time the forbidden fruit of Port Murdock.

How easy will it be for them all to fall in love? How quickly will their reflexes match their hormones?

They are not aware, poor fools, that time is watching them, waiting to drain their libido, release their embraces, stoop their shoulders, decay their bones, hasten their steps. Before they know it, an embrace will be a nuisance to them. A joint invasion to get things flared up and interfere with the aging process.

Iva hears soft footsteps approach. Margaret is as regular as a prune. She steps up to where Iva is standing and looks about.

Margaret mentions the danger that has been abolished, the fear of things that could have flown off the old barn and nailed you in the head. Danger is always on Margaret's mind. Perhaps it always settles deeper in the minds of spinsters and nuns who wear that "private property/no trespassing" look in their eyes.

"At our age, Ivadoile, a board to the head would be a disaster."

"A mosquito to the head, at this time of our lives, could be a disaster, Margaret."

Margaret shrugs her shoulders. She knows that Iva will always go the stretch for the last word. She dare not mention how happy she is to see the old barn gone. She was always a bit cautious to pass by it when it was windy.

Iva is in a sour mood when she catches Margaret observing her like a road kill.

"I used to like barns when I was a child, Margaret, until..." Margaret turns and looks down the lane waiting for Iva to conjure up something that will drive her to Tums. But Iva goes very quiet. Almost too quiet, as the wind brushes her hair from her face and her eyes sink further back as she grasps for a memory that she let off the hook temporarily. A complete thought is hard for her to hold onto at any given time.

She never wears a hat now or forgets to most days. She appears much smaller under a face that the wind and sun have tinted a gritty brown.

Margaret looks up towards the old inn and wonders if it is repairable. It has a lonesome, weather-beaten look itself, an atmosphere of abandonment.

Left voiceless.

Left loveless.

Left without music.

Left without time on its old clock.

Left drafty and angry.

The roofs are still well structured. They had been replaced ten years ago or more. Some of the windows could be replaced. A slow mean draft is not good for the bones.

Margaret has used this old wives' tale on Iva a few times, giving her a gentle warning about her health. Iva whistles a prolonged "frig off" Margaret's way. She is crafty in her approach, as if Margaret is the carrier pigeon she must send her message along with, to whomever is waiting in the wings.

"A new window is not going to stop my bones from getting older. You can deliver that message to your watch-dogs!"

Margaret is cautious now in her approach to Iva. She not only has the sarcastic remarks to pay heed to, but Iva has added a free tongue to her dialogue.

An image of Gladys flashes in Margaret's mind. Swearing came out of Gladys's mouth like a raspy breath of dirty air released from her lungs.

Dead and gone more than ten years now, Gladys rests in the Black Spruce Cemetery beside her husband. They puffed their way to paradise. To the left of their graves, an old smoke stack (used by woodcutters) chain smokes at alternate hours of the day.

"Oh where are my manners, Margaret," Iva's voice inter-jects. Margaret turns towards her and is surprised by the meek look on her face.

"It is about time I put the tea on." She moves towards Margaret and locks her arm in hers as they walk towards the inn like two school girls on their way home from school.

Margaret moves along slowly. In all the years she has known Ivadoile, they have never been physically connected. She feels rather timid and shy, baffled by Iva's gesture of open affection. Margaret feels in her sweater pocket for her roll of Tums. Thank heavens she has not forgotten them. Her freshly baked banana loaf is tucked inside her shopping bag. She is hoping she will have time to check the condition of the cups while Iva makes the tea. The last time they had tea, she found money folded in the bottom of her cup before Iva poured the tea.

"You should be more careful with your money, Ivadoile," she'd cautioned playfully. Iva smirked over her tea as she stared directly at Margaret.

"You can have all the money you want, Margaret, if that's what you are implying. I haven't made up my mind who to leave my bundle to. Perhaps it will be you."

Margaret chastised herself for saying anything. That's all she'd need, was to have people think she wanted Ivadoile Spears' money.

Margaret felt like a school child at her desk with the teacher asking if she wanted a strap for insinuating instead of asking for something directly.

I have plenty of straps left, Margaret. To insinuate is weak, a voice cried in her head and when she looked up she could see Iva's lips moving.

Margaret remembered the small parcel that arrived by registered mail to her from the States shortly after the death of Mr. Kalabash. It contained the medal of St. Margaret that she had given him in memory of his mother when he left the Tides Inn. In his will, Mr. Kalabash stated that he wanted it to go back into the hands of a kind friend. Included in the parcel was a certified cheque for a few thousand dollars and a brief note written by Mr. Kalabash himself.

"For you, dear Margaret. I ask that you do as you please with my blessing!"

Margaret blessed herself on the way to the bank. She took this as a sign that he, Jimmy, was looking down on her in her little house that needed repair. One has to be obedient to kindness. Two weeks later, her little house presented itself to the village under a pale blue roof and siding. "Money and prayers can change the colour of anything," Margaret smiled.

Iva places two cups on the table and turns to cut into the banana loaf. Margaret does a quick inspection. The cups are clean and empty. Iva sits facing Margaret square on. Her eyes are more alert, as if she had just risen from a restful nap. The banana loaf sits between them cut in slices so thin one could read through them. They lay unevenly on the plate like broken shingles. The cup in Iva's shaky hand has a painted mourning dove below the rim. The dove's beak is tilted upward, as if it were watching for something approaching. Iva drops it back on the saucer and wipes at the splatter of tea with the cuff of her sweater. She is watching to see if Margaret has noticed the spill.

"I never used to be this careless, Margaret. There was a time I could creep along the plank of a barn like a cat."

Margaret breaks a slice of her loaf into small pieces as Iva watches her.

"Of course, I was much younger then, a mere child, and that's when I took a dislike for barns."

Margaret sips her tea slowly, washing down bits of cake off her tongue. She is aware that this story is going to grow longer. Iva is making sure that she has an attentive listener.

"I always liked barns myself, Ivadoile. My twin brother and I played hide and seek in our barn. We had a swing made from an old tire." Iva has not heard a word she's said. She interrupts Margaret again.

"My father and my mother's Methodist cousin, Opal, played in our barn, but it wasn't a game of hide and seek. No, no, Margaret, they found what they wanted in a hurry. Nothing was hidden. They might have danced, but I missed that part. They were raw naked and then came the blood when my cat attacked. Cousin Opal cried out for repentance. Oh, the blood. It made him swear. I'd never heard my father swear before. My mother swore when he left Port Murdock the following year. I read the word she formed on her lips. My mother swore like a mime."

Margaret lets this statement roll around in her head for a minute. She coughs to delay a response, because this, she knows, is what Iva waits for. She is not sure if this is a game Iva is playing or something that has fermented in her head from a dream and she is splicing stories together to make them fit a pattern of everyday life. She rarely spoke of her parents, if at all, in all these years. Everyone knew Rory McLaughlin had left for the States and never returned and that poor Nettie McLaughlin was adrift on a leaky barge until her death.

"In the name of the Father, the Son, and the Holy Ghost," Margaret smothers the trinity under her breath. *This has to be something off the top of Ivadoile's head.*

When Margaret looks up she knows that what she just heard is the truth, so rounded up from the rim of childhood, so damned by adult obscenities, so crucified into Ivadoile's blood, she must have tasted it all these years without sharing a drop with another woman until this day.

Margaret, in all honesty, does not know how this story is going to end, after the hurting barns have been torn down.

The one Iva's father entered changed her life, and the one Ambrose Kane entered changed the lives of two women.

Oh, if only the swallows could speak. She would not have to reveal the good story to Ivadoile Spears. The fact that she had not been jilted, that Ambrose Kane gave a dying young woman her last wish. Life may have had a different outcome for Ivadoile Spears.

There is everything and nothing in Iva's eyes. Everything that she remembers and nothing that she can forget.

Memory thrives on everything and nothing to mount its terror. It is necessary when the tangibles have come crumbling down. Margaret is witness to Ivadoile Spears when the walls come tumbling down.

Again the cup is in her shaky hand. She does not take a sip. Iva is too busy whispering to the mourning dove pressed up against her lips.

THIRTY-FIVE

A NEW LIGHT had been cast on Ivadoile Spears after her revelation. A swell of pity rose like a moral tide in Margaret and butted at her conscience like a ram in a spring field. This pity was fresh and at its most vulnerable peak in the early summer of 2007, after each visit.

In all the years she had worked for Iva, there was never a hint that adultery could pull a child's curiosity to the height of a barn beam. Seemed impossible a view even for Ivadoile McLaughlin. But it is still there in her eyes after all these years, still scorching inside out, outside in. It dwindles out if you are lucky or forgetful for a time, and straddles your madness on someone else's shoulder for the ride. But it will return. It always does. The return has with it a different edge, like a fresh dog bite, a new found contempt for Sunday afternoons.

Atonement can be hard on the soles of the feet. She

added extra visits to Iva's old inn. Margaret's guilt, in part, lay in her judgement of the woman over the years.

The McLaughlins didn't live in her neck of the woods when she was growing up. Their magnificent home, surrounded by silver maples and apple orchards, stood at the end of a long lane. A house set amongst the trees can hold its secrets deep. Very few people saw its inner walls.

As children, Margaret and her brother feared to venture down the dark lane looking for treats on Halloween. The house was always dimly lit. Two large lanterns, disguised as pumpkins, glowed on either side of the big barn door. The kids who ventured near reported that Nettie McLaughlin was in the barn with her strap and a spelling book. You had to spell a word correctly or you were denied a treat and sent scurrying down the lane as she held up the strap.

Margaret and Ivadoile attended different schools and churches. This, in itself, in a small village, is often the straw that breaks the social camel's back.

Margaret remembers Nettie McLaughlin as a rather stern individual who watched carefully over her shoulder as if she were being followed by a sniper. Her husband, a tall quiet man who never believed in idle chatter, walked behind his wife smoking a pipe. What conversations people heard between them came out of a haze. Iva usually trailed behind, head down, as if she were looking for something to rise up out of the ground like an earthquake. A thin line of smoke divided them, the hazed family, in a straight line walking as if they headed straight for their own execution.

Margaret imagined the scene in the hay loft, the muscled Opal, the stern Nettie McLaughlin, off to a church meeting (the snipers closer than she thought), the pipe smoking father. Words were not required for such matters. Flesh has a language of its own.

It was hard to imagine the nakedness of it all surrounded by such physical beauty trapped amongst the trees. And Iva, a child in the wings, watched and heard her father swear for the first time. From her perch on the beam, she could hear a choir of maples through the trees in the distance.

Margaret made two weekly visits (weather permitting) to the old inn, instead of one, after hearing Iva's confession. She took with her, like Little Red Riding Hood, a yellow basket filled with food. It was the least she could do for the child witness who still carried visions of youth in her eyes like a disease. There are no words available to a child when the eye provided all the facts.

In her climbing age, Margaret took pride in being in fit shape. Good health kept her active.

She was surprised that even Iva, being eight odd years older than she, maintained herself in good form, despite the landscapes where children hide their terrors until age releases them to the tongue and they came crawling through her own set of teeth. To be told and not repeated. She had sealed it somewhere in the back of her mind since such an early age, perhaps to let it settle like a fruit cake in a dark cellar for future use.

No heart problems or diabetes have Iva and Margaret, just the occasional kick to the bones that everyone else would be subject to sooner or later. She wasn't quite sure if her moody behaviour was from old Iva or if it was something old people went headlong into to aggravate youth.

They were non-drinkers and non-smokers, although she had watched Iva swill a few glasses of wine at dinner like a rocking horse and stay steady on her feet. It wasn't a daily habit when Bowzer was gone.

No wonder Iva tilted them back now and again, Margaret worries to herself, with the weight of her parents' marital conspiracy on her shoulders and the voice of a muscular, naked Methodist crying out for redemption in her ears.

THIRTY-SIX

BOWZER HEARD THE story of her father and cousin Opal over several glasses of red wine to Iva's four. They were sipping until midnight in Bowzer's room. Picasso kept a bulging eye on Iva as she spoke. A full moon highlighted Bowzer's brassy red hair, sifted through it in slow motion like a laser beam from a space ship.

Bowzer grabbed the wine bottle and poured himself another drink when Iva got to the hayloft part of the tale. He inhaled the climax, coughed it up as a red bubble burst on his bottom lip as if he could see the scene directly in front of him. The innocent child on the limb of a beam getting her full view of real life way, way too early.

"The nerve of the dog," he spit across the room. "You'd think he'd have kept it in dry dock until they were off the property." Humphrey growled in her cage and broke in on the conversation. "Nerve of the dog. Nerve of the dog."

"She wasn't much better, Bowzer. She knew where they were and whose husband she was baring it all with at the time."

"Whose husband? Whose Husband?" Humphrey questioned as if she knew the parties involved personally and wanted to expose them to the public.

"Love is the most dangerous of all illusions, Ivadoile. I read that somewhere. Sex is something the fed-up heart keeps in reserve for a temporary thrill. A thief in the night, in this case in the afternoon. Some thieves never want what they steal. It's the thrill of never getting caught that they seek."

Bowzer took a deep drink and looked over at Iva's feet. His head appeared too heavy to lift.

"Sex is invisible. It's the easiest thing to steal," he told the floor.

Humphrey swung slowly on her little swing and sang out, "Sex is invisible. Invisible."

Bowzer staggered over to Humphrey and draped her cage in what looked like a blue velvet frock from the eighteenth century.

"Goodnight, Miss Humphrey, you've had your say for the evening." He tapped the cage affectionately before sitting down and filling up his crystal wine glass to the rim and taking a long drink.

Iva looked up at Picasso, who seemed to be taking the conversation in quite seriously. His eyes looked ready to pop. She'd had her share of decaying men who followed her with their eyes that looked ready to swim out of their sockets.

"Did your father know that you had seen them in the loft?" Bowzer's voice softened. He looked like he was about to weep. He held a linen hanky close to his nostrils as he sniffed. Two red streaks raced each other down the sides of his chin.

The room was cool, yet Iva felt too warm in her green silk dress. She wanted to slip down to her skin, to unravel everything from her. Bare it all. She felt her blood rushing to her head, an end of a river rush waiting to be drained into something deeper. She had not spoken a word to anyone about her father's affair with Opal. She can't remember why she had not said a word to Cullie Spears. He probably would have suggested she go to the Bible to uproot an answer. In all his medical books there was no cure for adultery, he may have said. The stuffy old men who wrote those books would not have placed pleasure and pain in the same bone.

"Iva, did your father know what you knew about him and Opal?" Bowzer's question startled her like someone being shaken out of a deep sleep. He was leaning on one side of the chair in a frozen position as if he had spotted a cougar.

"Not at the time," she mumbled as she drooled from one side of her mouth to let Opal's name slide out as if she could drown her in the slide, "but I knew Opal did when I bribed her the next day. Nervous Opal was on edge. Her eyes were still naked."

Iva breaks into a hideous laugh as if she just realized her scheme had worked.

"The bitch, she was a real bitch," slurred Bowzer. "Carrying on like that with a child in the house." His arm rose like a preacher's and fell between his legs.

"I can't say I blame him for leaving my mother. She was as crazy as a bag of soot," Iva belched. "But I hated him too for what he did."

He looked over at Iva as if she were still a child.

"At least that woman had the sense to get out the next day. But your father should have come back to see you after he left. He wasn't in exile in China for fuck's sake." He paused as sentiment overcame him and his chest heaved in and out like a dying man.

"I never knew my own father. Never saw his ruddy face. My mother, a decent but naïve woman, told me that he was a shy Norwegian with a lisp. She believed it was his romantic accent that she fell for when they met. He said all Norwegians spoke like himself. Left the country before I was born, he did. She believed her aunties threatened him with the law." Bowzer went looking in his bureau for a portrait of his mother and father, but couldn't find it.

"Christ knows where I was conceived, it must have been on the sidewalk because the man was never allowed in the house." He stopped to blow his nose as he sat down again facing Iva. "We didn't have a lawn. Our family was so close to the street I could hear people fart as they walked by. My aunties always had their noses in the good book like witches in a vat, but they would have sniffed out a man in the house."

"My mother would never have allowed my father to step foot on the property in Port Murdock. She never mentioned his name to anyone," said Iva.

"Bull on him. He could have met with you on somebody else's property. He wasn't that far away."

Bowzer pounded his fist on a side table to make a point. David collapsed as if he'd fainted. Bowzer scrambled up and grabbed the king by the torso with both hands and apologized before placing the statue, facing the wall, back on the table.

A small voice emerged from under the frock. "Bull... bull...bull," Humphrey whispered as the room went silent.

THIRTY-SEVEN

THESE WERE THE choices Margaret made to be kind to Iva. A tisket, a tasket, a little yellow basket. Margaret is partly up the lane, stopping to shift the weight of the yellow basket's contents from one slim arm to the other.

Iva wants to go out and greet her, but this is not how Margaret wants things to turn out. Iva does not know why Margaret's visiting times have changed or why she brings along meals on her visits. She's become immune to Margaret's whims and desires over the years.

Margaret's picnic penance must go as planned. It is part of the penance imposed on herself.

Bless me, Father, for I have misjudged the misjudged. She is a woman just like me.

Iva does not remember ever relating her childhood story to Margaret. And Margaret has no plans to have her relive the story with her again. She will not bring up the subject, but she is not sure what Iva will ramble about at any given time in the last little while.

There will be enough food for two. There always is. Shapely chicken legs baked moist to the bone. Cubed potato salad in a round bowl in low-fat mayo. Green parsley clinging to each cube like the whiskers on a moon-faced giant. And to keep them both regular, Margaret packs a prune and plum pudding on ice. Regular women need these delicacies to get them going every day.

Margaret is a food planner. She goes for the heart and the bowels in one meal.

Iva watches her as she approaches the kitchen door. She can smell the chicken as she enters the kitchen. Rose scurries around Margaret as she stares up at her.

"Don't worry, I didn't forget you, kitty-cat. Margaret has packed you a good little lunch."

Old Rose drops her head in the bowl of salmon as Iva removes two plates from the cupboard and places them on the table with the knives and forks. She has pushed the box of old photos to the edge of the table. Margaret flips through a few photos and comes face to face with Angelo Pinotti.

The man looked thin in a light suit and tie, as though he carried his own secret weight somewhere within him. Margaret knows this picture was taken on a Sunday, because he had mentioned that he was going to early mass in the village. He had even asked if she would like to accompany him. Serenity dances between the lines on his face. His forehead is braced against the sun. The rest of his face has the contentment of a man in a hammock gliding through a breeze before sleep. He looks much taller than she'd remembered him. The picture is graced with a gentle smile from dear Angelo Pinotti.

A sudden stab pierces Margaret's heart. After all these years, sentiment can strike her at any moment like an unexpected storm. But today, at this moment, coincidence overthrows sentiment and drops an omen in her little yellow basket. She can feel her heart pounding like it had when she received the medal of St. Margaret along with the cheque from Jimmy.

Iva has been watching the contours of Margaret's face. From sorrow to elation, the woman looks like she's in the throngs of a charismatic revolution.

"What in the hell is wrong with you or is there something in your chicken that is not going to agree with us?"

Margaret pulls herself together to explain to Ivadoile what she has just remembered.

"Look at this picture of Angelo Pinotti, Ivadoile! I remember the day as if it were yesterday."

"So what, that box is full of the dead."

"It has to be an omen, Ivadoile. On the day this picture was taken, I served the dear man the same food I have brought here for us today. And what do I see on your table but the man's picture smiling back at me as he did that day."

"How can a chicken or a prune fit in with an omen, Margaret? I will never understand you Catholics." Iva smiles at Margaret. "What will happen if your Saint Peter is a Presbyterian, Margaret? You people could be eating your chicken somewhere else."

Margaret ignores Iva's remarks as she unloads the basket. Her heart is too light to be scorched by anything Iva can serve up. The two women sit down in silence and eat the delicious meal. Margaret eats in peace. She knows what the omen could be. Angelo Pinotti is relieving her of her penance for misjudging Ivadoile. He is releasing her from limbo where she dwelt and is stepping her up into a temporary purgatory where the greater odds for forgiveness are the rule. Heaven is within her grasp.

She looks towards Iva who licks her fingers like a cat and smiles for reasons known only to herself. She looks up at Margaret with her smile still in place.

"Has Ambrose had dinner?" she askes.

Margaret avoids Iva's eyes, her smiling face, and the bits of chicken on the front of her dress. Her hands tremble as she clears the table.

"Yes, Ambrose has had his dinner, Ivadoile."

Iva sits quietly at the table as Margaret washes her face and hands and leads her to her chair by the window. She's still smiling as she watches the sun sinking like a fiery crown on the sea's edge, as if it had been tossed overboard from a sinking pirate ship. The day shrinks away like a dried up dinner. Clouds gather in a convoy in the low sky.

Margaret returns the face cloth and towel to the old pantry and leans up against the cupboard to make a decision one way or the other.

Time and reflections are running out for Ivadoile Spears, who is now looking out (as if for the first time) over the grand paths and cliffs and cherubs as a small child would in a new picture book. A sudden chill rises in Margaret LaMae. She, without asking, is responsible for Ivadoile Spears. Her second instalment of penance will not be easy, she thinks, as she whispers a silent prayer to Angelo Pinotti for guidance.

She will have to find a gentle way of telling Iva that she had not been betrayed by Ambrose Kane. How do you tell another woman that you have known for years why the love of her life had gone? It is not hard for Margaret to imagine that day Iva asked Ambrose Kane to leave. She had seen something brewing in her eyes for a week, a *get rid of a man plan* as it turned out to be. And when it ripened on Ivadoile Spears' tongue, there was no stopping her.

Iva would leave no penetrable opening for him to fill in. She would hear no words spill from his mouth like a school boy caught looking up a girl's dress at recess. There was always the mistake that, if she listened, she may have left an opening for some kind of forgiveness on her part.

She would have made him spit out the colour of her eyes first. How far the silk rode up her body before he moved into her. Was she wearing red lace underwear? Women compete with each other about things like this in living colour before all else dies. Her mother would certainly have given Opal a run for her American money in her red lace and then made a noose out of her braid.

THIRTY-EIGHT

NGELO PINOTTI GREW a moustache and goatee when he left the priesthood. It was rather odd, he thought as he glanced at his image in the mirror, that now as a doctor he looked more like a prophet.

The ability to study both a man's mind and soul should make a man complete, give him a decisive stance on which he stood his ground and beliefs, yet he wrestled with a loneliness that roamed throughout his spirit and nestled in the sand along the shore of his Lac Saint-Jean summer home.

He always turned and studied his footprints after walking a distance along the hem of the waves. They were never even, his footprints. He noticed that unconsciously he had walked out of a straight path, his feet turning either right or left. A few times he had paused before moving on. Shuffled his feet like a dancer to get his blood fired up. But dancing was not his forte. The last woman he'd held in is arms was his dying mother. It could have been a form of

231

dance, the way he'd held her with her head tucked under his chin. One of her hands caressed his jawbone as her last breath slipped out like the ends of a song. She always said she could tell her sons by the shape of their bones. *Angelo, it is you.*

He watched the waves wash the small pebbles at his feet and the birds of the sky flew over the water as gentle as a kiss.

He looked up and basked in the comfort that always came to him as he watched the flight of small birds taking on a circumference of depth on their own. They called out to each other as they flew wing to wing.

Angelo Pinotti strolled back to his home at a leisurely pace. He made a small fire to ward off the evening chill and sat beside the window to open his mail. The pictures of the Tides Inn fell gracefully to the floor from a thick brown envelope. A rainbow of colours lay at his feet. He read his friend's note.

> *Dear Angelo,*
>
> *I send along the pleasures that surrounded me recently on my visit to Cape Breton Island, in Nova Scotia. I know that, as a lover of nature, a glorious paradise awaits you, should you decide to go. The Tides Inn offers its beauty up like a prayer and is in close proximity to the Marconi Towers, where a fellow Italian, Guglielmo Marconi, reached out above the waters and left the world his code.*
>
> *As you can see, the gardens are a work of art and the sea cries out below the rugged cliffs like a Gregorian chant.*

The lovely cook, Margaret, is a master at her craft, a rare delight to the palate. But I must caution you, Angelo, that the owner, Ivadoile Spears, is a force to be reckoned with at any time.

I hope, my friend, that you are feeling much better after your heart surgery last fall. I hear that you are back to work on a part-time basis. Should you need any more information, I will be available until I return to Rome in a few weeks.

In God's hands,

Ricco

Angelo Pinotti studied the pictures in is hand. Large sunflowers swung their heads to and fro like galloping show horses. Near the magnificent gazebo, a lone figure knelt before a rose garden. She was cutting flowers and placing them in the basket beside her. Her posture was given to one with a hand for nature. Draped in a white apron, she reached precisely for the finest rose and held it as an offering to the sun. Her long dark hair carried the wind down her back. In the last picture she was not present.

"This must be Margaret," Angelo Pinotti thought to himself and smiled.

He left for Cape Breton by train the following week and met Margaret LaMae as she emerged from the garden gate, a beauty like a rose herself in a fold of soft petals. She was much prettier than the pictures allowed. A smudge of soil spread across the bridge of her nose and rather than apologize for her appearance, she enlightened it with laughter.

"I'm usually dirtier than this, Mister, when I'm in the garden."

Angelo Pinotti reached for her hand.

"You must be Margaret."

"Have we met?"

"Not officially. A friend of mine stayed here at the inn and mentioned your fine cooking."

They walked into the inn together. Margaret directed Mr. Pinotti to the office as Iva emerged in a white cotton dress and a stiff upper lip coated with fresh gloss. Iva stared at the soil on Margaret's face as her teeth dipped into the gloss in her lower lip.

"I requested that you bring in some roses, Margaret, not the womb that cradles them." She turned to Angelo Pinotti with a look to let him know that the mud stopped here, that she ran a tight ship. She noticed the look in his eyes as he followed Margaret down the hall. Angelo Pinotti stood on the cusp of Iva's caustic bite. Her own feminine beauty sealed behind a round of puffed red cheeks that looked as if they were about to blow a whistle. He disliked the woman's personality immediately.

He smiled at Margaret in a way he had not let his mind wander to since he was a young man. His yearning for two loves was deep, that of his God and the beautiful creation of an innocent woman.

Margaret, smudged and insulted, made her way down the long hall to the kitchen. It was her safe refuge from Iva and her harsh comments, this room with its spicy warmth and flavours. She controlled it, all of it. This was one room in the inn that was a failure to Ivadoile Spears. It was Iva's Achilles heel and Margaret knew it.

Margaret was yet unaware that innocence and love could not be divided in the heart of the man she had just escorted into the inn.

THIRTY-NINE

Busy is a word applied to the young. Busy with work, busy with falling in love, busy with giving birth and the finale of it all, closing death over with a shovel. These are the things the young get caught up with until they reach a certain age. And then comes the day when they ask themselves, "Is this it?"

They may be standing still or lying flat out or, in Margaret LaMae's case, sitting in an old kitchen and looking closely at a woman she has known for years with drool drowning her bottom lip, her eyes as dry as sandpaper, and her voice mulching her words like a shredder.

In another five minutes, it is wine Iva is asking for as a night cap. "Make sure it's red and warm, Margaret! That is how we liked our wine, Bowzer and I. It slipped down the throat like a tongue," Iva informs Margaret with a much brighter outlook on life. "Dear Bowzer," she sighs, "I always thought of him as the brother I never had."

Iva smiles as she searches Margaret's face for a reaction from her, but Margaret keeps her face light and controlled. She is not about to let things get out of gear at this hour. Iva has another story up her sleeve and is just waiting to unfold it on her.

"I don't suppose you ever ventured under the cork, Margaret, did you?" Iva laughs deviously as if she were already full of wine.

"Poor Margaret, I don't suppose you had a go at anything red and warm except a poker." She throws a serious glance directly at Margaret. "I don't believe I ever told you that your friend, Angelo Pinotti, had a flare for you. Whether it was religious or physiological, I don't know, but it was there nonetheless. The doctor part wouldn't interest me, but the priest part in the man would be enough for me to fall in love with him. I'd have eaten him up without a potato."

Margaret turns towards the dying sun so Iva cannot see her face blushing to a fever pitch. Iva's change of moods can be exhausting to her. The idea of that lovely man, Angelo Pinotti, doing anything out of character made her bless herself and recite a novena in silence. She knew more than Iva would ever know about Angelo Pinotti's feelings. God rest his soul.

She will not bother to tell Iva about the afternoon that she and her twin brother found their father's full bottle of wine in the barn. Margaret's father hid everything (that flowed) in the barn, away from her mother. Liquor in a man or a bottle did not form a shadow in the doorway of their home, as was the rule set down by their mother. They were thirteen-year-olds.

Her brother opened the bottle and took the first gulp. He grimaced as he passed Margaret the bottle and told her to take a sip. The bottle went from hand to hand, mouth to mouth, until they were drunk with laughter. Her brother dropped the half-empty bottle and they watched its contents flow like a dirty river along the floorboards as they held each other for support.

It was Margaret's idea to go to confession, but she didn't tell her brother. She had been agonizing over something the Mother Superior alerted her class to when she gathered the girls one afternoon during lent, in a classroom next to her office. The Mother Superior was tall with broad rounded shoulders that always made her look as if she were holding on to something invisible. Her face came to a sharp point like a rusty spike protruding over her white collar.

"At your age, most of you girls will have the urge to use your lips in an inappropriate manner." Mother Superior's voice deepened as she continued. Margaret imagined her father's wine bottle sitting on her school desk.

"I speak not of gum smacking or blowing bubbles, or the licking of one's plate, but in a manner unbecoming of girls your age. Kissing boys can be as destructive as kissing a wasp. You will be stung and swell up like a balloon. Raise your hand if you agree!"

Forty-two hands went mid-air. Some of them trembled. The Mother Superior made her way down each aisle of the classroom to count the raised hands.

Margaret believed the nun was looking for wasp stings on lips as she looked each girl straight in the face.

After vomiting three or four times, Margaret finally made

her way up over the hill to the church. She was light headed, but in a jolly brave mood on this Saturday afternoon. She would ask the priest if it was a sin to kiss a boy. Surely he would know more than a nun. The Mother Superior had not mentioned the word sin in her talk with the girls.

Margaret's knees trembled as she knelt in the dark confessional. Her head felt as if it was going to leave her shoulders. Her mouth felt sour as she swallowed her bubble gum before entering the church.

The screen of the confessional opened and the face of the parish priest seemed to float towards her like a jellyfish. The side of his face looked disfigured and out of context for such a small man. Margaret held her hands over her sour mouth as she blurted out, "Kiss me, Father, for I have sinned!"

Realizing her mistake, she up and ran out of the confessional, past the Pieta, past the statue of Saint Theresa, past the statue of Saint Anne, under the ceiling above her head where the cherubs floated merrily, until she reached the bank near the shoreline and slid down. She was glad that she was the last person in the pews waiting to go to confession. She could not remember if there were others in the church doing their penance.

The following morning at mass, the priest did not seem to remember her. She vowed then and there, at the altar of God, never to let a drop wet her lips again. She became a teetotaller at thirteen.

"Margaret, have you seen my good crystal glasses?" Margaret is jolted at the sound of Iva's voice. It is childlike in its pronunciation, the softness of the vowels coming like that of a much younger voice.

Iva is standing with her back to Margaret at the china cabinet with her hand on the handles of the glass doors.

"What can I help you with, Ivadoile?" Margaret's presence seems to settle her and she turns and walks back to her chair by the window.

"I remember Bowzer putting them back in the cabinet. Oh wasn't he fastidious in his chores. The man left nothing upended. I, for one, sorely miss the man."

"He was quite the comic, Ivadoile. Everyone liked him I must say. He really was wonderful to Violet Summers. She found him quite delightful in her short stay here with us."

Iva is pensive before she speaks.

"She left rather suddenly as I recall, something or other to do with death, wasn't it? You would know more about death, Margaret, when your number is up. We Presbyterians don't dilly dally in numbers the way you people do."

"It was her illness. The woman was perfectly content here, Ivadoile."

"My mother was never content, Margaret. She was mad, although I suppose madness has its own form of contentment. It takes a lot of courage to be mad. Mad at the world, mad at the poets who slip life right under your nose with a few words. Therapy in a stanza didn't work for my mother. She threw all the bastards out of the house and burnt them to death."

Margaret doesn't like where this conversation is going, but she has to tire her out before she can get her settled down for the night, before she can call her neighbour to pick her up. She will not chance walking home alone in the dark.

Iva announces that she is cold, "Cold with life," she adds dramatically. Margaret turns on the oven as she wraps a throw from the rocking chair over her shoulders. She cannot find anything in this house that will warm up Ivadoile Spears' life.

"You'll be warm in no time, Ivadoile. I have things turned up." A smear of a smile crosses Iva's face. She is digging something up again.

"That's what Ambrose Kane said to me, Margaret, when we tumbled onto the cold sheets. I will turn things up. You'll be warm in no time. And he always did. I swear the man was made of starch when he got at it."

Margaret pretends that she doesn't hear her as she watches the cat scurry towards the heat coming from the open oven door and curl up in a ball.

Iva is lazy with heat now as she sits beside the oven door where Margaret has moved her chair, the throw wrapped around her shoulders like someone rescued from a storm at sea.

It will be easier for Margaret to get her off to bed before she leaves. She can feel a weariness settle in. Perhaps she had imposed too heavy a penance on herself. The care, at this point, that Iva needs is too heavy a burden for her. As she walks along the hallway with her to the bedroom and readies her for bed, Margaret feels that she must nurture her, cradle her frail limbs.

Iva's thin skin hangs in pleats as Margaret pulls the night-dress down over her head. Nipples as hard as brown stones slide against her hands as Iva clasps Margaret's hands gently and holds them to her breasts.

"Don't go just yet please, Ambrose. Will you stay a while longer?"

FORTY

"ANGELO PINOTTI HAD a thing for you, religious or physiological," Iva implies, and this makes Margaret ill at ease. Iva had suspected all these years and never mentioned it once to Margaret. But Margaret cannot judge Ivadoile Spears for keeping a secret. They are on the same playing field now. Why had she not hinted at this before now? Does she believe she knew something about Ambrose Kane that she had not shared with her?

"He loves me...He loves me not," Ivadoile Spears is still counting daisies. They still strangle her mind like a snake weaving through heavy grass.

What could a man like Angelo Pinotti have seen in me? Margaret agonized after his sudden death. I was a cook, a flower clipper, and a thief. He had not seen through me and what my heart was truly capable of doing.

She had been in Angelo Pinotti's room, seen all the intimate things men use on themselves, lotions and powders and shaving cream, without any desire to swipe them. He was too unwrinkled. The slick straight razor puzzled her, his face was so delicate. She would have thought an electric razor was all that touched his skin, removed his stubble in light strokes, without the possibility of a deep nick of a blade. Perhaps it worked easier along his goatee and moustache and angled them in the way women angled their brows.

And his hands, his gentle hands had written the words that fell from an open letter to the floor one morning when she was placing the roses on his bedside table. It was written to his dear friend in Rome. It lay flat and face up at her feet like the stretched out palm of a school boy waiting to be strapped. His penmanship was like a child's under construction, needing repair.

Why had she read as much as she did? She was fascinated by the formation of the Ts that looked like small crosses on the pages. And the awkward loops in the Gs in some words. Margaret read on, because she had to, felt he had left it in her path to let her know. And then she sealed it in the back of her mind forever and a day until now, when Iva opened the seal again.

> *My dearest friend Ricco,*
> *On the eve of my month's stay here at the Tides Inn, in*
> *Cape Breton, I have yet to unveil a solution or unmask the*
> *truth to myself or anyone else, as to the attraction that I feel*
> *for the beauty that has stirred me like none other. If anyone,*
> *it must be you that will receive my truth. My confession.*
> *You were accurate in your description of her, my dear*
> *friend. I long, not only for her smile, but the laughter that*
> *ripples with it, that smooth childlike innocence that spends*

*all its time in the heart of a good woman without the
aid of vanity to interrupt it. With the mask of a wolf, I find
small excuses to have her attend to my needs so that I can
penetrate her presence, the approach of her footsteps, the
sound of her voice, the smell of her hair. She is unaware of
my cowardice and it is a coward that I am. For years, I've
rallied around love and truth and yet when they are most
needed to round out the heart of a man, I am unable to
blend the two.*

*At this moment, I feel too, that I have abandoned my God
and all His mercy. I feel my prayers come back to me and
settle in my shoulders like the weight of a cross. I fear the
knowing of what I know and how I feel. How can a man
love God and fear to love one of His people? Perhaps this is
why He meant for me to be here to mend my broken heart,
to make my decision about the life I choose to pursue
without the pain of indecision.*

*Last evening, I watched her as she left on her journey
down the lane to her home. My heart sang with the terror
of a fool. The setting sun danced around her feet as it
abandoned itself to the coming night. I wanted to call out to
her, to have her return and hear my truth. I want to love
her physically, mentally, emotionally, as I fear she has never
been loved by anyone. I realize this reads like fiction, but I
am a true believer that fiction happened somewhere.*

*I am as awkward with women as I am with life at this
moment. I know I would have confused, perhaps frightened
the dear soul with such foolishness thrust upon someone
who knows little about me or my life, except for her own
innate instinct to trust me completely. I have not mentioned*

anything of a personal nature to anyone. I fear that my
physical health has not progressed to my advantage since my
open heart surgery. I will have to see someone about these
chest pains and therefore will be checking out soon.
I have no other place to put my secret, but between these
lines and hope that one day they will fall within your vision
and compassion.

Until,

Angelo

P.S. You were exact on your measure of Ivadoile Spears.
This island is too small for this woman. She belongs to a
large city where the soulless mingle in the cavities of their
own demise. My sympathy for her, nonetheless, lies in the
fact that she carries a primal fear like a torch and is hell
bent on keeping an open flame to her advantage.

Two days later, after the reading of the diary, Margaret found Angelo Pinotti dead in bed. He was fifty-two years of age when his thoughts ran out and he dropped his pen. He had made no recordings on that fatal day.

After her initial shock, she wrapped the diary securely in brown paper and wrote the message, "To my friend Ricco," in bold print and placed it amongst his personal belongings before they were shipped back to Montreal.

Margaret slipped into the empty church on her way home and watched the votive candles waltz in waves of colours. A burst of energy from a green votive candle flamed upward like the lead dancer separating from the others. Margaret held her hand up slightly towards the fire, as though she had been asked to dance and accepted gracefully.

FORTY-ONE

MARGARET IMAGINES THAT flames in perpetual motion burn the brightest in the fire world of Rome. The thought of Angelo Pinotti's letter reaching Rome and being read by his friend with her name canonized over a flame has always intrigued Margaret, even after all these years.

She is in a reflective mood as she readies herself for the day. The wind is cagey, howling from two different directions and caught in its own crossover, and the sharpness of the sun filters in the trees, revealing yellow streaks of twisted and broken limbs felled by an army of winter and spring storms.

Margaret has made up her mind. The story of Iva and Ambrose Kane must be uprooted and revealed. But not without tea biscuits, not without homemade jam, and not without the sweet delicacy of a blueberry pie (Ambrose Kane's favourite) to sweeten her tongue. Iva is expecting her visit in the afternoon, but she will pack her goodies and leave a bit earlier on this day. She will tap on her back door and enter as she has done for years. She will sit on the same kitchen chair and look into the face of the woman she can read like a slate, crawl between the pale cracks, and pick out what is left of her memory. Iva's words, when she gets them by the tail and flings them out like fish that are too small to keep for any useful purpose, are less threatening now.

Only in the crossfire of the changing wind does Margaret try to remember the words of Ambrose Kane so long ago. In what order had he revealed them to her? In what order should they be delivered to Ivadoile Spears?

"He loves me...he loves me not...he loves me." She could use this childlike line should Iva's mind be in a spin and she'd ease her back if she could, place her in a time when women ripened their sexuality and coming of age on something as simple as a daisy.

Margaret watches the slow shadow of Iva's face in the window as she walks up the lane. She is in and out of the lace curtain while watching her approach, a puppet-like figure drawing attention to the moral dilemma they render on children. They are clever puppets. They are full of solutions like all prophets of wood and string. They exist for smiles. They collapse when the giggles run out.

Iva's greeting is friendly.

"Oh you came back to visit, Margaret. But you always do, I must not forget that. You have not abandoned me."

"I come twice a week to visit with you. Do you remember my visits and our cups of tea?" She does not answer, but studies Margaret as a school child would focus on their first teacher's face.

Iva has the furnace turned up full blast. The old radiators heave and sigh along the walls and frighten Old Rose from her nap. She crosses the floor in a slant of fur and cries at the back door to be let out of the inferno of heat and voices rising from under the floor and along the walls. The cat crawls beneath the veranda in the shade. Margaret pours a large bowl of cold water and places it near the veranda opening.

Iva is sitting at the kitchen table in a blue frock held together by Velcro and strings. It is one of those hospital gowns that one of the nurses has put on her before going outside to cool off while Margaret is visiting. Iva's eyes are crusted over and weighed down by a salve with an irritating odour.

Margaret removes her sweater under Iva's watchful, crusted red eyes as she fills the kettle with water for their tea.

"How are you today, Ivadoile?" Margaret's words are hammered with anticipation. There is something in those red eyes that is still knowing. Up to this point, Iva is not rambling, she is aware of her presence through a blur of salve and salvation. The tangible beauty of life is hers by request. Ivadoile Spears is on at the moment.

Her head turns towards Margaret's voice, her face framed by its old strength, her jaw flattered by the sudden agility that she feels in her limbs.

"I want you to stay here with me. I don't care for the women my lawyer sends here to look after my needs. Come to think of it, I don't care for my lawyer either. He looks too much like John Diefenbaker. I've never trusted a man whose jowls outrun his mouth." Iva takes a deep sigh.

"I made a mistake by making him the executor of my will and signing over the power of attorney to him. He said I needed one because I have no living relatives to care for my interests."

"The nurses take care of you, Ivadoile. I am always available for our visits. And the cleaning woman is here twice a week."

"At my age, care is what, checking my ticker and cutting my toenails and wondering if I'm still able to piss on my own without hitting the floor? I want someone I can talk to, someone I've known for years. I want someone I can trust."

The singing of the kettle makes Margaret jump to her feet. She puts the teabags in the pot and lets the tea steep for a few minutes.

The word "trust" throws Margaret off her game plan. The thought of Angelo Pinotti calling her innocent scalds her mind like steam. Innocent people tell the truth when the truth is still fresh, when she knew Ambrose Kane did a dying favour for poor Violet Summers.

She has not answered Iva's request as yet. She'd have to have her own home taken care of for a time. Lord knows what was floating into the doors and windows these days off the roads.

Margaret pours the tea with a shaky hand. Iva's salve is melting down her face like tears as she bites into her tea biscuit. Who did Ivadoile Spears ever weep for in her lifetime? She no doubt wept like a mannequin for her husband when he died. And waiting for Ambrose Kane is what she has done now for years. Waiting can hold back tears. A holding tank in the mind, keep them handy for the right moment.

It is hard to tell how some women mourn. Margaret remembers her own mother wrapped in black clothing for a year after her father died. The radio was turned on to voice only the news and weather in their home. Christmas was cancelled. The blinds remained down. The house was as dark as a cave, as the black clad mother swept the dust under the mats.

Dust frightened her. *From dust you came and unto dust you shall return.*

She and her mother (after her other two sisters escaped to New York) spoke only at mealtime and when they prayed. How strange it appears to Margaret, in this day and age, that her father's name was never mentioned, nor her brother's as though death held that space in reverse. But grief is a determined emotion, it will always keep sneaking back. Margaret had delayed her grief for her twin brother, her other half, her parents' creation, their twin eggs, so alike in thought. Did he weep for her when death hijacked him from a cloud?

Margaret swallows her tea slowly. She had not thought about what she would do, if Iva would shed a tear when she heard the truth, as she glances over at her. She has not gone off track too far since she arrived. She could ask her something about her eyes. This way she would know if her memory is holding up. She doesn't have to because Iva is relating the whole process to her. A spectacle of yesterday's events spill out of her mouth as she chews.

"I had blurred sight, saw things doubling in size, the cat appeared as big as a lion. I had to claw my itchy dry eyes for some relief. I know who gave me the evil eye, brought it into this house to put a curse on me."

"Who would that be, Ivadoile?"

"The people looking after me. They are just waiting for me to croak. That is why I need you here to watch things for me, to keep an eye on my sheets. You can have Bowzer's room. He won't be back. There is a naked man in there named David, but he won't bother you."

"No, he won't be back. He died a long time ago, Ivadoile. Most of your guests and staff are all gone now."

"Do you believe the dead remember the living, Margaret?"

"I believe so. Do you?

Iva searches the room with her cloudy eyes as if she had heard someone enter the kitchen and she can't make out who has stepped in. She may not even remember his scent after all these years. But Margaret would, it's amazing what an empty aftershave lotion bottle will hold.

"There is just you and me in the kitchen, Ivadoile. The cat is outside under the veranda. Were you expecting anyone?" Margaret inquires.

"He won't be back. He's gone with the ballerina."

"Who won't be back?"

"Ambrose Kane." His name is slurred or dragged out intentionally like a row of tin cans behind a car. Margaret has her chance, it is easier than she had anticipated.

"He left on his own, Ivadoile. There was no ballerina."

"I saw them, Margaret, as plain as I see you now."

"You can't really see me now, Ivadoile. And you really

didn't see what you thought you saw back then."

It has been said. It has a life of its own, this truth that comes years too late for Ivadoile Spears. She is at its mercy. Her face is sinking in below the jawbones as her cheeks form an arch, each bone set in a locked position. Her thin mouth is quivering as if holding back the rest of her face from complete collapse.

"What did I see?" comes whispering out.

"You saw him teaching Violet how to dance. She had never learned to dance."

"What was he teaching her dress to do?"

Iva's red eyes are searching the room. Her mouth opens and closes like a bird grasping for the precious worm that fell from its beak by its own clumsiness.

"I saw her braid. It lay so still down her back like a tail on a dead animal."

"You saw your cousin Opal's braid, Ivadoile. Violet Summers never wore a braid."

"No, no, she didn't, the poor girl. She wore a brace on her foot."

"Yes, she wore a brace. You do remember her. She was ill when she arrived at the inn, but a very determined young woman."

"I never hated her. I was very fond of her. I admired her spirit."

"Everyone loved her, but Ambrose Kane was in love with you."

"But you loved him too, Margaret. I've always known that. He knew it too. He loved you like a sister. He often mentioned that to me. That's why you were never a threat to me and him. You should have told me why he left. I was always jealous of you because everyone loved you."

Margaret swallows deeply before saying another word. She is blushing as small patches of flames ignite on her cheeks, but not from shame. She is dealing with a slow anger mapping out a new route to her life. One she wishes she had taken years ago. She does not want to be just somebody's sister. She is a woman who was loved as a woman ought to be loved. Someone's sister be damned. She will not be identified as somebody's sister ever again.

"Ambrose Kane was a good man." She hears herself responding to Iva, because this is what she planned to say in a benevolent, sacramental manner.

"I'm sure many women loved him, Ivadoile. I didn't know until later why he left so suddenly. You never mentioned his name."

"That's what every mother who springs their sons from their loins hopes for, Margaret. They want someone to love their sons when their job is done."

Iva pauses and looks around. She needs a memory link to keep the conversation going, her mouth twisting like a riptide.

"I married a good man, once upon a time." She stops to listen to the voice in her head as if someone else is speaking her words.

"Every woman should try it once. But my parents should never have married each other. I'm sure of it. My father was as fragile as broken glass between the sheets. I suppose kissing him must have been like kissing a blade. You should have seen the pecker on him that day in the hayloft,

Margaret." Her face is jailed in thick moisture. "He looked like a two-legged bull."

A mouthful of tea from Margaret's open mouth forms an arc in the air. Margaret is laughing so hard the cup goes crashing to the floor. Iva is oblivious to Margaret's outburst as she continues to talk.

"I was always jealous of you, Margaret. Everyone remarked on your great beauty. People not only loved you, they liked you as well."

Iva, with her head turned, is speaking to a shadow on the wall. Shadows never answer back.

"I don't think many people ever liked me. Cats liked me. And Bowzer liked me. Cullie Spears shortened my hatred for my name, called me Iva, I believe. That's why I married him, isn't it? Is that why I married him?"

Margaret is still smiling as she sweeps up the broken cup.

"I don't really know, Ivadoile. I'm sure Dr. Cullie must have been very fond of you."

"Fondness makes poor marriage material, Margaret. One can be fond of rattle snakes, but they don't sleep with them. Did Ambrose Kane tell you he loved me?"

"I'm sure he did."

"Then why didn't I marry him? Did I love him? I sensed he didn't love me in the same manner. I can't recall him ever talking about marriage. Did he leave me for another fool?"

"You sent him away because you believed he was cheating on you. And yes, you did love him."

"I'll be damned. Is that right? And he wasn't cheating at all, just dancing?"

"Not at all," Margaret half whispers, "He knew that Violet Summers was sick and he granted her a dying wish."

"I did love him. I'll have to find him and apologize to the cowardly bastard. Why didn't he stick around and fight it out?" Her voice is agitated as she rubs her eyes, her fingers dancing around her thoughts as she scratches at her scalp.

"Why can't I remember how to do things? I get everything all wrong. Why does a person have to surrender to old age through stupidity?"

Margaret gets a warm cloth and soothes Iva's sad eyes. She clings to Margaret like a lamb at play, bunting her head softly against her shoulder. "Probably we should go away, Margaret."

"Where would we go?"

"Anywhere, can you find it on the map for me, Margaret?"

"Why would you want to go anywhere, Ivadoile?"

"He could be there waiting for me. He was a marvellous lover. Did I ever tell you that? Some women only love parts of a man, Margaret. If they tell you they loved the whole thing, they are lying to you. Men never surrender it all. He told me that one night, but it was too late for me. I had already fallen for all of him."

"We can wait here."

She looks up at Margaret with a painful, puzzled look.

"Who are we waiting for?"

"We are waiting for the past, Ivadoile. But I believe we are too late."

"You are such a pessimist, Margaret. You need a little get up and go. You have to reach for the humps. I'll help you."

"I should have gone away years ago, Ivadoile. I always wanted to see the world, not just feel it. I wanted to be a pilot like my brother, if you can imagine that one."

"I'll buy you a plane if you want one."

Margaret laughs at the image of her at the controls of an airplane, yet she has never felt so in control of her life.

"I have no need for a plane these days. I couldn't steer a wheelbarrow down a path, but I thank you for the offer."

"What offer, Margaret?"

"It doesn't matter, doesn't matter at all, Ivadoile. It's just idle chit chat."

"Is the ballerina dead?" Iva inquires out of concern.

"Yes, Violet Summers is dead. She died many years ago."

"Did she ever learn to dance or did the swallows frighten her away?"

"She learned to dance, Ivadoile. Nothing frightened Violet Summers. She was her own woman. She learned to dance with one lesson."

In the white heat of the afternoon that Ivadoile Spears learned that the ballerina was Violet Summers, she sat like a spectator who refused to leave the scene of a tragic event. She stared straight ahead keeping her head on a slight angle as one would pose for a camera. The strife in her mind concentrated on one scene. She blinked occasionally, shutting out the trauma that claimed her speech. Her hands lay on the edge of the table in a quiet disorder. They spun awkwardly like a broken top then formed a small fist. Margaret placed a fresh cup of hot tea before her on the table. It went cold before Iva reached out for it.

FORTY-TWO

T HE CLEANING LADIES washed down the walls of Bowzer's room the day before Margaret arrived with her personal belongings. Iva's lawyer pleaded with her to move in for the sake of the three nurses who threatened to quit.

The poor man sounded desperate as he spoke. He offered to double Margaret's pay, have her driven wherever she wanted to go day or night.

"You will never be alone with her. A nurse will be on duty around the clock. A male nurse will be assigned the graveyard shift so that you will have extra protection at night," he stated firmly as though he were speaking of a convicted felon.

"You may have to dig out the nurses now and then from their hiding places. Your job really, Margaret, would be that of a peacemaker."

Margaret smiled behind the receiver as he spoke. He knew Ivadoile Spears as well as she did over the years. She had seen him at the inn on more than one occasion.

"You are the only person who can handle the old woman," he continued. "I realize it is a lot to ask of you, but she is in failing health and may not last out the summer. She's in the early stages of dementia, her doctor says. The rest homes have waiting lists. I've tried everywhere. I know she was adamant about not being put in a home, and she certainly has the means to be cared for in her own home if the staff will stay with her long enough."

Margaret made arrangements with her neighbour to look after her little house plants. Before she left, she had something that only she could take care of, something she should have done years ago. She watched as the garbage truck rounded the corner with the picture of Ambrose Kane tucked inside a cardboard box.

Margaret shook her head at the thought of going back to work again, at eighty-four years of age, for Ivadoile Spears.

"You can't cry over split milk," she frowned, "and had you spoken up years ago, Ivadoile could be living in Georgia all these years with the man she loved."

Bowzer's room smelled of Pine-Sol and fresh wax as she hung up her clothes in the closet. Margaret chuckled at the old wool sock placed over the naked statue of David by one of the cleaning ladies. She imagined what Bowzer's reaction would have been to find his beloved David stuffed in a sock like a sausage. Margaret removed it and placed the statue back on the stand. David stared across the room with a plastered, grateful look on his serene, beautiful face.

Down the hall, she could hear voices or a voice pleading, coming under the door in a muffled, agonizing height like a soprano who has forgotten her next line.

The afternoon sky was covered in a crust of bubble clouds and the fading sun ran out like a yellow draining sore.

Margaret opened the door slightly to find Iva thrashing along the walls to the sound of the dinner bell she believed was ringing. A rusty wind chime, on its last breath, wheezed outside the dining-room window.

She stopped when she saw Margaret and smiled approvingly. Margaret motioned to the nurse that she would take over from here.

She led Iva to the kitchen and settled her into a chair. She had ripped open her gown held together with Velcro and put a heavy wool sweater under it. It clung to her shoulders like an oversized collar.

"I made some soup for you and me, Ivadoile."

"I don't like chicken soup."

"Yes you do, it's your favourite. You used to have me make it for you three times a week for your guests at the inn."

"I know what you're up to, Margaret. You will say anything to get me to eat your meals."

"Why would I trick you, Ivadoile?"

"People are always trying to get a stab at rich people's ambitions. You know how wealthy I am."

"Rich people like chicken soup. Most of the rich guests who stayed at the inn loved chicken soup."

"Did they like me, Margaret?"

"I don't know, I didn't serve you up in a soup bowl."

"I'm going to the show tonight as the Savoy, Margaret."

Iva's face is mixed with anticipation as if the show had already started without her.

"Are you now, and what are you going to see?"

"I'm going to see *Gone with the Wind*. Do you want to come with me? I'll buy you some popcorn and a cold drink."

"I've seen it already."

"Stay home then. I can go by myself. Frig off!" A cold indifference crossed her face. Who did Ivadoile Spears need to escort her anywhere.

Margaret placed a warm bowl of soup and a slice of bread in front of her. She hoped this meal would be uneventful and that she wouldn't have to bother the nurse to settle her in for the night.

Ivadoile ate slowly and delicately with an air of social charm and grace, with her shoulders squared back into the chair. She dabbed in small pats with her napkin at her thin mouth that emitted a draft of sour breath from some drug along with a slang of French dialogue. She held a conversation with an empty chair. She called for the maître d' to view the dessert tray. She ordered a special imported wine. She spoke with a crippled French accent. She mentioned an auction she'd attended in London and was outbid by an Englishman by a few mere pounds, because of her accent.

"They'll do it every time, the English. They'll never get over their battles with the French."

By the time Margaret got Iva back on her feet and to her room at the Ritz (where she said she was a guest) she claimed to have been in Paris for a week after her London travels and would be leaving for her home in Cape Breton in the morning.

Margaret bid her goodnight at the bedroom door as she looked in at the resting Ivadoile. She was mumbling words from an Edith Piaf song. It was something to do with a bird.

FORTY-THREE

MARGARET LAY AWAKE for hours wondering if she had made the right decision in returning to the inn. All of the friends she'd worked with are gone, locked in a box that Iva keeps on her kitchen shelf. And the place, albeit in sturdy condition, is in dire need of cosmetic work. The character of the inn has been replaced with antiseptics and strangers and out of control weeds, and a woman who cannot answer to her own name most of the time. Margaret knows that this could be deliberate on Ivadoile's part, because of her dislike for her name.

Margaret leaves a nightlight on beside the bed should she hear Iva wandering down the hall for something or other. Margaret likes the young nurse who comes in the morning to relieve the male nurse. Someone has set a single bed in the parlour for the nurses to sleep on. But she cannot yet make a full judgement of the other three. The male nurse, in his late thirties, a rather cool and dismissive type, eats jellybeans by the handful as he reads. He sits for hours in the parlour reading *In Cold Blood*. He hadn't even looked up when Margaret offered him a cup of tea, his first night on duty.

Margaret let Iva know that she is down the hall and that she can call on her if she needs anything. But she knows Iva had probably already forgotten that Margaret is here at the inn, before she even left her room.

"I'm such a light sleeper, Ivadoile. I can hear the stars falling," Margaret smiles.

"I'm not stupid, Margaret. You can hear no such thing as a star falling. You poor Catholics will believe anything the atmosphere throws your way, out of your heaven one supposes. Heaven has always been your greatest commodity, but your stars could be shooting at you."

Margaret grins to herself. Iva is back in the grove for a time. Her thin little mouth growling like Humphrey's used to. She is her own alter ego. She has no Bowzer or Humphrey at her side to carry her along. There is no one here to repeat her words.

It's a tiring pleasure when Iva is balanced. Her mind comes and goes into its secret sphere, but she is someone to talk to. The male nurse buries his face in his book when she enters the parlour at night to ask him something. Margaret is not likely to do much talking with anyone more interested in murder than an ordinary conversation.

"Should the stars fall like dust, where do you suppose they'd land?" Iva ponders aloud, her face framed in concentration as if she understood that her mind had hit the correct circuit, that her thoughts were unscrambled, and life as she knew it, climbed up hard and cold and was still directing her life from a beam.

"I don't know, Ivadoile. Perhaps the angels collect them all and polish them up for another night."

"There is no such a thing as angels, Margaret. Your God is not that generous. Cousin Opal believed in angels and ended up with Rory McLaughlin. Where do you suppose they are now, in your purgatory? I hope they don't have any hay lying around for all those sinners to lounge on or they'll never want to leave."

Margaret avoids the bullet on this comment.

"It's possible the cherubs collect all the stars and shine them up again," Margaret proposes lightly, waiting for another caustic response about her religion. She dare not whip Iva into a confrontation on anything with wings.

"My cherubs can do that," comes from Iva's drooling mouth, a little sad, a little happy, a little young, and way too late for her to get the full brunt of her own fairy tale.

"Yes, your cherubs can do all the shining, Ivadoile, indeed they can."

Margaret has decided there will be no war of words with Ivadoile Spears again. She will let her ramble on. Whether she is aware of it or not, Iva has made a truce in her heart towards Margaret. Her words are woundless against her. She has a charitable gleam in her eyes when Margaret is present, despite her outbursts.

Margaret is aware of it, in the childlike movements Iva's hands form as she reaches out to hold Margaret's hand and brings it to her mouth to suckle. Once, she had undone the braid in Margaret's hair and combed it out down past her shoulders and tied it back with a ribbon. Margaret had been in her room talking with her when Iva came up behind her with her brush.

She is like a child in need of a mother, thought Margaret, as she watched the ribbon slip to the floor. Iva picked up the ribbon and tied it on top of Margaret's head and smiled.

FORTY-FOUR

THE CLOUDS HANG dark and low in the thunderous summer of 2009, a heavy brow mounts a stern warning, a meteorology god stirring a curse above their heads. A few scarecrows stand in silence in Port Murdock's gardens, these ambassadors of the fields pay close attention to the reels and rumbles in the western sky. Not a breath of wind worms along their threadbare attire on this Sunday morn. Ivadoile Spears is sound asleep. It is nine-twenty in the morning. She is naked under her quilt. Stripping naked to the bone is something she has taken to in the last few weeks.

"I was born naked as a blue jay and I'll die in a naked form," she says with a wry smile. Margaret glances at her quickly and realizes she is held together by bones and confusion, as she removes her clothes from the floor and puts them in the hamper to be laundered. A woman from the village will be in on Monday morning to do the laundry.

Old Rose sprawls at Iva's feet. Now and again, she will twitch one eye open, direct the eye's focus on the sleeping Ivadoile, and close it again and summon sleep on her back.

Margaret roams throughout the silent Tides Inn as free as a kiss sent by a hand. She feels invisible. She opens up the parlour drapes to let the room breathe. The old chairs cough up dust like a miner. The cleaning ladies will vacuum them out and air out their inners on a windy day. If she is going to be here while things are settled with Iva, she will not live in dust. She moves slowly up the stairs. At the top landing, she turns and looks down at the footprints she's made. They remind Margaret of being followed on a snowy path.

Old Rose hears a familiar sound in her ear and jumps from the bed to the window ledge to investigate the source of the melody. A bird is singing in the garden. It stops and starts as if being directed by a maestro to get the correct pitch. And then, its voice ripples and soars higher than the window ledge, higher than the pitch of the roof and straight up towards the converging clouds, before flying into the darkness of a branch.

Outside the windows, the grass is an obscene green. Its colour formed from a spit of rain here and there. There have been no real downpours to get straight to the roots. The storms come by day and night, the most dangerous of thunder and lightning storms with no rain to quench the thirsty fires should the lightning strike. Light raindrops make a path down the salty windowpanes like peeling skin.

Iva stirs in her sleep and calls out for someone to close the windows. She is dead set against drafts. Drafts are a danger to your hide. Who told her so? She can't remember but she believes it was an old graveyard curse. "They caught the draft," the old people said as they walked away from the graves of the drafty dead who died beneath their windows.

Margaret can hear Iva's voice calling out, but decides to ignore it. She can tell her sleep voice from her awake voice. The nurse can see to her. Margaret, standing in the long hall window, surveys the scene below. A rotting clothesline prop clings like a thread to the old line once used for dishcloths and drying towels. Further to the south, the line that Gladys hung the bedding on dangles to the ground. Margaret imagines Gladys tangled in the white sheets with her arms braced against the line and her mouth full of clothespins to tame the white beast she battled for so many years.

Old Rose leaps from the foot of Iva's bed like an acrobat and heads to her bowl in the pantry. A flash of lightning, like a curtain call, fills the pantry window. She listens for the approaching rumble with perked ears then dips her head into the bowl.

It is raining harder now. Ambushing crevices and eaves and uprooting their decaying fabric. The wind joins forces with the rain. An army of elements spreading havoc. Unarmed, the old inn sheds its skin of shingles and boards along the sun porch as a flash of lightning highlights the fall.

Iva tosses her foot towards the spot that Old Rose always claims. She is not fully awake, but moves her limbs out of habit, a lover making an ambitious move that would require urgent sexual attention from someone close by.

You have to pay love for it possibilities, even when they are not possible.

"Who in the hell said that?" she asks in a drowsy mood.

Perhaps it was Ambrose Kane or poor Bowzer. She is not sure. Somebody's mouth had to form the words. Somebody's lungs exhale them into the atmosphere. She drags this thought back with her into sleep. A slight smile slides from her mouth onto the pillow and drowns in a pool of saliva.

Margaret is standing outside of room number Seven. It is so much easier to turn the door knob today and walk in. She is not sneaking anymore, just browsing. The room is hers to explore at leisure. The three windows are victims of neglect from both land and sea. The bed is covered in a white sheet. There are no pillows on the four-poster bed. Everything else is in its place. Folded in the dressers are full-length slips and camisoles. Two pairs of seamed nylons lay unopened in their packages. A pure white girdle has the price tag still attached to the left leg. Margaret opens the closet door.

A few old garments hang from dusty hangers as limp as wet fur. On the top shelf, pushed to the back of the closet behind the hat and shoe boxes, is a large cardboard box. Margaret pulls up a chair to reach it and pulls the box down and places it on the bed. "The New York Dress Shop, Gottingen Street, Halifax, Nova Scotia" is written on the cover.

Its contents are wrapped neatly in blue tissue paper and tied with a white ribbon. Margaret unties the ribbon gently as though she were unravelling it from a child's curl.

Inside the box, a wedding veil with a Juliet cap is spread out over an ivory wedding gown of sheer illusion and lace. The date-of-purchase slip reads October, 1953. The price tag lies at the bottom of the box. Margaret reads the handwriting on the paper. "No alterations required!"

Outside, the thunder is violent in nature, bursting and splitting up the clouds. Clapping and spreading its applause above Margaret's head. Lightning streaking a route of destruction to follow as something is hit. Port Murdock is powerless.

Iva knocks over the alarm clock on her bedside table. It is too dark to tell the time when she reaches for the clock on the floor. Its face is twisted like a round knot, reminding Iva of Gladys when she gave her an order to do something on the spur of the moment. She calls out to Rose and gets no response. She reaches for the chain on the lamp and yanks it. Its light is dead.

Margaret, walking through her own footprints, descends the stairs with sheer illusion and lace in mind. Something troubles her mind like the thought of an unfinished prayer, a candle left burning in an empty house, a wedding dress that was never worn. The ecstasy of the first waltz rising from the hem of the gown to a Juliet crown. She had missed it all with Ambrose Kane, poor Ivadoile. She had one illusion too many.

Old Rose walks leisurely down the hall, her tail outstretched and rising up over her back like a crooked twig. She is licking her lips as if she were watching for an audience of mice to come in out of the rain. There is a moment of silence between a flash of lightning and the galloping of thunder. What do people think about in this lull: fear, pardon, death, inventions, or possibly creation?

Iva pulls the quilt back up over her head and waits for time to clear its face again. She smiles remembering what she had overheard in a conversation between her parents. She was conceived during a thunderstorm. She laughs out loud and calls out, "Mother dear, it was probably rape." Her mother was terrified of storms.

All the downstairs lights are off. Margaret flicks a few switches before she realizes that the power has gone out. She thinks Iva is out of bed playing with the light switches, turning daylight into darkness. It matters not to her now which side of the sun is up. Margaret will heat up the left-over stew for lunch if the power returns before then. If not, she can muster up a thick sandwich with cheese and grapes on the side to fill the bill.

The cat leaps up on the bed, purrs down on Iva and licks her chin and her sleep smile before she moves to her favourite spot at the bottom of the bed. Old Rose can find her meal in or out of the dark.

The rain has left secret codes on the window panes in bold dots that, when deciphered, might read, "Rain, rain go away, come again another day!"

IN IVA'S BEDROOM, daisies lean over the edge of an antique vase like a bride's wilting bouquet that was never caught. They have been there for three days. Iva looks like a dying carcass of quilt and flesh. The quilt has slid down exposing her breasts. They are sprawled out over her folded hands as if she were about to summon a prayer. There is a sense of beauty in this scene. Her fine white hair is shapeless, resembling ruffled dove feathers resting against the pillow's lace. Her mouth is pouting small bubbles like a child discovering the body's magnificent abilities in a time of need.

From the doorway, Margaret checks in on Iva. A decaying mermaid comes to Margaret's mind as she watches Iva sleeping. She has wrapped her legs up in the white quilt. For a brief moment, Margaret imagines her in the ivory gown and veil, until the lamp comes on suddenly and Iva's face is caught in a harsh glare of the bulb. She is gold and white, a streaked version of a stranger in cold slumber, a painting, a faded bride, a diva with a dream in her head that makes her smile outwit her demons.

Old Rose winks at the light. She looks towards Iva and sniffs at the quilt. Beneath the cover she picks up the scent of fresh lavender hidden deep in a field of flesh.

The wind has changed voices, gone from tenor to alto. An odd rag on the line is twisting to its rhythm. Whose voice is giving it directions?

Iva's feet tap the floor. There is no noise when she unravels from the quilt and lets it fall. A snowdrift at her feet, she is aware that her feet are cold. Right foot first and she is on the bare floor. Someone has removed the mat from alongside her bed. She can't remember giving anyone permission to remove anything. She grabs her cotton robe from a chair and slips it around her shoulders and makes her way down the hall towards the kitchen with its lunch aromas. Her robe is flowing like a bride's second-hand train.

Margaret is startled for a minute by the image standing in the pantry doorway. Iva is smiling in at her. Her opened robe is sliding off her shoulders. Margaret immediately buttons it up, hiding wrinkles of nakedness behind each button. She sits Ivadoile in a chair near the kitchen window and returns to stir the bubbling stew. She has lost her appetite for the chicken stew and coconut cream pie. "Oh dear Lord, forgive me, but the woman looks like a plucked chicken in the nude!"

Old Rose sits at Iva's feet like a foot warmer. She paws at her blue veins, a wizard at casting a spell, stopping long enough for Iva to stroke her with a long nail, a slow petting along the length of her spine, a lover's scratch that ends with a purr.

The darkest of daylight is brightened by a yellow break. The sun is healing the lives of the remaining cast in the Tides Inn.

Margaret is suddenly hungry as she places two bowls of stew on the table. She hurries out the back door and pulls up a handful of wet daisies, sticks them in a vase and places them between her and Iva. They catch the attention of the returning sun. It lingers above their petals as if they are in need of warmth.

And Iva, where she sits at the table in the sun's pure light, is now completely naked. Her head is bowed over her coconut-cream pie as she gleefully licks off the cream with one finger. Her legs are spread outward as if to make room for the falling cream dripping from her chin to the chair. Old Rose is standing on her hind legs for this feast.

Margaret, returning from the pantry with fresh iced tea, is mortified by the scene in front of her. The pitcher of iced tea slips from her hand and crashes to the floor. The cat rushes out of sight. Margaret stands in a pool of ice and tea, wondering what her next move will be.

Old Rose keeps a steady eye on the cloudy stream floating under the chair. She moves slowly towards it and sniffs. This cool liquid is not her cup of tea. She retreats to her spot under the cot and watches as a mop swings in and out.

The sun takes a dim view of the present scene. It floats behind a cloud and leaves a tail of beams coasting along the window like brightly coloured strings.

The table creaks under the sound of Iva's pounding fist. She demands another glass of red wine after her imaginary first glass. Cream clings to her mouth like froth. A prop used by an actor for the real anger effect.

"I am going to have to hire a new server," Iva shouts. "You can't have your guests waiting this long for service."

Margaret places a long-stemmed wine glass full of warm tea in front of Iva to pacify her. She devours it like a drunken sailor.

"I'll get more wine when I go into town," says Margaret, watching Iva licking her lips and getting ready to ask for more.

"Who drank it all?" she demands. "Are you into my wine again, Margaret?

"I never drank, you know that."

"How do I know what you did or didn't do?"

"Trust me, Ivadoile!"

"Trust and I have been cruelly severed. You, above all people, should know that. I trusted pain, it was the only thing I knew for sure that would surround me."

Margaret is sure she has hit a chord somewhere with her. Iva is rational at the moment. Naked and rational is better than naked and off in limbo.

Times like these give Margaret breathing room. Woman to woman conversations. The sun sifts through the old lace curtains in the pantry, sprays the walls with a pattern of a flower as it appears on a cupboard door. Time was as time is. Margaret is remembering the inn in the image of the flower, in the stir of a cloth in the wind, in the song of a bird, in the ringing of a bell. What stranger appeared at the door? Whose marriage started off between Ivadoile Spears' white sheets? Whose faces the mirrors once imaged? Whose fingers found a song in the old piano keys?

Rose moves out from under the cot with her shoulders rising, her eyes focused like a swimmer who has made it to safety out of troubled waters.

The sky looks broken with chipped edges of clouds. The sun rides in and out, looking for a soft blue spot to lounge on.

Iva calls out for more wine. "Fill her up, s'il vous plait!"

She is standing in the back doorway smiling, her naked body caught in the summer breeze. She is swaying to the rhythm of an old French song she heard Margaret sing many times.

Margaret tugs at her arm gently and brings Iva back to the chair beside the window as the song runs out. She fills up her glass with more tea and returns to the pantry with the pitcher. She swipes at her own perspiration, despite the fact the kitchen is quite cool, as she pours herself a small glass of iced tea from the refrigerator. She can feel the cool rush in her throat going down and backing up like a river against its own banks. She leans against the cupboard with the empty glass in her hand. A figure of white flesh is calling out her name like some visible ghost in the kitchen. Her voice is alive and alert. This ghost of Ivadoile Spears is hungry for sex. "Stew is for old people. Sex has more flavour," she shouts, demanding a cigarette dipped in fire for dessert.

The cat is hunching again, its eyes full of wonder, its whiskers full of cream, and its head full of forgotten old songs. A horizontal string of skinny clouds float over the inn. Someone (a guest) once left the name of these clouds at the dinner table like a tip.

Iva is buttoning her housecoat carefully as if the buttons are fastened from broken twigs. She is buttoned crooked. Oh, a sure sign of a jealous person the myth has it. They might as well be daggers on Ivadoile Spears.

Watching carefully, Margaret walks casually into the kitchen and wipes off the kitchen table and chair.

"Are you cold?" she asks without looking up.

"I thought I saw someone walking up the lane. Did you see anyone, Margaret?" Her face on the verge of anticipation and excitement.

"There's nobody walking up the lane. The nurse won't be here for a while. She went off for a short walk."

"What nurse are you talking about?"

"The nurse that takes care of your medical needs, that is the nurse I'm talking about."

"Do I like her?"

"No."

"Does she like me?"

"No."

"Then what in the hell is she doing here?"

"Her job, that's what she is doing here. She checks your blood pressure and heart and whatever is required medically for you. You have four of them coming here at different times around the clock."

"Four at different times? I have only one heart. I am paying three of them for nothing. Get rid of them! I know things are missing. One of them stole all the sheets off the line. What is it about sheets that make women turn into thieves?"

Iva stands erect taking a lap around the kitchen, her fist in mid-air. A boxer warming up for the first round. Anger keeps her steady on her feet. A woman has to defend her titles as her robe slides down to the mat.

Rose has made it safely to the landing of the stairs before she stops and listens. A crash sends her up to the top floor as she finds the nook at the end of the hall. She keeps one cautious eye on the stairs. Noises can travel.

A hostile clap of thunder overhead. Is there a need to fear what one cannot control? The old inn is drowning in rain once again. All its windows are weeping.

Iva is propped up against her pillow in her bed counting something or other before the nurse arrives. She orders Margaret to hide all the sheets in the inn, as she takes inventory of the room with her glasses clinging to the bridge of her nose.

Margaret takes a break and lets the nurse take over. The older nurse looks weary, as if she were being led to the gallows. Margaret meets Old Rose in the hallway as she reaches the top of the stairs. Margaret moves along slowly until she comes to room number Three and opens the door with a squeak. The cat runs in between her feet and curls up on the floor.

Memory may have labelled this room her favourite of all with its direct link to the setting sun. Its ghosts. Its rose garden that she believes still beats a pulse in this room. Something is always alive in this room. Margaret is comforted not by its stillness, but by its dead memories.

She is in love with dead memories. She sits on the edge of the bed and looks towards the spot where she'd picked up Angela Pinotti's letter. A piece of his soul lay between the lines with his love for her. She had hidden this knowledge away for so long it's a surprise to her that these feelings emerge now on this particular day. The idea of it all touches her deeply. Oh, the heart can teach you more than you can ever teach it. "Angelo Pinotti would have loved me safely, elaborately," she smiles. She understands these things now like a prayer that closes down for the night.

"Meow," squeals Old Rose, voicing her independence. She is up on one of the window ledges listening for sounds. The air is loud with bird lyrics. It has stopped raining and the birds no longer need the leaves of the trees for umbrellas.

The sea, the sun, and the wind have combined forces over Port Murdock for the moment like the lead performers in a grand parade. All the wildflowers are marching.

A new isolation begins to take form in Ivadoile Spears. She looks about her bedroom as if she had been robbed of the delight of artistic sensibilities. She had acquired Bowzer's sensitivity to colour's magnetic pull, with greens and blues taking the head of the class on the emotional scale. They were, he noted, great appetizers for calming life's clutter. He'd lived his life between their hues. As Iva looks around her room, she believes that her grey walls (a faded green) are closing her in. Her drapes (bleached yellow) are ready for the flames. Her four-poster bed is a dark crate. She climbs out of the crate while the nurse has gone for water and makes her way to the window. The garden cherubs are still. So, so still that they hold summer on their shoulders like a grey cloud.

Margaret takes her leisurely stroll break down the lane towards the village. She has refused a ride. An acquired snobbish air to her gait makes her smile. Undaunted, she has placed herself on a stable path where the leaves applaud as she goes on her journey.

Old Rose sniffs at the nurse's shoes and is quickly shuffled off into the corner by an unfamiliar sole with the moral force of a mad dog.

The wind, at the tail end of an embrace, hurries out from under the skirt of a young woman standing facing the sea and whistles down the side of the cliff.

Iva, watching from her bedroom window, calls out to the young woman fading in the distance. She pounds with her fists on the glass, but the woman is moving further along the cliff and ignores the summoning fist behind her.

"Come back, Violet, you are going in the wrong direction."

The nurse, hearing her cry out, pulls the screaming Ivadoile back into bed and wraps the sheet tightly and roughly around her and clips it down before sedating her.

"She is out there, I saw her," Iva protests. "I saw Violet at the edge of the cliff." The nurse leaves the room shaking her head.

Margaret removes her shoes at the back door when she returns and walks down the hall towards the room that was reserved especially for Bowzer. She will take a little nap before her evening meal, after checking in on Iva.

Iva is wild-eyed under the sheet tucked under her chin with plastic clips.

She resembles an old rag doll hung on the line to dry with her hair in dampened clumps like unravelled string. Not a word comes from her voice, only a small ripple, a brook drowning into the earth as it dries up. Her head is thrashing on the pillow like an old book cast out into the raw wind with its pages flipping to the rhythm of their own decomposing knowledge. Margaret releases her from her bondage and throws the clips in the closet.

The cat crawls into the room and looks towards the bed with fearful eyes, moves backward and yawns, before curling up in the doorway as if to block anyone's entrance.

Margaret pulls up the dark window blind to let daylight back in. Wind and grit sift in between the screen and dirty the freshly washed roughly before going out again. The two women are shaded between the soft day's rays. The elegant shadow of the tall spruce pine juggles its fingers along the back wall like a green giant in a children's story book.

Iva's hand is shaking as she holds onto a fresh glass of water. Sitting on the side of her bed, she is unsure what is to be watered. A plant with a purple head is drooping for a sip. "Everything is dying in here," she mumbles, "mother told me to water the plants, but to hell with her. Let her believe that I've fallen in the well. She always makes me water the plants with water from our old well. I won't answer her when she calls out again."

Margaret reminds Iva that she is going to take a short nap before she will prepare their evening meal. "I took a nice jaunt into the village, Ivadoile. The weather is ideal for walking."

Iva closes her eyes on Margaret's conversation and is smiling at something behind her lids as if she were taking inventory on some past excursion at the end of a jaunt.

Rose follows behind Margaret's familiar heels. Curls up at the bottom of the bed and drops her head. Margaret slides the bedspread over to the side and lays her head on the pillow. Pieces of light float in the room and create a deep shadow on Picasso's self-portrait. One round hard eye looks anxiously towards the bed as if seeking out its former tenant.

Iva is watching a parade of people going past her open window. She believes they have passed this way before. A small child with a limp is carrying a rabbit in her tiny arms. It is missing a paw. The child stops and looks in at her and smiles. Her soft mouth cornered by regret. The other three are sultry looking adults, two women and a man. The man's face is blistered in scorn, his eyes hard and broken like scattered gravel.

A blond woman walks behind the man with her head bowed as if she is searching for something she's dropped along the path. Her hair is full of sun streaks and wind stirs.

The other woman, following closely behind, is dressed in black. Her eyes are small and mean, shivering in their intimate darkness. They are gone when Iva reaches the window. She calls out to the tiny armed child and the rabbit, but they do not return.

Margaret is surprised to find Iva almost fully dressed when she goes into her room. She has put on three sweaters and two different socks and shoes. She is not wearing any underwear or slacks.

"Are you going somewhere, Ivadoile?"

"I'm looking for the little child. She has a rabbit."

"I'll help you get dressed and we can go out together."

Margaret helps her into her underwear and slacks. They walk leisurely towards the edge of the cliff towards the sea. Iva leans on her cane for support as Margaret points out the scenes surrounding them.

"Look, Ivadoile, there's a sailboat in the distance!"

"Who cares?"

"You like ships and boats, Ivadoile. You always liked to watch them pass by the inn."

"I was lying. I hate anything that floats, even soap. I hate soap."

"Would you like a little stroll in the garden near the inn? You will see a hardy group of perennials at their best."

Margaret walks her to the bench overlooking the land and sea, before they return to the inn.

"Did Bertie prune the lilac bushes as I requested him to do?" Iva asks as Margaret settles her on the bench.

"Bertie died in a car accident."

"Why didn't you tell me, Margaret? How is he going to

do what I've requested now that he's dead?" Her skin is pale under the yellow sun, a mass of transparent blue veins detouring under her skin like a badly sketched map.

"He died many years ago," says Margaret, her words dragging and sorrowful like someone delivering a death message to herself. She can't remember if she had ever spoken those words aloud.

Margaret removes her shoes and lets her feet play in the cool grass. A secret wind circles along her flesh in a rotating motion. She hasn't done anything like this in years, not since she and Gladys sat behind the barn for a breather in the summer months out of Iva's sight and Bertie gave them a slight wave whenever Iva came outdoors.

Ivadoile is bent over with her hands in the grass. She is spreading it between her fingers like someone looking for lice. Margaret watches her carefully, her long white fingers gallantly spreading each blade within her reach. The sun dips into each opening, revealing deeper, healthier blades of grass. Iva sits up with something clenched in her closed fist. She stares towards the silver sea with fading blue eyes.

This sudden chill of remembrance of her friends throws Margaret into a melancholy state. She takes a deep breath and pulls from her roster of saints the patron saint of sorrow, Saint Mary. She still dreams of the dead, calling to her softly and appearing in their full forms with engaging smiles. They always appear happy, yet when she wakes, she mends her loneliness with a silent prayer.

But something is different on this day, the idea of Iva believing that Bertie is still here is very unsettling to her. "At my age, dear Blessed Mother of Sorrows, I hadn't expected to be here at the inn with Ivadoile chasing a fairy tale about a child with a rabbit. Heaven knows who will appear before this is over."

Old Rose is under the veranda when Iva and Margaret return from their walk. Pensively, her green eyes stare out at their approaching feet. She moves out from under the boards and crawls between their legs with a noticeable limp.

A light haze of fog tumbles in below the cliffs and up the side of the banks. It covers the old viewing bench like a secret shroud.

Iva pays particular interest to the plate Margaret has placed before her. Several cattle are grazing in an open field. A man stands at a distance leaning on a stick and looks over towards the cattle. A dog stands at the side of the man with the stick. There is a slight chip on the edge of the plate. She has seen this plate before on someone's table.

"Where did you get this plate, Margaret?" Iva's voice is hostile in nature.

"They are your plates, Ivadoile." Margaret's voice is calm and reassuring.

"Look at it!" cries Iva, "Opal chipped it when she fired it on the shelf after drying it. Mother would never let her wash the dishes. She said the Methodist was too intense. Put her near water and she'll baptize everything and anything."

"That was a long time ago, Ivadoile. She is not here now to baptize your dishes. I'll wash them for you myself."

"She baptized my father in the hay bin, the wooden whore. She used blood when water was not available."

Margaret tries to alter her agitation with a lighter conversation.

"Bowzer's bed is very comfortable, Ivadoile. He sure had a flair for décor."

"What are you doing sleeping with Bowzer! I had the decency not to take advantage of my dear friend."

"Bowzer is no longer with us. He's been gone a long time."

"Where did he go?"

"He died, Ivadoile, quite a few years ago."

"Who died?" she asks vaguely while looking out the kitchen window.

"I think we should eat now before dinner goes cold and the tea will settle into a stale brew," Margaret adds, covering Iva's plate with fresh meatloaf and vegetables.

The two women eat in silence until the man with the stick and the quiet dog reappear on Iva's plate. Margaret is in the pantry putting bread pudding in the bowls when she hears the sound of breaking glass. Iva is standing in a pool of broken plate pieces smiling as she looks down at the floor.

"Why did you do that?" Margaret inquires, exhaling. "You could have hurt yourself in that broken glass."

"I didn't do anything. Opal broke the plate. She hates dogs. They all bite into her solid ankles. She told me so herself, the conditioned bitch."

The angry nurse pulls at Iva's arm and yanks her from the puddle of glass. Iva leans forward at the sound of Margaret's voice and grabs her hand. The nurse is mumbling under her breath when Margaret cuts her off at the pass.

"I understand what's happened here," Margaret addresses

the nurse in a terse voice. "I'll take care of things if you care to sweep up the glass." Margaret settles Iva into bed before she offers her the bowl of bread pudding. She has softened it with ice cream and let it melt to make it easier for her to swallow.

The swelling bruise on Iva's arm moves in rhythm with her spoon. Arm and hand go upwards and the melting ice cream drips off the spoon and spirals down her bib. Her eyes have lost their hard bondage. Glass dogs and Methodists are forgotten. They have softened into the vulnerable stare of childhood and the soft purr of a hungry stray that she reaches out to pet.

Old Rose is purring at the closed door and rushes in on her limp paw to find a spot under the bed. She sneaks a peek upward as her owner is nodding over a white bowl. A spoon slips to the floor close enough for Rose to get the last lick of ice cream before her nap.

Margaret makes sure not to use any dishes with prints on them at this point. All the dishes that she will serve Iva from now on will be unbreakable and plain.

Rose appears in the pantry with a dusty green look in her old eyes. Her fur coat is thinning and patchy in spots. She is falling away from herself too. She takes little notice of the parts of herself dropping off in corners, and on the stairs, and under the kitchen table, to be collected by the broom and whisked away to the wind. Living in fur for seventeen years, she still maintains her degree of independence and charm, despite her shedding decline.

She looks around with her whiskers groomed of the ice cream she lapped up from Iva's spoon. Posing an elegant stance, Old Rose stares up at Margaret and raises a paw like a frayed wool mitten that requires mending.

Enough daylight is left for the cloudy sun to glorify the property in short sequences, spot check the legacy of the old gazebo frame. The hide and seek paths leading to and from its octagon steps. The dusty lane leading to the front door of the inn is shedding its last coat of paint. The brass lion's head is tarnishing, with its eyes downcast, as if it were watching the paint as it falls.

Iva is happy to see Esther Neulands again in her mind's eye and she beckons her to come closer to her bed as she slides in through the bedroom window. A cobweb is titling on her head like a twisted crown. Iva notices that the wine stain has been removed from her red kimono. Esther, the lady of the book, manoeuvres around the room in a daze like someone who has crawled in for shelter from a tornado or an abusive husband. Thank heavens none of them followed her into the room. Esther is not interested in a conversation or Bible quotes. She inquires about one thing and will answer no other questions.

She has come for the one thing that will make her happy, the beautiful doll with the little white teeth and the spruce green eyes. She is buzzing around the room searching for the doll, under bed, in the closet, in the bureau drawers. Iva shouts at her to leave her doll alone.

"You will not take Victoria away from me, now go away and don't come back!"

Margaret is alarmed by the growling coming from Iva's room as she goes to check on her. She believes the nurse is arguing about something or other with her again.

Iva is bolt upright in her bed like an old spring about to snap. Her fists carving circles in the Sunday dusk when the male nurse enters with his book beneath his arm and places it beside him like a pistol.

"Having a little trouble are we?" he directs his question to Margaret, as if Iva were not in the room, as he sits on the edge of the bed. He checks her pulse and pressure with a deep sigh. "Did you have a bad dream?" he asks Iva without looking up at her.

"Who in the hell are you asking about my dreams?" Iva's voice is laced with fury. The man's jaw arches like a pit bull's.

"I am on duty for the night," he answers with a snarl.

"Why are you on duty here, Mister?" Iva inquires. "I don't fancy young men crawling along my sheets like a cockroach, unless I've invited them here for my own good."

Iva is not aware of Margaret's presence until she hears her voice. "He is the nurse on duty for the night, Ivadoile. It is safer to have a man around the place after dark."

Iva begins to laugh in a haunting voice. "Men are never safe, in or out of the dark, Margaret. Look at the muscles on him, they were honed for lust!" The male nurse coughs up a snicker.

"Margaret, make sure you bring me my doll for safety before Esther Neulands finds her and runs off with her!" shrieks Iva.

The nurse is about to inject her with a sedative until Margaret protests and offers to sit with her until it is time for a sleeping pill.

"I'll carry her over with a cup of green tea," she assures him as he walks off with his book.

"She's your headache," he adds, as he turns to Margaret with a look of self-defiance, as though he considers Margaret a headache to a lesser degree.

"One minute, young man. I would assume in your line of work, a headache along with many other maladies are your bread and butter. Believe me, you will be old someday yourself," Margaret rifles at the male nurse. The suddenness and the anger in her voice startles her. This is one person, of all the help here at the inn, whose feathers she doesn't want to ruffle.

She is aware of the indifference the nurses hold towards Iva, their impatience with her (except for the young one who comes in the morning for the day shift) yet there is no way Margaret will let the others abuse her.

"Dementia is not arrogance. It is life going backwards and colliding with its past self," she adds in a softer tone of voice. She'd seen Iva's bruises from their rough handling of her.

Margaret hears the slamming of the door as the nurse makes his way down the hall towards the parlour. She hears Old Rose let out a yelp in the distance. Margaret calls out to the cat as she makes her way to the pantry. The cat crawls along slowly as she follows Margaret's voice and flops at her feet. Margaret hugs Old Rose and brings her to her room for safekeeping.

The cat purrs as she stretches out on the bed. Margaret is still trembling as she pours two cups of green tea and goes back to the room. Ivadoile, stretched full length on the bed, is oblivious to the last few minutes of life. She is totally naked with her legs crossed like a bold X and is puffing away on a make-believe cigarette.

"I love this brand," she smiles up at Margaret. "It's an after-making-love brand, the flavour is intoxicating. I bought them in Europe for Ambrose to drool on. He loves them."

Margaret pulls the quilt up over Ivadoile before giving her the mug of tea. She sits beside the bed and drinks her tea with Ivadoile, as Ivadoile throws her imaginary cigarette to the floor.

"You've brought me my favourite wine."

"Yes, I did."

"Did you find it in the wine cellar?"

"That is just where it was, Ivadoile. I had no trouble finding it on the shelf. I'd know my wines from green tea any day. I brought your doll downstairs the other day. She was upstairs in one of your rooms. You told me her name was Victoria. Would you like to see her? I put her in the drawer where you asked me to hide her. She's a real antique doll, Ivadoile."

"So am I, Margaret."

Iva is silent as Margaret places the old doll in her arms. She watches as Iva rocks back and forth tracing the outline of the doll's small cracked face with her hand, the curvature of the fingers and toes, the stuffed body, the cry coil cried out years ago, the musty hair and delicate little yellow teeth. The dress comes apart in her hands before she places its small mouth to her broken breast to nurse.

Old Rose is stretched out on Bowzer's bed a few feet from the eye of David. The ageless king is very observant. He is surrounded by the masters of the art world, Picasso, Monet and the like. And the Queen of the Hunt, the old master Rose, is sculpted out in a soft, pliable sensual mould of thinning limbs, worn paws and fur, and eyes that have lost their shine.

WHO REMEMBERED THE next morning that a full moon had followed them the night before on their walk? That the moon shadow boxed the whole event and the big dipper appeared like a fill-in-the-dots sketch over the cliffs. Old Rose was caught in silhouette with her tail in the air like a young feline out for a midnight stroll beside her beloved Ivadoile, who had spit out her sleeping pill like sour milk when she burped.

She had no idea that by staying awake, she could go to the lover who called out her name. He called to her in song, Ambrose Kane did. He was so close to the window his voice trembled through the curtains. She thought he was behind the blind like a bat looking for a way into the house.

Iva had no trouble fitting her small frame out the low window, or placing her feet on the grass that swam in its own dew, as she followed his voice towards the purple path.

Margaret, still awake, saw a shadow pass her window. She watched for a moment its slow pace, its stalling and awkward sense of direction when it moved again. Old Rose followed closely behind her as she made her way to Iva's room and saw the open window.

Both Margaret and Old Rose made their way outside through the window. Margaret saw Ivadoile as she moved slowly down the lane, past the spot where the old barn had stood for so many years. She did not call out to her for fear of frightening her. Old Rose was at Iva's side as Margaret neared them. Iva was singing as she moved towards the purple path. Margaret called in a low voice, ever so grateful that Iva had not removed her nightdress. She turned slowly when she heard Margaret's voice.

"He is here, I heard him singing."

"Yes he is, Iva, but he wants us to go back in now."

"Why?"

"He brought us a bottle of red wine. He wants us to celebrate, Iva." She thanked heaven silently for having had the courage to go into the liquor store a few days before.

Margaret wrapped the quilt around Iva's shoulders. She had pulled it from the chair before leaving the room.

"Who wants us to celebrate?"

"The man you heard singing, don't you remember?"

"I heard a bird, Margaret. I know a man from a bird. Birds sing with happiness. Men sing for its possibilities. Mother always says so, when she is in a foul mood. I never really liked that woman. She hates men and poetry."

Margaret smiled. Here in the moonlight, Ivadoile Spears was giving life and Nettie McLaughlin one last shot.

"Perhaps Humphrey was singing, Iva. She liked to sing."

"Did you hear Humphrey singing?"

"Is she singing now?"

"I don't know. If you believe she is, she is singing for you."

"Yes, she is, I can hear her. Bowzer is singing too. He is in the lead. They are singing my favourite song."

Margaret wrapped her arm in Iva's as she led her back

towards the inn. "It's time to go in, Iva, the singing has stopped. They want you to go back. The song has come to an end."

They walked along the grass towards the open window of the bedroom. Old Rose strolled behind them. They were clever and secretive, this trinity of females threading softly on the carpet of night. Almost daring should anyone know what they were up to.

Margaret could not chance having the male nurse hear them enter the kitchen door. They would be both carted off somewhere. She helped Iva enter the window, as she held onto her arm for safety.

Old Rose slipped in like a white shadow with a dark secret. And then Margaret entered the dimly lit room and closed the window with a soft blow to keep it closed.

Calmness settled on Ivadoile Spears' face like a hazy sun spinning gold through a filter. The scent of fresh grass was rooted in the floor between the floorboards. They had brought the outdoors in with them. The four-poster bed looked like an old barge marooned on a calm sea.

Iva sat on the edge of her barge stark naked as if she were contemplating a midnight dip. Her head looked down towards the shiny floor. Enough light on one spot to have her imagine a warm pool of slow water waiting for her. Margaret slipped her nightdress back over her head as she stretched out her arms like a scarecrow. She covered Iva's feet in pretty blue socks and got her under her quilt against two white fluffed pillows.

Margaret went to her room and returned with the bottle of red wine and two crystal glasses. Iva had not moved. She sat in her old bed holding her doll in her arms. Victoria's eyes stared at the closed window, as if watching for an intruder from behind the blind.

"A toast," said Margaret, holding up the crystal glass as she poured a drink for Iva. A white feeble hand floated towards the glass like a spotted moth. She made a suckling sound as she swallowed. She hadn't tasted real wine in years.

Margaret poured herself a drink and sipped slowly as she watched Iva take another swig. Margaret took another drink from her glass. It lingered in her throat like a lost word before it settled down deep and a feeling that had died in her spit itself up like fire.

"A toast," she said looking down at Iva who smiled up at her. Iva responded in a light and airy voice. "A toast," she said, holding the doll in an upside down position. Her aging face aglow beneath the surface, beneath its chiselled edges that unravel to let in the light.

"I love the flavour of life," Iva laughed heartily as she tipped the glass to her lips. "More! More!" she commanded holding out the wine glass.

The doll falls from her hand and tumbles to the floor. Margaret reached for the doll and placed Victoria back on the bed with care.

Old Rose sniffed at the rim of Iva's glass and licked greedily at the contents running down the sides, as Margaret poured with a shaky hand. The cat found a spot at the bottom of the bed and stretched out like a piece of taffy. Margaret crawled beside Iva at the back of the bed and poured herself another drink as she leaned back against the pillow. Something fermented in her head. It would have been out of reach before, a trip to Italy, even the thought of it so far removed from her life. She could feel the marble of the Pieta tremble in her fingers at that moment. There was something else she imagined may still exist, the old letter that may have reached Angelo Pinotti's friend. Frayed and yellowed at the edges, no doubt, asleep between the pages of Rome.

The half empty bottle of wine fell from her hand and landed behind the bed with a thud. The noise startled Iva. Margaret laughed hysterically, releasing within her the memories of her brother and their father's stolen wine. Her sister's over-fashioned clothes that still arrive for her from New York. She will have to tell them the truth, she announced to no one in particular. She always hated the damn things.

"New York fashions clash with country roads and confession boxes. I'd rather be seen and absolved in a potato sack," she blurted out.

Iva stuffed the doll under the quilt. She had an urgent need to protect something, to love someone. She removed Victoria from under the quilt and smiled at her. Iva could hear Margaret breathing beside her. The sound of life so close was pleasing. She had never slept in her own mother's bed, had never been invited in. Another woman had never shared her bed with her.

Once, while in the back woods with Ambrose Kane, she believed she heard a thud, as if something was moving like a pendulum against a tin object. She had glanced up quickly and thought she saw someone standing still in the distance along the dirt road. When she and Ambrose Kane moved out from under the tree, there were apples all around them on the ground, but the road was empty. Iva glanced over at the sleeping Margaret. She was smiling against the pillow. Iva pulled up the quilt and covered Margaret as close to her smile as she could reach.

EPILOGUE

TWO YOUNG GIRLS found the photograph near a briar in the fall of 2010. Ivadoile Flora McLaughlin was neatly written on the back of the sepia toned photo taken in May of 1928. Her letters were perfectly formed. They assumed it was her handwriting because of the clarity and style it embraced. Girls could really write back then, they thought. They were forced into perfection or else were strapped raw for sloppy penmanship.

Ivadoile is wearing a long form-fitting brocade coat and high laced-up boots. Her hands (in light gloves) form a small arch mid-air as if she were praying. She is hatless. Her outfit is one of great beauty, like the old movie stars wore. Her blond hair is full of wind. A cat shaped like a comma is at her feet. The girls take several guesses at the possible colour of her coat. "American Beauty, or Cherry Red, or maybe it was a Sky Blue," they swoon.

Ivadoile is glaring at someone or something behind the

picture taker. Something turbulent has caught her attention. The girls do not question the look of determination in her young voice. They are more interested in the clothes worn back in the twenties, the cumbersome price a girl their age had to pay for beauty. And a beauty she was, at a young age.

They giggle at the thought of the crazy cat woman who lived in the old Tides Inn who was carted off to a hospital somewhere.

They can't imagine her having ever possessed such feminine beauty. One of the girls shreds the photograph into small pieces when they become bored of admiring the photo. Up it goes in one toss and scatters in the air like confetti.

They watch as the torn photo swirls lightly towards the ground and scatters like seeds carried by the hand of the wind. The pieces gather in small mounds beneath the briar and circle about in the dried mud before being stilled.

ACKNOWLEDGEMENTS

TO MY DEAR friends Alistair MacLeod and A.L. Kennedy and my brother Roddy MacDonald for his professional input. I owe a depth of gratitude to my dear friend Donna for her sharp eye and grammar skills. To my son, Greg, who was at my side for the duration, much thanks. To Dawn and Sheldon Currie for their insight and encouragement and to all I may have forgotten who offered a kind word along my journey, I thank you for your support. And I wish to thank Breakwater Books and my editor James Langer for his careful and diligent observations.

PHOTOGRAPH BY KATHERYN GORDON

BEATRICE MACNEIL is the bestselling author of *Where Wild Horses Gallop*, *Butterflies Dance in the Dark*, and *The Moonlight Skater*. In 1999, she received the Tic Butler Award for outstanding contribution to Cape Breton writing and culture.